Praise for the Base Branch Series

"Megan Mitcham's books are well-paced, well-plotted suspense novels edged with stunning sensual intensity. Her lovers are cold and deadly--except when they are skin-to-skin. I can't wait for the next book in the series!"

- **DELILAH DEVLIN**
New York Times and USA Today bestselling author

"Nail-biter all the way to the end."

- **Michelle**, MsRomanticReads
Adult Romance & Erotic Book Reviews

"This is a fresh and exciting story with lots of great characters."

- **5 Star Amazon Review**, Enemy Mine

"Megan now joins my elite team of must read authors. I fell in love with her work in *Enemy Mine*, and it just gets better the more I read."

- **TNT Reviews**

BOOKS BY MEGAN MITCHAM

BASE BRANCH NOVELS
ENEMY MINE
JUSTICE MINE
STRANGER MINE
WARRIOR MINE
DANGER MINE
PRISONER MINE
SURVIVOR MINE - 2017

BASE BRANCH SUB-SERIES
VERSIONS - updated 2016
VIRTUES - 2016
VARIATIONS - 2016

BUREAU NOVELS
FOR ALL TO SEE
PAINTED WALLS
FORD'S BOOK - 2016

ANTHOLOGIES
ANTICIPATION
CONQUESTS
ROGUES
SEX OBJECTS - 2016
COWBOY HEAT
HIGH OCTANE HEROES
WILD AT HEART VOLUME II
benefiting Turpentine Creek Wildlife Refuge

Warrior Mine

Base Branch Novel #4

Megan Mitcham

Published by MM Publishing LLC

Edited by Lacey Thacker

Proofread by Tina Rucci & Lynn Mullan

Cover Design by Deranged Doctor Designs

Warrior Mine
All Rights Are Reserved. Copyright 2014 by Megan Mitcham

First electronic publication: January 2015
First print publication: January 2015

Digital ISBN: 978-1-941899-06-9

Print ISBN: 978-1-941899-07-6

To the warriors who defend our freedom. Soldiers. Past. Present. Future. Your sacrifices humble and will not be forgotten. Thank you for your service, your honor, and your heart.

Prologue

Today the universe slammed the book on Vail's existence. Most people didn't know the day they were going to die. And perhaps that was the kindest thing. Awareness of one's impending doom could go one of two ways.

The most often applied method allowed just enough time to pine away until the definite end, and make everyone around him sad and miserable.

The second approach, Vail's personal favorite, involved seizing the time left. Living life to the fullest. Strapping on a bomb, running into the center of a terrorist cell, and sending all their asses to the fiery pits of hell.

Many failed to realize everything ended. Death spared no one. Sure, some believe it's just the beginning, that pearly gates or hordes of virgins await them on the next plane of existence. When, in fact, to Vail's way of thinking, a mound of dirt was as good as it got.

People should be damn happy to receive a proper burial. So many didn't. Many met death in the sea, in the incinerating flames of a bomb, by the hands of fuckers so irreverent they left you on the sidewalk, gasping as your lungs filled with blood. Left you fighting the inevitable end, their bullet lodged deep inside your chest cavity assuring it. Left you scraping, filing your fingers to bleeding nubs to reach the vacant blue eyes staring back at you.

Vail Tucker had died that day on the roasting Jamaican concrete. So, dying today wasn't a big deal. He just wished he'd gotten that last jewel of information Carlos Ruez held back. He knew it would be important. For him. And for others.

His cheek lay on the gray concrete where he'd spent so many days over the last ten years bulldogging information from the earth's most maniacal beings. Fight fled him, dripping out of the single bullet hole that split his abdomen. The puddle of red crept forward, a slowly advancing battle line. For the second time in his life, he expected to lose the war. For the first time, he didn't much care.

This time, pain didn't exist. The numbness that had settled into his heart nearly twelve years ago grew tentacles. They coiled around and clung to his middle, then stretched over his shoulders, down his thighs. Only the chill of lying on the freezing floor disturbed his indifferent peace.

He and Base Branch Agent Sloan McCord had both been called cold, arctic, even heartless. They weren't heartless. They'd just lost everything dear to them, and lived through the nightmare that time and again refused to change its ending. When you experienced your own emotional death, the stolen beat of all you loved, and then lived, it was hard to get excited about anything ever again. Especially your own end.

Chapter One

"We're thin at home base," Tucker admitted. The place normally whirred with the hustle and chatter of agents. "But I can reroute an incoming team. Consider it done in twenty-four. Then wrap it up and get back here. I have a mountain of paperwork for you to complete on this joyride of yours." The corner of his mouth twitched with the first trace of a smile in days. The Boy Scout had finally spread his wings.

"Yes, sir. I earned it," Base Branch Agent Ryan Noble, a.k.a. the Boy Scout—to Vail, anyway—agreed. The boy's backbone snapping to attention translated in his tone.

"And then some."

Though Noble had gone off mission and Tucker would give him hell for it for years to come, pride for the kid's ability to think on his feet and save lives while still completing the assignment straightened his drooping shoulders.

"You heading back into the room?" Ryan asked.

The ten-by-ten square of concrete had been his home for the majority of the last four days. Aside from showers, grub, and the occasional piss, he'd mapped several constellations of air bubbles in the hard surface—and in the tiny circles of blood speckling the floor from the cuts in Carlos Ruez's face.

"Seems I'll be in there for the rest of my life. He's let off a lot, copped to knowing about the cargo load you intercepted and two others at a northern site. I had to send teams there too. But he's holding something back."

"If anyone can get it out of him, you can."

Right.

"Quit kissing my ass, Noble."

"Yes, sir."

Vail set the phone back in its cradle and wondered why this high tech, highly funded organization still had corded phones. The tangled curlicue looped round this way and kinked that. His cell wouldn't work in these thick walls. If that wasn't enough, the Base Branch installed jammers to keep the top-secret information floating around the air classified. His gaze jumped from the twisted cord to the sashay of a feminine shadow through the frosted glass of his office door.

It grew more imposing the closer she came, even though the frame that knocked while simultaneously opening the door and peeking in only stood a couple of inches over five feet without the added height of heels. Sandy blonde hair swung about the curve of her chin, bracketing apple-rose cheeks. Rhonda Merk, his secretary for the last six years, gnawed on the inside of her lower lip before reluctantly smiling.

"Can I get you something, sir?"

"No, thank you, Rhonda." He nodded her dismissal, but she didn't budge. The lip chew started up again. "Is everything all right?"

"No, not really." Apparently tired of being a doorway sandwich, she stepped into the office. Her petite hands smoothed the starched front of her suit coat and the sides of her charcoal skirt. "I've never seen an interrogation take this long." She stalled.

"And?"

"And...I think you might need to," she winced, "take a break."

"In the real world interrogations can take weeks. This facility is conducive to prying information from people. The mystery. The sterility of the environment." *The tools and drugs did a bang-up job too.* But he didn't say it.

She patted a perfectly ordered strand of hair. "I think you have a lot to do with it too."

"I have plenty of experience."

"Your build helps too." Her eyes bugged wide for a split second. She curled her lips and rubbed them back and forth. "I just meant you're imposing."

"You're just short." He smiled to set her at ease.

She shook her head. "I mean, yes. I'm short. And no, you're not the biggest guy around here, but it's in the way you carry yourself. Like nothing and no one can shake you. It's in your eyes." She huffed. "Anyway, I need to talk to you...when you have a minute or ten."

He didn't point out that she'd already taken two with all her fidgeting. She didn't usually squirm. No way he could have taken it, if she did that every time they talked. But when things got frantic around the office or when she had something on her mind, she wiggled and wormed all over the place.

"I thought," she added without giving him time to speak, "you could get me squared away now, then go back to interrogating Mr. Ruez, and eat while you listened." Her slender shoulders shrugged and her head cocked.

His stomach whined for food. The sound echoed in the empty cavern, doubling the sentiment. He could out-maneuver snipers on a battlefield, but somehow women always knew just what to say to outflank him. "Women. You always know when to drop the F-bomb. I'm dying for some food. Do you have any? I wiped out my stash two days ago."

Her head bobbed and she smiled in triumph. "Ordered pizza an hour and a half ago. I'll be right back. Do you have sanitizer?" The question came with a hike of her brows.

"Yes, ma'am."

"Good. Use it and I'll be right back."

Vail sat in his chair for the first time all day. By now the sun dipped low toward the western horizon. Not that he'd seen it all day. He wrenched his arms into the sky and kicked his legs wide. A groan condensed in his throat as his muscles lengthened then cinched before elongating just a bit farther. The scars on his chest tugged like they always did and—like he usually did—he ignored them. His cuffs, still rolled over his forearms from his time with Carlos, stuck around his elbows as he sagged into the chair.

When the clack of Rhonda's heels rang the dinner bell he rallied. He sat forward and tugged the white fabric over the dark hair of each forearm.

At least those hairs aren't gray.

The silver tones on his head appeared in his late twenties, when he was still an active duty SEAL. His brothers, the bastards, had called him grandpa. They should see him now. At forty and some years it nearly consumed his head. It didn't really bother him, except when people assumed he was feeble because of the color of his hair. The mandatory suits he wore and the accompanying desk that came with his job as the commander of the US Base Branch, a Special Operations Division of the United Nations' military force, added to the assumption of age and, with it, sedation. On the other hand, it gave him the advantage of surprise.

"Here we are," Rhonda crooned like a mother hen, which incited a pang of sympathy for the henning he'd done to Sloan after she'd been stabbed in the gut. "Did you sanitize?"

"Sure did." The last time she'd made him.

"Good. The way these superbugs are flying around, you never know what you'll catch."

He held his tongue, not mentioning the reason superbugs were so prevalent was peoples' overuse of sanitizer and antibiotics, and that a bullet or knife was far more likely to kill him than a case of H1N1.

On his desk, Rhonda deposited a plate with four slices of combination pizza, a bottled water, and several napkins. He snagged one before the plate fully landed and tore off half in a bite.

"My goodness," she gasped. "Your knuckles are redder than a stop sign. Do you want a cold compress?"

"Thanks for the pizza," he said around another chunk of cheese, peppers, and meat. "No thanks, to the compress. They're fine."

She plopped onto the leather seat opposite him, her mouth still ajar.

"So, what'd you want to talk about?"

Her mouth closed and then opened. Then it closed again. She repeated the process several times, while he polished off the first piece and two thirds of another. "I love my job," she blurted, finally. "But I'd like...more responsibilities." With the brunt of the difficulty out of the way, she pulled her shoulders back. "I answer the phones, take care of your calendar and files. Lieutenant Commander Slaughter won't let me near her stuff, and I'm not complaining, but just saying—trying to say—I have a good bit of free time. I'd like to do something more meaningful. Not that my current duties are unimportant."

On her breath, Vail jumped in, afraid she'd rattle on all night, and he had a load of stuff to do. When she'd first started working for him, she'd nearly shaken his ears off his head, sashaying her petite frame around his office and filling the air with flirtatious chatter. It didn't take her long to realize those were waters he'd never wade into. There was nothing wrong with her. Him on the other hand... "That's perfectly reasonable. I'll start the process of upping your clearance. It will take a few days. A week at the most."

Instead of using the back of his hand like he would've were he alone, he plucked a napkin off the pile and wiped his mouth, content to leave the last piece where it lay, grease spotting the thin paper plate. Both Rhonda's hands migrated to her mouth, half pressed together in mock prayer, half pressing her lips. He tossed the napkin into the wastebasket beside his mahogany desk. He'd moved the thing they'd called a desk out and brought his own for the space, needing a bit of warmth in the severe confines of concrete and glass—and something sturdy enough it wouldn't shatter with one false move.

"Thank you so much, sir."

"Vail or Tucker. After the first two years of trying to get you to call me something other than sir, I gave up. But if you want this promotion, can the sir."

"Yes, s..." She smashed her lips together. "Just yes."

"Great. Thanks for the food."

"Do you want me to take the plate?"

"Leave it. I may need it after the next round."

"You're going back?"

"We all have our jobs. Mine isn't complete. He's given a lot, but there's something he's holding back, and I intend to push harder."

Rhonda nodded and left with an efficiency he'd come to appreciate.

It gave him that many more seconds to complete a task. And in his experience those few moments tipped the scale toward success. He shoved the pizza aside and eyeballed the various piles of paperwork accumulating on his desk. Yeah, interrogating in an air-conditioned room a short walk from operational plumbing was great, but jungle interrogations didn't have near the administrative commitment.

Carlos Ruez's file splayed like a yawning, food-filled mouth on one side. Two light-red sheets of paper lay atop it, covered with his soldier-straight block letters, giving a timeline and near word-for-word reciting of the Q & A for the first two days. The first page held significantly less than the second, since the bastard refused to open his mouth in response to any of his questions and Vail couldn't get too physical until other avenues had been explored, unless it was an emergency greater than a handful of Base Branch Agents' lives. And boy, that hacked him.

A day without food and water loosened Carlos's lips enough to fill a page, but not enough to satisfy Vail. Efforts ratcheted up on day three. And today, well, his knuckles ached, and that said something for a guy who worked a heavy bag for at least an hour every day. His hand hovered over a new red page, but stilled. The air shifted almost imperceptibly. Head still bowed over the stack, Vail's gaze flew to the door. No one stood in the doorway. No shadows approached.

He stood, hand automatically reaching for his sidearm. If he knew anything, it was the ways of the room and his instincts. The air only moved in his office when someone opened the door. But no one had.

The Sig's cool handle nestled home in the web of his thumb and index finger. No windows graced his dungeon. Still, he turned, surveying the placards and commendations Rhonda had commissioned and had installed on his gray rock walls. Nothing was out of place.

Four strides had him through the door. He studied the short corridor and found all as it should be. "Rhonda?"

"Yes, sir? I mean, Vail?" His name sounded like an ugly word on her lips. She poked her head out of the first door to his left.

"Did you just come back in my office or even toward it?"

Her bottom lip poked out while she thought quickly. "No. I've been at my desk. Is something wrong?" Her eyes hopped to his hand and gun.

Vail exhaled long through his nose, and then dropped his hand. "Not that I can tell. Guess I'm just jumpy from lack of sleep and exposure to a human fungus."

He returned to his desk, walking with heavy footfalls to get his blood pumping. When he rounded the thing he didn't sit, but instead shook his arms out like a boxer in the ring. Hackles rose on his nape and his breaths sped. Hand on his gun, he waited. For what, he didn't know.

Chapter Two

The digital numbers on the sleek desk clock his mother had given him when he took the job as desk jockey marked the passing minutes. *One.* He hunkered down, obeying intuition that had saved him more than a dozen times. Though it was February in Washington D.C., the person operating the building's HVAC units seemed oblivious to the fact. A moment after the low *whoosh* began, cool air kissed his face, carrying with it the hint of lilac. *Two.*

His brow quirked. Many smells had poured out the old ventilation system over the years, but none so sweet. He turned and surveyed the exposed silver ductwork with its two-by-two square grating and thin layer of dust hugging the top curve of metal before it disappeared into the ceiling. If Rhonda were tall enough to see it, she'd have a heart attack. Next, his gaze roamed the bookshelf, its metal racks dipping slightly under the weight of thick directories, three-inch binders, and the boxes of information on each active mission.

He pivoted back toward the door and eyed the clock. *Three and a half.* When the faint blue light showed he'd been on guard for five minutes without a single hint of movement, Vail shook his head. He let gravity crash him into his high-backed chair and his elbows pillowed on the mounds of paper. Silver hair tickled his fingers and his still nearly-black stubble poked his palms as he rested his head in his hands. The blank red paper stared back at him.

Vail moved his right hand toward the ball-point, but shoved the thing off with his big elbow along with a few errant sheets of paper. If they'd just move to computer filing, his life would be infinitely simpler. But they wouldn't. Ever. Too many critical details lay in the depths of the Base Branch's vault. And even the thickest firewalls wouldn't protect it as assuredly as the security system installed in this building. With a bit of a groan, as much of one as he could muster for the minuscule inconvenience, he leaned to retrieve the fallen objects from the floor.

Metal scraped metal, light and tinny. Not that of a racking chamber. Not from the wheels of his chair. But enough that every muscle in his body sang with a burst of energy. Abandoning the writing tool for a more useful one, he shot to his feet and turned in time to see two black boots hit the ground beneath the opening where the vent grating had been unfastened. Hand on the grip of his gun, he began to draw.

"The building is rigged to explode." A melodic voice poured through a balaclava. The only part of the woman not covered in black was the oval cut-out around her eyes. Even the pistol in her hip holster and the detonator in her gloved hand gleamed onyx in the severe office lighting.

In little less than a second Vail had a decision to make. Option one, continue the draw, shoot her in the head, and hope he could grab the detonator before she depressed it. Option two, leave his gun where it hung, attack with bare hands, get the detonator before she depressed it, and then find out who the hell she was and why she'd broken into his office. Deciding on option two, he released the gun and coiled slightly to strike. But a closer look brought that train to a grinding halt.

A long lever compressed between a slender metal box and her palm. That, combined with the distance she put between them, railroaded a surprise attack.

"Listen carefully," she demanded in an even tone. "I do not wish to harm any of you nor steal your secrets. But, if you push me, I will lay waste to us all and have completed my task all the same. Do you understand?"

"Yes." He held his body loose, waiting for any opening, while he catalogued the intruder.

Five-eight, maybe five-nine. Slender frame. Full breasts.

Not important at the moment, Tucker.

Still, he couldn't help but notice how the thin cotton fitted the pretty mounds and dipped at the sway of her waist.

He moved on. Belt with extra magazines. Knife strapped to thigh. Bulge at ankle, probably a small cannon. Dark, sad eyes. Light caramel skin. Smooth. Long lashes.

Again, not important.

Heedless of the warning, his body stirred.

"Open your left desk drawer."

Tracking his options, he did as she asked, knowing what came next.

"Remove your gun with two fingers, place it in the drawer without putting your hand inside, then close it."

Her gaze didn't rove like his had, but speared him in the solar plexus. A nice trick to watch the surrounding area and your target at the same time.

"What is it you hope to accomplish with this misadventure?"

"Secure your sidearm. Then we'll talk."

"I don't expect talking ranks high on your to-do list," he said, dropping his weapon into the shallow drawer and pushing it closed.

"It is my list."

"Really?" For a reason completely concealed from understanding, the words, *'I think we'd fare better with action,'* tickled his tongue. He swallowed them, but his brow and smirk refused to fall in line.

She surged forward one brimming step. The gloved hand not holding the key to their possible doom snapped to her hip. Her gaze rose and lanced his own.

"Yes," her sweet voice lashed like the end of a whip.

Vail remained still and watchful, a ready predator to his unsuspecting prey. She calmed in stages, as if summoning all her strength to rein a simmering rage. Again he inspected her eyes. There was no more accurate tell about a person's mental state than the eyes. They were windows all right—he just didn't think soul described what they revealed. Intent. Sanity or the lack. Direction. Fear. Malice. Truth and lies. If only they'd differentiate the lies from the truth.

The hue of her big rounds matched his coffee—devoid of cream or sugar—and the eyes that stared back in the mirror every morning. Only where his gave nothing away but the chill of earth's poles, hers revealed everything. Passion. Fear. Determination. Stability.

"Don't make this more difficult than it has to be."

"For you?" he asked.

"For me. For you, Mr. Tucker. For your agents and organization. For your secretary."

She'd done her homework because she knew just how to tweak him to get the desired results. His people and the security of his organization trumped it all, even his own wellbeing. Most of his people were currently on mission, but the lives of the few who remained were in his hands. Plus the lives of those on the thirty-one floors above them. Yeah it was late, but more and more people put in grueling hours, striving for that next corporate rung or avoiding home life. He couldn't make a move without endangering their lives. So he'd ride this wave a bit further and look for a safe break for land.

"How can I do that? What's your name?"

The mask moved around her mouth, but she didn't speak. A smile, maybe, or a frown. He hated not being able to see her face. The tiny gestures lost behind the knit also gave vital clues to a person's intentions.

"Pick up your phone, hit only the top left button for your secretary, tell her you need a boost and this coffee isn't doing the trick. You need her to go get you a triple shot espresso."

"Would you like anything?"

"I'd like for you to quit being a smart ass."

"Fair enough."

He put the receiver to his ear and Rhonda to task. Sure the request was odd, but she'd been trained to do as he asked—no questions—from covert work to coffee runs. It also meant one less person in the building.

"Good. Now, lift both pant legs to mid calf with your thumbs and forefingers only."

Sorry for him and unlike her, he didn't have an artillery launcher strapped to his ankle. Once again he complied, concealing slight irritation at the prolonged situation. He'd expected her to move in close for a pat down or to talk. Yet, she maintained enough distance between them to limit his options.

"Pat your pockets," she ordered.

He slapped his hips and upper thighs, since he rarely carried anything in the front of his pants save for the occasional hard-on. Wouldn't you know, the beat of his hands on his lap provoked his burgeoning erection. Like this was even on the same continent as an appropriate time.

"Hands in the air. I want a slow 360."

When his back faced her he tried to wither his cock into submission with a scowl, but then he met her gaze again. What little progress he'd made reining himself in died under her gaze.

"The first two buttons on your shirt, open them."

Vail swallowed, and licked his lips before setting to work on the buttons. "If you're trying to check me out, there are easier ways. Knock on my front door and tell me to strip. Better yet, knock on my front door naked, and—"

"I'm sure you're quite used to that reaction from women, Commander. But you are not my type."

"Exactly what type am I?" he asked with a grin, pulling the separated fabric of his shirt wide.

"The kind to shoot me in the heart the moment I take my eyes off you." She maintained a level gaze, refusing to look at his bare chest.

He'd sweated through his undershirt in the first session with Ruez today. "And now what would you like me to do?" A satisfied smirk quirked his lips.

"Bring me to Carlos Ruez."

His smile fell, and he began refastening his shirt.

"I'll detonate this place myself before I let you take him out of here." He hadn't thought it possible to spring the man from this place, but up until ten minutes ago, he hadn't thought it possible for someone to breach their security and drop through the rafters.

"He doesn't deserve an easy death. I prefer he slowly rot behind these cold walls."

"Then why risk your life to break into this place, if not to rescue him. To kill him?"

"I told you already. To talk. Though killing him isn't outside the realm of possibility." The masked woman tossed the detonator above her head. She snatched it from the air with her other hand with the speed of a striking snake before Vail could even think about closing the gap between them and the end of all their lives. "Are you really willing to give your life to protect his?"

Chapter Three

"His? No. Others? Yes." The man's sturdy jaw flexed.

That she could handle. Just barely. But her cheeks still heated from his words combined with the slabs of muscle and taut skin. Thank goodness for the balaclava. No way could she allow this lethal man an ounce of leverage in his favor.

"Just think of those other people, then, while you take me to Carlos."

He turned and walked to the door, pulling it open and proffering her ahead with a hand.

"Put down the door stop, and go first."

"It was worth a shot." He shrugged, toeing the stopper with a black wingtip. The move accentuated the athletic globes of his butt.

Carmen raised her scrutiny and followed the commander's wide shoulders down the corridor. He slowed at the first door and peeked his head around the corner. The secretary must have gone on her errand because he powered on with sure, ground-eating strides. She didn't have to work hard to keep up. He stood a good six or seven inches taller than her five-eight, but seemed well-proportioned, while her legs accounted for a larger percentage of her body. When she was young her brother's friends had teased her mercilessly about her tarantula legs. Over the years, their taunting grew explicit with ugly details of what they'd like to do with her extra-long legs. Accustomed to ignoring their needling, she hadn't let the hideousness of their words near her heart. But it only took one touch for the bravest among them to lose three of his teeth.

They hadn't talked about her legs again.

At the main corridor—she assumed, because it was a good three feet wider than the other—he eased again, checking the space. His large hand raised in a fist. She stilled and held her breath, waiting for the all-clear signal, glad he didn't want to run across any of his people any more than she. Talk about complicating matters. Then her gaze drifted over his thick forearm revealed by a rolled sleeve, dusted with generous black hair that crept and thinned at his hand.

Strong. Powerful. Sexy. Dangerous. A warrior.

Carmen took a silent step back, switched the detonator to her left hand, and firmed her grip. Five seconds more and his hand dropped. He moved quickly left around the corner and past two frosted-glass doors that looked like the main entrance. She finally exhaled. He hadn't attacked. A small weight fell from her shoulders. She must have convinced him not to jeopardize the lives of his people over a simple conversation. If he planned to attack, it would have been the perfect opportunity. For the briefest of seconds she'd been preoccupied with the possible occupants of the hallway and stood far too close. Though practiced in hand-to-hand combat, he could take her. Years, experience, and at least eighty pounds weighted his favor.

Ahead, two long walls of bare glass and two short cement walls centered a long wooden confer-ence table surrounded by twenty or so high-backed chairs. Before they reached it the commander veered right down another slender corridor. Toward the end, four thick metal doors lined the left wall. Each hosted a small, square window scarcely low enough for her to see through and a silver metal keypad.

He stopped at the farthest door. The fingers of his right hand hovered over the numbers. His gaze slanted, and then his head followed. "I won't hesitate to kill you both, if I need to. Bomb or no bomb. Y'all go or we all go. It makes no difference to me."

"I understand, but I vote for none of us. Just stay out of my way and I won't get in yours more than I already have. Ten minutes should get me what I need."

The commander, Vail Tucker, laughed. Not a, "*That's really funny,*" chuckle, but a deep, rumbling, "*You really are insane,*" roar. Despite the offensive notion, the sound warmed her belly, and she found it suddenly impossible to remove her gaze from the bracket of his mouth and the swell of his full lips. He sobered and smoothed a hand over his close-cropped salt-and-pepper hair. The gesture struck her as very personal.

Up until that moment he hadn't wiggled his brows, scratched an itch, clenched his fists, nothing. He exuded cold composure. But that simple brush of hair gave a bit of personality to the stalwart man. And that she didn't need one little bit.

"When we get inside, stand in the corner I direct you to and don't interfere. Open up," she commanded. "And don't block the code. You can change it when I leave. And don't even think about sounding an alarm." She pulled the compact Beretta from its holster and drew on him. "You'll only create a body count."

He turned to the panel and ticked off a ten-digit sequence she catalogued immediately. "Once we're in, close the door behind you. We don't want him to escape, now do we?" Then he opened the door and walked inside. "I'm back, Carlos. And I have a friend who wants to chat."

A man sat facing away from the entryway in a high-backed chair. Unlike the ones in the conference room down the hall, this one was formed of gleaming metal and was bolted to the concrete. Leather straps held the captive's head to the unyielding frame, thwarting his efforts to see his visitor. Still he struggled.

Fighting until the end, huh, Carlos?

Bolts, chains, and cuffs secured each limb independently to the floor. Amazingly, a bright orange suit, covering his petite frame, signaled him a prisoner more than the bonds. They could leave every door and window in the place open, but this chump wasn't going anywhere. Regardless, she closed the door. The metallic *clack* echoed in the confines.

Carmen surveyed the room. Concrete floors. Concrete walls. One window in the door. One door. In the corner opposite the door sat a metal cart on rollers with four small drawers and two large ones on bottom. Pliers and two bloody fingernails crowned the box of horrors.

She wanted the commander as far away from the door as possible, but that would put him at her back, if she stood in front of Carlos. A place infinitely worse than having him where she could easily see to shoot. Using the barrel, she pointed to the corner opposite the cart, at the captive's back, farthest from the door...except for the corner behind her.

He sauntered to the wedge of the walls, folded his arms, and leaned his shoulder blades on the unyielding surface. The stout things took up nearly three feet. But much more important things than his breadth and intriguing eyes were at play here. One thing more important than even her own life.

Keeping Vail Tucker in her periphery, Carmen walked boldly between the cart and the prisoner. For all the blood spattered on the floor she would have suspected his face to possess a tenderized quality. Save for rub-reddened skin about his forehead where the restraint held him, the light mocha skin lay smooth and unblemished across his cheeks. His upper lip still speckled with an attempt at growing a mustache, which required a bit more testosterone than the bastard had to offer. One cut split his lip and another, his nose, but nothing like she'd expected.

"You think a bitch in a mask can scare it out of me, Tucker? Think again," Carlos boasted. Spittle rained on his chin and lower lip. He looked directly into her eyes and then raked her head to toe with his sandy brown gaze. A sneer rippled his mouth. "You know what I do to bitches?"

Neither Tucker nor Carmen responded.

"I put them on their knees. Make them gag on my cock until I cum down their throat." He smiled at his own crudeness. "Is that what you're going to do, Tucker? Suck the information out of me?" A laugh, high and incensed, shrilled from the man's nasal cavity.

The sound sent a shiver of gooseflesh over her skin, which stoked the embers of her ever-present rage.

"You can try," Carlos laughed louder. "But it won't work."

Carmen stripped the rubber band she'd hidden below the sleeve of her left wrist, worked it down her hand, and fixed it around the detonator. Both men's gazes followed the movement as she leaned to her right and placed it on the concrete between herself and the cart.

"What is that?" the captive asked.

Again she didn't speak, and, as ordered, neither did Tucker.

Gun still in hand, she dropped to her knees between Carlos's secured legs. Wisely, he eased his ass back in the chair, using as much slack as the chains allowed. It wasn't much. Fresh sweat beaded on his forehead and his Adam's apple bobbed as though in an ocean of water.

He cleared what sounded like several layers of phlegm from his airway. "I like it when they start gentle," he rasped. "Get me good and hard, then take me between—"

With the safety on, she flipped her grip to the barrel, and hammered Carlos Ruez's penis into a pancake.

The chains tensed. A gurgle bubbled in Carlos's throat. His wide eyes wrinkled and then pinched shut. The round of his developing paunch concaved. His face reddened as though slathered with paint. Soon the gurgle grew into shallow gasps. Over the column of his neck, muscles she'd never before noticed strained. Tendons and ligaments holding his head to his body protruded just beneath the skin.

"You stupid bi—"

Whack!

The squish of his sex beneath the force of the blow churned Carmen's stomach. She longed to drop the gun and wipe her hand on the leg of her pants, but she showed no reaction—not that either of them could see.

Carlos sputtered and wheezed much like he had the first time. Tucker didn't squirm in his corner like most men would, but his eyes alighted with newfound interest. When the chained man recovered enough to curse her she rewarded him with another driving blow. One more clobber and the foul language dried right up. She struck twice more in quick succession.

Wise man that he was, the commander maintained his post. He had crossed his legs at the ankle, assuming a leisurely pose. From comfort or empathy, she wondered, but didn't dwell on the matter long. Raising the pistol in the air again, she prepared to strike.

"No more," Carlos moaned.

Wham!

When he could breathe he heaved deep and ragged. Again she levered back. This time, wrenching sobs shook him. Were it not for the manacles he would have crumbled into a heap on the floor. What a complete and total shame. How different things could have been. Carmen found herself shaking her head in a slow back and forth, and stopped.

She'd used up all her prayers, all her breath, and all her tears on this man. None of it had helped. They only seemed to drive him further in the opposite direction.

"I will continue until your penis is a pile of bloody tissue, unless you give me the coordinates."

Carlos's eyes widened, as she'd known they would. It took a few moments more for his weeping to cease. "Carmen?"

"Yes, brother." She removed the suffocating balaclava, combed the hair from her face that had worked free of its loose tie during her efforts in the yards of duct, and glared.

Tucker straightened, his fists balling at his sides.

Smack. She dealt Carlos another shot to the nether region to bring the realization full circle.

"Don't move," she warned the commander.

His thick chest filled out his white button-down and he released a deep growl. Every muscle in her body tingled with awareness. Not the kind she welcomed. She moved her hand over the gun and willed the wildness away. A matter of life and death. No place for the faint of heart. No time for the flutter of appreciation. Carmen stood, ignoring the throb in her knees.

Tucker wedged himself in the corner with a scowl.

"The coordinates," she reminded.

A ball of spit sailed from the prisoner's mouth, but it lacked the velocity to meet its target. The glob flopped onto his bare foot. "You would at-tack me? While I'm unable to defend myself? I should make her pay in kind for your disrespect."

The words were choked and low, but he may as well have yelled them through a megaphone di-rectly into her ear canal. Carmen's vision tunneled. The surroundings grew dark with a halo of red cir-cling Carlos. She envisioned her sweet Sophia at the hands of his lackeys, as she had been for the last two weeks. The only difference was now she had an outlet for her fury.

She holstered the gun without realizing it and sank her fist into his soft belly. The hot breath she forced from his body wet her cheek. Her right hook plowed his jaw. She longed to uppercut the bastard into oblivion. With the pounding of her knuckles, the haze of hatred dissipated. Reason crept in. If she killed him or even knocked him unconscious, she wouldn't get the information she needed.

He spat again. This time something hard hit her cheek. She wiped the spit away with her glove and looked at his tooth on the floor. She stared at the jagged, bloody bit for far too long.

"How did we come to this?" she whispered. "I protected you from the monsters under your bed. Cleaned your cuts when you fell. Held a rag to your head when you were sick." Her stomach twisted like a wrung washcloth. "You should have told me when you found out about Father. I would have protected you still. We could have set out on our own. We had money from Mother, and we had our training."

A raw chuckle vibrated up his throat. "If you think he'd have let us go, you're dumber than I thought." He tongued the gap where his left canine used to fit in a row of straight white teeth.

"You never had faith in us. You. Me. You signed on with him and look at what it's gotten you." Her gaze flashed to Tucker, who leaned on the wall observing the drama. "You can have my inheritance. Give me Sophia and you'll never have to worry about us again."

He smiled, but winced. A faint bruise already stained his cheek.

"Why take her in the first place? We were home just like you wanted."

"Carmen, you really shouldn't buy fake identification from someone I own."

She tried to quiet her reaction, but he may as well have taken a sledgehammer to her chest. He knew she'd been planning to take Sophia and run away. In an effort to save her daughter from the ugliness of her brother's work, she'd placed her in greater danger.

"I want your loyalty. After all, sister, isn't that what family is about?"

Carmen pulled the Beretta from the holster, flipped off the safety, slid one into the chamber, and leveled it between her brother's eyes. Tears clouded her vision, but she refused to set them free by blinking.

"You will never have my loyalty. But I will have Sophia. You will tell me, if with your last breath, *brother.*"

He didn't look at the gun, which froze her heart. His gaze trained on hers. "If I die, they have instructions to kill her. If you don't return in one month's time from the day you left in your futile search, they have instructions to sever a piece of her each day until you return or she dies. Whichever comes first."

Dread slashed her belly and threatened to drag her back to her knees. How had this gone so wrong... This family. This fight for freedom. This search for the only person in the world she loved. How had he turned the table when his balls were almost literally in her hands?

Leverage.

He had nothing to lose. She had everything. And one way or the cursed other she would keep it.

Her tears fell, *plopping* in the puddle of her soaked shirt. "I hate you."

"And I love you. If only you'd see that I'm trying to protect you. The world is a cruel place for a woman."

"And I stare into the face of the merciless."

"Hurry home now. By my estimation you don't have long. I'd say take me with you, but Tucker doesn't have the key and I'm fond of my limbs. Fond of my dick too. If it doesn't work right, you'll pay." He gestured as though brushing her away with his gnarled fingers. "Go, run things in my absence. Prove your loyalty. Then I'll send her to you. But...if my men even think you're leaving, they'll end you both. Tell Javier to go ahead with the deal. And I'll be home soon."

Chapter Four

"The fuck you say," Vail barked. "Where you're going from here, they don't make daylight."

He'd held his tongue way longer than he could stand. The shit spewing from Carlos Ruez's mouth made him sick—and it took a damn lot to goad him. And, maybe, it wasn't the bastard's words so much as it was the woman's gut-rending reaction to them.

As if she'd know he was thinking of her, she scored him with her gaze. Her wide, wet eyes begged his words to be true. He could plainly see the thought of Carlos free terrified her almost as much as the thought of losing Sophia. Their sister? Her daughter? Her lover? He didn't yet know. He had boxes of files on Carlos and his associates, but his blood relations had been thought dead.

Apparently not. One was alive and kicking. Or punching and hammering, as the case may be.

Vail's arms were crossed. His fists wedged in the crook of tensed muscles. And despite every-thing—his unwilling detainment, her relation to Ruez—he nodded his promise to keep that piece of shit locked up for all eternity. Not that the man would live long in the prison where he was headed.

A token of relief settled her shoulders. She wiped the stream of tears from her face and swatted back the long, dark tendrils crowding her brow. He would keep his word, just as she had to him. An accord among strangers with a common enemy seeking justice. The woman hadn't gotten what she wanted. Not even close. The least he could give her was that pledge. The reassurance.

She turned her gaze on Carlos. Her thick lips pressed in a line of rage and her head shook once. "Goodbye, brother."

Something about her resignation, like a fine animal beaten into submission, seared his insides in a way nothing had in a very long time. He'd give her case a closer look, use his considerable re-sources to track this Sophia. If for no other reason than it would annoy the hell out of Carlos. Then again, he could always drink that coffee he'd sent Rhonda for and continue the man's torture. It was all a matter of leverage. And now he had a bit more than he'd had an hour ago.

It didn't matter how tough the bastard was, if he didn't receive medical treatment shortly, he'd walk with a permanent limp and never get off again. When faced with the decision of forever-de-fective goods or a little information dump, any man would cave.

Carmen swiped the detonator from the floor, flipped the rubber band around her left wrist, and glanced back at him. He couldn't discern the ex-pression in her round, lash-rimmed eyes. Regret? Appreciation? She'd planned this little fiasco beau-tifully, knowing she'd have to threaten more than just his life to get his compliance. He had no doubt that she'd find a way out from under her brother's thumb. With or without his help. She'd chosen the perfect spot in the room to make him completely worthless and unable to strike an attack.

They bowed their heads toward one another. A bit of a truce. She spun on her heels to go and he let her.

"Before you leave..." The tone of Carlos's choked voice razed Vail's nerve endings and pulled Carmen to a stop.

"What?" She regarded him over her shoulder, her eyes narrowing to slits.

The son of a bitch's mouth spread wide and curled at the edge, despite the swollen part he could see. "Show me you mean to run the family business. Kill him." The thumb he'd pried the nail from earlier hitched in his direction, as if there were any question to which *him* he referred.

Son of a fucking cock-sucking whore! Screw torture. This guy needed killing.

Carmen's gaze darted from Vail to her brother and back. The thin line of her mouth morphed into a snarl. She yanked the compact gun from the holster. The barrel rammed the side of Carlos's head. Her jaw flexed. "So help me, brother, you'll die before he does."

"I'm surprised you'd give his life for Sophia's," the scum provoked.

"He's innocent," she retorted.

"Please, he's killed more people than I have."

"Your causes are very different," Carmen ground out.

"Make your choice, sister. Who deserves to live? Him or sweet Sophia?"

A scream, feral and pained, ripped from her throat. She bore down on the grip. Her arms shook. The shriek pitched high then rumbled into a growl. "One day, brother, your sins will come for their retribution."

She lifted the barrel, aimed at Vail's middle, and fired once.

Chapter Five

Carmen dropped to the ground, happy to leave the blackness of the ducts. She just couldn't escape the blackness of her mind. She sprinted toward the vacant building where she'd left the rented sedan. Though the standing water in the pitted alleys she fled through crystallized in the chill, the flames of hell licked her cheeks. Sweat suctioned the front of the black shirt to her stomach. In the dark of night and the gleam from the street light it looked like blood. She smacked the moisture from her eyes with the hand she'd used to pull a trigger. She imagined Vail Tucker clutching his abdomen, fighting to stem the flow of blood as futilely as she tried to dam her tears.

"Damn you, Carlos. And damn me too."

Up two flights of stairs she found the white car she'd left four hours earlier. Retrieving a key from a lower cargo pocket, she unlocked the indistinct wheels, opened the door, and tossed herself into the back seat. She hurled the detonator in the small confines and released her disgust in a yell so loud her throat burned and her ears rang. With a limited wind-up the dummy mechanism did little more than *tink* off the dashboard and then plummet to the floorboard.

"Fuck!"

Her brother hurt people. She didn't. She hadn't intended to harm anyone, only learn where Carlos's men held her daughter.

In her search for Sophia through the family's Mexican holdings, she'd heard murmurs about her brother's capture in the States and little more than a whisper about the organization that had taken him. Not FBI. Not CIA. Similar, but much more shadowed with a much broader reach.

Carmen pulled civilian clothes from the duffel on the seat next to her. She peeled the wet and all too conspicuous clothing from her body, slamming it into the bag with vicious slaps of her fist. One week. They had been one week from leaving. She'd gone for her five a.m. run as usual and returned to find her daughter missing. Sophia's sheets spilled from her bed, her closet was ransacked, and a note lay in the middle of the floor.

One way or another, I will have your loyalty.

Your adoring brother,

Carlos

She'd been so high on the thought of holding Sophia in her arms again. So wrapped up in the nearly impossible job of breaking into a building so heavily secured she half-expected to be tossed into a cell with her brother for the attempt. So stupid. She'd been so stupid to overlook the possibility that Carlos had planned for his capture on his first border crossing into the US as leader of the cartel. Floundering these days, the Arellano-Félix Organization had maintained its status on federal alert systems thanks to the early work of her treacherous extended family and father.

And now it seemed she'd never be free of her cursed family.

She climbed into the driver's seat, stuffed the Beretta into the center console, turned the car on, and headed for the exit. At the street level, she stared at the empty road, unable to move. West to the interstate. East to the tall dark building with a man bleeding to death inside.

So help her, she couldn't leave him to the worms. Not him, of all people. The sadness, heat, and depth in his eyes deserved life. Deserved happiness. She'd pulled the shot as far right as she could and still hit him. But the building had been deserted. That made her entrance and escape easier. It would make his dying all the more probable.

If he died, he couldn't plaster her face on the Most Wanted list.

Rubber burned onto the parking garage floor as she turned right—back to the scene of the crime.

Chapter Six

"Home at last," Oliver yawned from the back row of the Tahoe.

"You live in the parking garage? Ah, it explains your perma-stench," Hunter prodded from the middle.

From the rearview mirror Khani Slaughter watched Oli whack Hunter's yoke. Curses and laughter filled the vehicle and rocked it on its wheels. She smiled in spite of the hour and the number of hours strung together she'd been awake. By now it crept toward the fifty mark.

"All right, ladies," Tyler's voice rumbled from the passenger seat, "let's thank our LTC for getting our sorry asses back in one piece."

"Ever grateful, Lieutenant Commander," Hunter said, tightening his hold on Oliver's throat.

She slid the SUV into the parking space, shifted to park, and turned to regard the overgrown children in the back seat.

Oli—still restrained, but making headway with a twisting grip on Hunter's ear—winked and flashed a wide grin. "Thanks, LTC."

"Get your gear and get out of my sight. I'm tired of staring at your ugly mugs," she ordered.

"Yes, ma'am's" rained all around and they— some of the most ruggedly beautiful and extremely capable men of her elite Base Branch team—hustled out of the Tahoe.

Tyler opened his door, but turned and offered his hand across the console. "An honor, Lieutenant Commander."

"My duty and pleasure to return you to your misfit lives." Khani accepted the large hand with her equally firm grip, shook, and released his hand. Only, her subordinate's fingers remained wrapped around her slight hand, detaining her with gentle pressure. "Release my hand or lose yours, Tyler."

Her English accent thickened along with her anger. She'd crossed an ocean to get away from this kind of puppy-love shit, and she wasn't about to move again. Last time it had been her bad judgment, and the puppy in question. Now she was older, wiser, and a hell of a lot meaner.

"Sorry, ma'am. I just—"

"Get your gear and go home." A little more loudly she added, "It's been a long few days for us all. Right, guys?"

"Yes, ma'am," Oli and Hunter called from the back hatch.

The men scattered to their respective vehicles, but Khani sat staring ahead. The level sat full of Base Branch transportation. Commercial grade utility vehicles. Police cars. An ambulance. A hearse. Beater cars. Fancy cars. Blacked-out SUV's like this one they'd had at the airfield at the edge of the county. You never knew what you'd need to complete a mission.

Khani dragged her sorry arse from the seat, collected her gear, and trudged halfway up the ramp to her dark-grey Benz. The sight of the prowling little car eased the weight of her load and her bone-deep weariness. It was just like the one she'd had back home. Sleek. Fast. Ticketed?

"What the hell?"

A rectangular piece of paper lay pinched between the clean windshield and wiper blade. The parking level wasn't impenetrable, but it was blocked by a thick lift gate, a pass code, and spikes. Automatically on alert, Khani's gaze swung left and right. She catalogued the classic Chevy in the space to the right of hers—Tucker's truck—the empty space to the left—Rhonda's spot. Nothing stirred in the otherwise deserted section.

She dropped her gear and herself to the ground looking for trip wires, bombs, or boogiemen, but found none. Maybe it was no more than a note placed there by a member of her team. Tyler. If the paper pimped that man's signature, his next mission impossible would be cleaning the locker-room johns for the next six months.

On her feet with a hop, Khani neared. Still watchful, she plucked the small sheet from the car and read.

Your commander is shot and bleeding out in the interrogation room with Carlos Ruez. Help him. If he lives, make certain Carlos believes he is dead.

Hurry!

Whether from her grogginess or the shock of the note's content, she read it again. And once again, she looked around but saw no one. Adrenaline rushed her veins like football fans storming a World Cup field. With the click of a button she popped the trunk and placed the note deep in back for analysis. Next she slung the duffle. It clattered and the car's chassis gave under its bulk. She screamed the zipper open on the bag.

Over her black T-shirt she strapped her vest. She slung the M4 over her head and right arm. Sidearm in holster, she slammed the trunk and took off for the stairs. Khani beat them into submission with her powerful strides. One flight up, a large metal door blocked the way. To the right a silver keypad built into the wall. She tapped off the code, distinct to each member of the Base Branch, opened the door, and then threw herself through it.

Down the sight of the assault rifle she cleared the entrance foyer. Elevators. Main entrance. Stairwell. Not much to behold. She sidled up to the hazy glass double doors, hating the exposure, also knowing no way around it. Millimeter by millimeter the door opened under her slow, steady force. Using one eye, the dull, drab corridor came into focus. Walls. Glass. But no bodies. Alive or dead.

She flung the heavy thing wide and rushed across the hallway to the corridor to Tucker's office. No bullets bit her rump and no one moved to gain better ground on her. All good there. Five silent, hungry strides brought her to his door. Like this was any normal day she knocked twice. "Commander Tucker?"

Silence. From inside. From all around. Nothing moved.

Khani shoved the door wide with her hip and confronted an empty room with the tip of her M4. The chair sat far back toward the wall. Above it hung a dull silver vent grating. Her insides—not prone to drama—danced about as though they'd never seen battle. And they hadn't...not on their home turf.

Khani bolted down the hallway, into the main corridor, and hooked a right at the prisoner's wing. All the while she scanned the offices she blurred past, the conference and break rooms. All sat vacant. She skidded to a halt at the last chamber. Her fingers slammed in the access code, slipped as the sweat and nerves got the best of her, and she was forced to clear and reenter the digits.

She inhaled one long, fortifying breath and opened the door.

Or, at least, she tried to open the door. The damn thing only gave an inch. In that inch a streak of wet blood seven inches wide and nearly five feet long sliced across the floor, as though a body had been dragged. Khani heaved again, but only gained two inches. One of Tucker's wingtips showed in the crack, along with the end of a pant leg. She ground her boots into the concrete and shoved with every honed muscle she possessed, knowing that the commander's body blocked his own rescue.

A chuckle started and grew into a cackle. She stopped and drew her pistol, but the noise didn't change position to hide or jump at her. The vest added width to her chest, not allowing her access. So, smart or not, she shucked it and the rifle before slipping through the crack.

Carlos Ruez sat chained with his balding head glistening under a layer of sweat. The cackle grew louder. "You see what happens...when your great leader...messes with me."

Khani cleared the two steps to Ruez and slammed her pistol against the side of his head. The laugh still rang in her ears, and when she saw Tucker's prone frame laid out on the concrete, it roared. But the bastard no longer made the noise. Her father did, in the cold recesses of her mind.

"Tucker, it's Slaughter. If you can hear me, say something." She slid on her knees to Tucker's big shoulders. Gun holstered, she went straight to the carotid. She repositioned her hand. Pressed harder. And finally found a pulse. Weak, but there.

She sat on her heels and looked him over. Blood soaked his lower back and pooled around his torso. The exit wound blew a nice hole in his shirt. She would hate to see what it had done to his flesh, but she'd have to. Looking left, she followed the track of red twenty feet to the far corner. Every two feet the line of blood-covered forearms and smeared handprints showed Tucker's fight to save himself.

Now it was her turn to fight for him.

One hand on the shoulder, another on his hip, she pulled. He rolled like a rag toy, slack and life-less. But there was life left in this bloke.

"Tucker, if you can hear me, I need your help. Just a little, all right?" She moved as she spoke, standing over him at the tops of his shoulders and securing her grip in the hollows of his armpits. "I'm going to lift your big arse. If you can hear me at all, when I get you up, lock your legs for as long as you can."

His lids fluttered. "Yep," came dulcet between his dry lips.

"Great job, Commander. Let's get you out of here."

Khani hefted him to a sitting position. A groan rumbled beneath her hands, the most reas-suring sign. Pain equaled life. She hugged him close, locked the tips of her fingers around his chest, and drove her legs and all the weight they held toward the sky. "Lock 'em," she grunted.

Bracing his back with her body, she grabbed his right wrist with her left hand, and spun around in front of him—like they twirled on the dance floor of a honkey-tonk, as Tucker had called it. She crouched, shouldered his right thigh with her right arm, wrapped his left over her other shoulder, and bore his body mass in a fireman's carry. Her legs shook under his weight, but held firm. She'd never been so happy to be a member of the 300 Club in squat max.

"All good, sir. Here we go."

"Slaughter," he whispered, his head lolling beneath her pit.

"Yes, sir."

The door was a bitch and a half, but she made it down the maze of hallways at a swift walk, leaving her vest and rifle by the interrogation room and hoping like hell she didn't need them. Khani leaned their backs against the double doors and eased through them without a problem. She opted for the elevator to the lower parking garage with all the Base Branch vehicles.

With another tap of her ten-digit code, she tugged the keys for the ambulance from the box and prayed her quivering legs would hold out long enough to get him inside the thing.

"You still with me, Tucker?" She gritted the question in an effort to turn her mind outward, where it needed to be.

Nothing.

Thankful it was close to the door she veered right for five more grueling steps, unlocked the back doors, and opened them wide.

"Damn it." She panted at the nearly two-foot step up.

A growl breached her clenched teeth as she boosted them through the door and over to the gurney. The judges would've given her a three on dismount. One of his arms and one of his legs hung off the edge, while she landed atop him in a knotted heap. With a wiggle and shove she righted them.

The interior light illuminated his pale complexion. She clapped and spoke louder than her norm—unless she was pissed, and, now that she thought about it, she was bloody pissed. "Tucker! What the hell happened?"

While she hoped for a response, but didn't expect one, she extended the IV rod and combed the drawers and bins for the supplies she needed.

"Commander, I'm putting in an IV drip, and then I'm going to wrap your wound to stem the bleeding."

Khani did as she said, glancing every few minutes at the clock that seemed to speed with her growing fear that she'd be too late. It might be far too easy to convince Carlos Ruez that Commander Tucker had died, because the Reaper hovered just over her shoulder, waiting for him.

She fished her phone from a pocket only to have the thing slip from between her fingers and slide across the floor. For the first time in a long while she looked at her hands and found them slick with blood.

"Tucker, who shot you? Why did they shoot you? Is everyone in danger?"

While rattling off the questions, she soiled a towel wiping his blood from her hands and then snagged her phone from the floor and cleaned it also.

"No." His eyes remained closed and his voice, a nearly imperceptible rasp, hardly penetrated her eardrum.

"No, not everyone is in danger?" she asked, while depressing the speed dial for the Base Branch doctor.

"No, she didn't...want...to shoot."

"Who?" Khani leaned so close she could feel the waft of his shallow breaths on her cheek.

"Don't...kill her...or Carlos."

"Don't kill who?"

"Hello?" On the speakerphone, Doctor Williamson answered.

"Operative: Lima. Echo. Oscar. Papa. Alpha. Romeo. Delta. One. Nine. Nine. Four."

"How may I be of assistance, Lieutenant Commander?"

"I need a miracle, doc."

Chapter Seven

The earth must have shifted a few million miles toward the sun during the night. Beams of light blazed through the tiny slits Vail managed to pry between his eyelids. They pierced through his cornea and lodged in his brain, calling forth tears. Moisture welled and overflowed hot on his cheek. The harder he tried to blink them away the more clouds gathered. He lifted a hand to wipe the bleariness away, but lost the will to move them somewhere between one and two inches from the scratchy cotton beneath his fingers.

For a while he closed his heavy lids, content with the easy rock of the sea, though he inherently knew he wasn't in water. He'd be at home in the water. Here, wherever here was, was far away from home and far too close to a memory. Sorrow, tight and unyielding, gripped his chest, weighting him, sinking him below the nonexistent surface.

Ellie.

I'm sorry.

Ellie.

Forgive me.

All at once the pain ripped at his middle, a hungry wolf making a meal of him. His eyes shot wide. A wash of white assaulted along with the multiplying pack. White walls. White curtain. A four-

strip rectangular fixture with blinding white flores-
cent bulbs.

"Welcome to the land of the living," a voice
came from across the gigantic room.

Vail gave gravity his head, letting it loll to the
left, away from a large window white with the fury
of day. Not such a big room and not so far away.
His lieutenant commander, Khani Slaughter, sat
two feet away, long limbs knotted in the confines of
a ridged recliner. The high-backed monstrosity
looked more like a plastic box. Its footrest, wedged
only a few inches from the frame, provided rest for
nothing at all.

"Is that what this is?"

"Yep. As good as it gets." Her mouth kicked
into a half smile.

He blinked, struggling to pull color into focus.
Khani's lips were always the craziest hue of
orangish-red he'd ever seen, her eyes usually an
electric shade of green or blue to really set her face
alight. But his abused lenses refused to see color
on her porcelain skin.

"Well damn," he muttered.

She unfolded her legs and arms and he found
color—albeit a hideous one—in the mint green of
the scrubs she wore. His eyes worked okay. She
just didn't wear any make-up. He blinked again,
locking his gaze on the tiny, ultra-white scars that
tarnished her otherwise impeccable complexion.

"What happened?" he begged.

"Doc Williamson called it a class III hemor-
rhage."

Quite the evasion. He smiled and his skin
seemed too tight for his face.

"And you smile about almost bleeding to
death. Men, I'll never understand you. Not ever."

"I meant, what happened to you? Not me," he swallowed against the raw dryness of his throat. "And men are easy. Eat. Sex. Sleep. How simple is that? Women..." His mind conjured Carmen Ruez. Her big, sad eyes. The small, round barrel of her gun. "Y'all are complicated. To put it mildly."

Khani crossed her arms and narrowed her gray gaze. "You happened to me." Her head kicked to the side. "So, was it your eating, screwing, or sleeping that got you into this predicament? Or are you willing to admit that men are slightly more complicated than you thought?"

"Maybe, slightly, but nowhere near as complicated as women."

The scratch worsened with every syllable he spoke, but too prideful for his own good, he didn't say anything about it. He tried to ignore the rhythmic, stabbing throb in his side as well.

"You stubborn man." She poked the red call button on his hospital bed. In the seconds it took for someone to respond, she glared.

A speaker behind his head crackled. "Yes?" a woman's voice asked.

"This is LTC Slaughter. The commander is awake and could use something for pain and some water, please."

"Yes, ma'am," the nurse said.

"You never tire of that, do you?"

"What?" she asked Tucker.

"Having people ma'am you."

"Not a bit. Is it that obvious?"

"The side of your mouth twitches, like you're holding back a smile."

"I suppose I am. It took a hell of a lot of work to earn that ma'am." She folded her arms and settled back against the plastic. "You came from a military family. Probably heard and said, 'yes ma'am, no ma'am, yes sir, no sir' a thousand times a day. Where I came from...the words were nowhere near as civilized."

Khani's clothes crinkled as she turned toward him. Instinctively he knew that was all she'd say about her past. It was more than she'd said over the last year she'd been working for him.

"I'm wearing these obnoxious clothes and have not an ounce of make-up on my face because I found you face down with a bullet in your gut, hauled you over my shoulders, and lugged you here."

"Thank you," he croaked.

"Stuff it." She waved a hand to shoo his words off. "Just don't ever bleed on me again and we'll call it good."

"Deal." He nodded. "How bad was it?"

"The shot? Not bad. Struck mostly muscle. Did nick your large intestine. Williamson performed surgery practically in the hallway. You were pretty out of it by the time we arrived. The blood loss was the biggest concern. He gave you a transfusion. Do you remember the shooting?"

Again his mind called Carmen into the forefront. Her long tousled hair blanketed her shoulders, corkscrews weaving this way and that. The rage in her eyes directed full-force onto the chained bastard. Then they turned on him, the hatred shifting to pity. For him. For her. And finally, the shot. The air it stole from his lungs. The strength it zapped from his legs. The cold.

"Yeah," he squawked.

"Where the hell is that nurse?" Khani slapped the fringe of her dark bangs from her forehead and shot to her feet. "Good, hold that thought. I'll be right back."

He tried to call her back, but he'd completely run out of everything. Saliva. Energy. Brain power.

***

His eyes opened without melodrama. The same white room, ugly chair, and knotted Khani greeted him. But this time a half-melted cup of ice sat on a tray hovering over the edge of the bed. He stared with a wiggle of fingers. When they obeyed he moved to the wrists, rolling them and stretching his forearms. The things burned as though he'd walked a mile on his hand. And boy, hadn't it seemed that way. It had taken extreme effort to gain only inches in his attempt to reach the door.

All or nothing. Vail reached for the cup, levered the thing over his lap and then to his lips like it were a ninety-pound dumb bell. Sweet relief washed over his stale tongue, down his abused throat. He reached the end too soon. The ice sloshed forward.

He cursed softly, but still Khani jumped, her right hand automatically going for her sidearm. "Go home," he ordered. "You've done enough."

"Answer me one question, and then I'll go," she yawned.

"Ask."

"Last night, you didn't say much, but you said, 'Don't kill her.' So, I'm assuming your shooter was a woman. A highly skilled woman breaks into the Base Branch's US headquarters, places a bullet so the shot won't kill you, escapes undetected, only to turn around and leave a note on my car, telling me to save you, but not let Carlos Ruez know you're alive...why?"

In the minutes leading up to the bullet in his belly and during the trudge across the never-ending floor, he'd thought a lot about the who's, how's, and why's of that night.

"Because Carlos has leverage over her. She attempted to get it back."

"But failed?"

"Yes. He has the one thing she can't live without."

"What?"

"You said one question, Slaughter, and you've surpassed that limit."

"Fair enough. You need some rest almost as much as I do." She stood and grabbed a red plastic bag.

Vail hauled the cup back to the table and set it at the edge. "Do me a favor. Don't let anyone interrogate Carlos until they release me, and have a courier drop his file and all related info this afternoon. Also—"

"Not to be insubordinate, but you're in no position to give orders, Commander."

He hitched a brow, or he tried to. "See, that title says I give the orders."

"I see your sense of humor has returned." She walked to the bed and placed a hand on his forearm. She felt a thousand degrees hotter than him. "You need to stay out of sight and recover. You're looking at four to six weeks here."

"Those words hurt worse than the bullet hole."

"Trust me, I know."

He sighed as much as the burn in his side would allow. "One order then. Have dogs run the building. She had a detonator and said the building was rigged to blow. I don't know if the threat is real, but check anyway."

"I'll get it done before I go home."

"Well, looks like you have a Base Branch to run, LTC. Just keep me in the loop on this."

"You know I will." She patted his arm, slipped behind the curtain, and then he heard the latch catch on the door.

Six goddamned weeks. They'd be lucky if he relaxed at all. His brain certainly wouldn't comply. Not even to his own directives. He appreciated Khani's help. Was only alive because of it. But now he wanted to be alone with his thoughts. Like newbies fresh out of the recruiting office, they wouldn't fall into an orderly line. One second he whirled about memories best left covered in dust. The next he envisioned beating Carlos Ruez to death with his fists. More than anything though, Carmen consumed his thoughts like no other woman had. Not since Ellie.

Two women had never been created more opposite. Ellie had been light in every way. Soft, slight curves topped with short, straight hair that appeared nearly white in its blondness. She was the party life threw in celebration of all things pure and lovely, always quick with a smile and those brilliant blue eyes. Ready with a song or dance to brighten even the dreariest times.

Carmen was the funeral of life's let-downs, the embodiment of all things that could have been, but never would be. Her long black spirals and eyes a deep, swirling torrent of darkness sucked him in, whirled him about, and refused to let him catch a breath. The ever-present sneers and scowls warded off the barest inclination of a red-blooded man, but her ample contours raised even the most unlikely flags. And the proof tented his hospital issue gown.

Chapter Eight

"I don't know how the hell I let you talk me into this in the first place. I bloody well hate the cold and we both get plenty enough adventure with our jobs."

"This isn't about adventure, Zeke. It's about slowing down, living off the land, becoming a part of nature," Khani cajoled, craning her neck toward the hands-free microphone, as if those few inches would help her case. An express delivery truck wedged between her Mercedes and the cab she'd been tailing for four miserable miles like it were no bigger than a Vespa. "Fuck you too, bastard."

"Well, hell, sister. You're abandoning me on a vacation I didn't want in the first place. You don't have to cuss me too."

"Oh, shut up. You know I wasn't talking about you."

"Ah, hoped not, but you never know."

"I haven't cursed you since the day you took that stupid job of yours and left me in your dust halfway across the world," she reminded.

"Did it ever occur to you that I moved to get away from you?"

"No."

"Figures."

"I still don't know why you wouldn't take the job I offered. It pays well, you'd love the work, but it's more than that. You'd be doing good. For the good guys."

"I'm doing good, Khani."

The growl in his voice should have warned her off this beaten path, but she plowed ahead anyway. "For private sector asshats who only worry about lining their pockets, not for honor or duty."

"Before you're left talking to a vacant line, why don't you explain to me again the reason you're abandoning me, your only flesh and blood worth a damn, to traipse around a barren wasteland, get frostbitten, and die at the mouths of hungry wolves *all by myself.*"

"Even as a child you were dramatic. Not much has changed, has it?" But neither of them commented on her ill-chosen words. Their lives were night and day to what they'd been. Though they each saw unimaginable things and did unimaginable things in their work, these days were the light, the good.

"My superior was gunned down in our secure facility. It's my duty to take over his post until his return, but it's my desire to catch whoever did it and bury them under the slab."

"So, he will return?"

"Yeah. It'll take a while, but he won't even let a gut shot slow him down for long."

"Bet that hurt."

"You should know." She sang the words.

"Lower obliques aren't considered the gut, thank you."

Damn she missed him and all his smart-ass ways. She weaved around the truck, sped in front of a mini-van, and made the exit to the private hospital. "I am very sorry to have to cancel. I know he'll want to take over in two weeks. Hell's bells, he wants to take over now, but he won't be ready by the time our flight leaves."

"Let's reschedule," Zeke suggested.

"And when exactly are you going to have leave again? Next year?"

"So? What good will it do to stare at my toes as they fall off? It'd be much more fun to watch yours fall off instead."

"You're sick."

"Your fault."

"Not."

"You raised me. You've only yourself to blame."

"Don't I know it. I love you wider than the river and taller than the trees."

"I love you more, you sappy sucker." His rumbling laugh filled the line.

"What?"

"If only your underlings could hear their fearless leader."

"Goodbye, Zeke. Call me when you get back. I want to hear all about it."

"Only if I can move my blue lips."

"Zeke," she admonished.

"I will. I will. Later, sis."

The line clicked and quiet filled the car. They'd planned the trip while he'd been recovering from the bullet wound he'd sustained only three weeks after moving across the world and taking a job as a glorified gun for hire. She hated more than anything to miss the trip. She hated it more than she hated the number of times in a day her mind drifted to thoughts and images of the other major reason she'd left England.

Khani parked on the third level of the garage and made her way to the bank of elevators. Through the thick wedges of concrete pillars and walls, the sun shifted toward the horizon, calling all the orange and red hues to the sky. She slung the large purse over her shoulder and pressed the button for the sixth floor. Only five o'clock and she'd already put in thirteen hours at headquarters.

She'd spent the first five on the phone answering questions from the higher ups, the next two answering questions from the agents and setting them to task collecting evidence. The next had been spent on paperwork. Day one in the full-on role of commander and she already saw one of the other reasons she'd transferred from commander of the Base Branch's London headquarters. She despised paper work, pandering to men who had no idea the types of things they accomplished on a daily basis. That, and she loved the thrill of down and dirty missions.

After reaching the sixth floor, just to be sure no one followed her, she took the stairs up two more flights to Commander Tucker's room. She knocked on the heavy wooden door and waited. And waited. With a hand on the door, she gave him to the count of ten to call out before she barreled in, fanny out or not.

"One moment," a male voice not belonging to Tucker hollered.

Two minutes later a burly man in scrubs opened the door, nodded, and turned down the hallway. Tentatively, she eased the door open. Tucker's feet tented a thick layer of covers. Instead of lying flat on his back as he had yesterday and the night before, he sat upright with pillows wedged on either side of his torso.

"Your lover? I mean, I could have given you two a few more minutes for wrap up."

His head shook, the stubble from the previous day gone and in its place a sharp, smooth jaw. "I wish. That's much less embarrassing than the real reason Damien and I have gotten close today. Can't even take a piss by myself."

She breathed to speak, but he continued on his little tirade.

"You know, I was held captive for two weeks by Cambodian rebels. I tolerated that better."

"It was them holding you down. Not your own body."

He just blew a breath between his lips.

"On the bright side, you don't look like you're knocking on the pearly gates begging for entrance anymore."

"There's that." He gestured to the most uncomfortable chair in the world. "Take a seat in the ugliest chair in the world?"

"Most uncomfortable, if you ask me. I've seen more horrid than this."

"I'm amazed you still have your sight."

She sat on the edge of the chair and folded her legs toward him. Her pant leg stuck on the back of her Tamara Mellon spiked heel. With a wiggle of her foot the suit's material smoothed. "Are you scared of death?" She didn't know where the question had come from. It was just there and out before she could think it through.

"No."

"What are you scared of?"

He sat quietly for a long time. The minutes ticked by on the large digital clock across the room. Intent wedged the center of his brow. "Life."

She gave a pitiful attempt at a smile. "Me too. It seems a common theme among us covert types."

Her crooked lips fell into a flat line and his followed suit. "Why do you think that is, Commander?"

His wide shoulders shrugged and a gritted groan slipped through his teeth. His breathing came harshly for a four count. "Why so many questions?"

"Figured you might know the answers."

"Older and wiser, huh?"

"Something like that."

"I'll let you know when I figure it out." His watchful eyes shifted from her face to her oversized purse. "Are you going to give me that file or just torment me with it?"

"You've suffered enough." Khani reached into the bag, extracted the hefty file on Carlos Ruez, and handed it to Tucker.

"Thank you."

"Do you have anyone you want me to call? They'll release you in a few days and it might be a good idea to have someone around."

"I think I'd rather bleed out on my bathroom floor than let my mother hover over me for a few weeks and my dad carry on about how I should've taken charge of the situation and not gotten shot in the first place."

She opened her mouth to speak, but he stopped her with a hand.

"And don't think for a second you're going to come waste your time watching me toddle around. I have a cleaning lady and a grocer. So, I won't starve or sit in squalor. And if I happen to rip my stitches open, I'll call the doc. And if I can't make it to the phone, the cleaning lady will find me before the stench gets too bad."

"How often does she come?"

"Twice a week."

"Seriously? It's just you in the place, right?"

"My parents are both military. What can I say? They messed me up."

"Whose parents didn't?"

"Yet another question I can't answer."

"I'll give you one you can...probably. Why not take her out between your office and interrogation room?"

"She held a pressure release detonator and kept me far enough away I couldn't close the distance without risking the lives of the people in the building." He paused as though to add more, but didn't.

"You said you didn't think the bomb threat was real. At what point did you know there wasn't a charge in that entire building?"

"The dogs didn't find anything?"

"Nope."

He pursed his lips. "I knew when she pulled the trigger. She didn't want to hurt anyone. She said it, but her actions said it more clearly."

"But she shot you."

"Not because she wanted to."

"Ruez's leverage?"

"Yep."

"And then she left the note."

He nodded.

She stood. "Look, know that if you need anything, I'm here. And try not to obsess over this." Purse slung over her shoulder, she tapped the file laid out on his knees. She headed for the door.

Vail cleared his throat and she paused with a hand on the crisp knob. "It's because we can't unsee the things we've seen, unknow the things we know. We're scared of what life could give us to lose."

Chapter Nine

Three weeks, two days, nine hours, thirty-four minutes, eleven seconds, and Vail could not take one more hour of lying low. The sterile white of his building's stairwell threatened to rupture every vessel in his eyes. Heaves of stagnant air inside the echoing column of metal and concrete shaved another year off his life. Gunshot wound or not, he hadn't been able to sleep past 0445 since he'd enlisted. And here he was, up before the sun. Not that he'd seen it lately.

He kicked his knees high on the fifth floor, refusing himself the break he'd taken yesterday on the last of three sets of the entire staircase. As workouts went, it wasn't much. But it was progress. It had taken a week before he could walk the ten flights to his condo. Another week to do it without expecting his lower half to completely separate from his top half. And it beat the hell out of staring at the wall all day.

Sweat tickled his forehead and dripped from his chin on to his sopping shirt. The cold refused to leave no matter how hard he pushed or how many layers he added. The chill of death clung, reminding him of that night. As if the darkness of his persistently drawn curtains and agent detail at the front and rear entrances of his building—both Commander Slaughter's doing—weren't enough to do the trick. That combined with his wayward subconscious and it was all he thought about.

Right. She's all you think about.

True as it was, he couldn't yet admit it.

His mending muscles burned from the abuse. A cramp stitched his right side from overcompensating for his weak side. One more flight and he'd be home.

Home.

Vail laughed at the notion, but it cost core strength he lacked. Especially after fifty toes-to-bar, two miles on the treadmill, seventeen-hundred meters in the pool, and then the stairs. His left hand shot out to the cold metal railing. The sweat-slicked fingers didn't do much to help. He met the concrete with his palms, shins, and knees. He sprawled to the side and then rolled to his back. Slowly the rise and fall of his dark grey T-shirt reached a functional rate. He braced one hand on the rail—after wiping it on his athletic shorts—and the other on the stair close to his rear. He'd learned quickly it hurt less to get vertical this way.

Upright, he used the rail and tugged himself up the remaining steps. Across the hall and down two from the stairwell. The gray front of his door looked like the others. The only difference nestled above the door's knob. He punched in the code to his self-installed security system and shoved his way inside the cave.

Normally, unobscured windows lined the space, framing out the living room, office, and two bedrooms with the radiance of the sun. Normally, he ran through the city and hoofed the steps of the various monuments littering the National Mall. Normally, he didn't notice the emptiness of the space he referred to as home. But now the only thing that felt comfortable to him were the pages scattered across the granite of his kitchen counters.

Vail peeled the shirt from his torso, opened the closet off the entryway, and hung the wet thing over the edge of the washing machine. After toeing off the black Mizuno's, his socks, boxer briefs, and shorts, he added them to the clutter. He closed the door, and then he grabbed the small towel he'd set on the foyer table. Draping the cloth over his head, he lumbered to the sink for a glass of water. Or three.

The stacks of paper called to him and, like always, he went. Naked. Sleepy. Confused. Hungry. Horny. Sweaty. Pissed. Time and again he returned to the information he now knew better than his own name and aliases. His persistence—obsession, really—had paid off in the darkest hours of the night.

Twenty years ago the Arellano-Félix Organization had been Mexico's most powerful and feared cartel, controlling Tijuana and its lucrative border crossing with merciless tyranny. Carlos's full name, Carlos Félix-Ruez, revealed his connection to the organization. He was the only son of Ángela Arellano-Félix-Ruez, the world's first female drug lord. Though his mother hadn't been long for the earth it seemed she'd passed the lust for violent authority through her genes.

After Ángela's death her husband took control. Carlos Hersio-Ruez lacked none of the ruthlessness the business required. He did, however, lack the family name to bear the weight of leadership. The remaining Arellano-Félix brothers, Ángela's brothers, wrestled her husband for control. The organization cracked, allowing the US government to capture some of its top tier leaders and the Sinaloa Cartel to gain footholds in the foundation of their rival. Little by little, the Sinaloa overwhelmed

the AFO, took control of Tijuana, and set the remaining members of the once prestigiously infa-
mous family scurrying to the corners of the country.

Carmen's entire family was remnant of cartel
history. Carmen, with her sad eyes and surprising
knack for stealth, torture, and precise aim. She'd
placed the bullet just where it needed to go to show
Carlos that Vail was a goner, while simultaneously
doing the least amount of damage and giving him a
fighting chance. Though the rage and regret etched
into her face said she didn't want to kill him, had it
not been for the note she'd left Khani, she would
have sealed his coffin.

How she fit into the puzzle he couldn't yet
tell. Carlos Félix-Ruez aimed for the top office, his
father be damned. He apparently hadn't been satisfied with his rich but powerless life of exile in the
small fishing town of Puerto San Carlos in the
southern Comondú Municipality. Five years ago the
bastard began buying up real estate in Tijuana,
Sonora, Chihuahua, Sinaloa, and Durango. An
alias protected his identity, until Vail had coaxed it
out of him. La Muerte. The name spoke of forebod-
ing. Vail thought about the man, the malice in his
stare, and knew if left to his deeds Carlos would
ratchet the level of death in Mexico's streets. Ruez
had bought enough land, black market weapons,
and people to mount a war.

His agents and contacts had heard the name
La Muerte whispered over dark beers in even darker corners of rowdy cantinas. And though he'd suspected The Death to be one arm of a cartel falling
away to become its own entity, as so often they did,
it was good to know exactly who they were dealing
with.

Three and a half weeks ago Vail unbound the file and separated the last five years of documentation into piles. Five in all lay in their respective heaps. Real estate. Known associates. Weapons. Income. A cabin in the wilderness of Kentucky.

The cabin stack had started as a single sheet. A buyer's agreement between two men—Hank Higgins—an old guy being placed in an assisted living facility closer to his children in Lexington—and Charlie Ranger—a false front. The Base Branch system had flagged the transition because its routing number matched the routing number to another of Ruez's aliases. Nothing about the cabin had fit into the equation. Not until Carmen dropped through his ceiling and started making demands.

If you needed to hide someone and had a sister willing to rip Mexico from its bedrock and toss it across the ocean to find that person, what better place to hide the person than somewhere she'd never think to look?

Carlos had been stopped in Tennessee on a simple traffic violation. The officer had hauled him in after running the license of one Charlie Ranger, which showed a federal warrant for his arrest. Those two pieces had been enough for Vail to move, but accustomed to checking and rechecking facts for his teams, he dug deeper.

Yesterday's search yielded several other properties the good Charlie Ranger purchased in the States. Houses in San Diego, Tucson, and El Paso tipped the scale from likely to definite in Vail's mind. Carlos Ruez had been planning something big. And from the way he ran his mouth before Carmen had left—before ripping a hole in his belly and screwing with his mind—he'd guess the crazy son of a bitch still hoped to carry it out. It made sense. He'd given them vital information, which allowed the Base Branch to take out several key Sinaloa facilities. And he bet the information dump had been another strategic move on Carlos's part.

Vail placed the glass in the dishwasher and then pulled the topographical map of Kentucky and the cabin plans from the stack. Stiff after being still for only a couple of minutes, he shuffled around the high bar—the only thing that separated the kitchen from the living room, and dining room for that matter—past the fancy sofa and chairs with their accent pillows as the decorator had called them, and stopped at the eight-top dining table he'd never used. Well, he used it. Just not for its intended purpose. Most often he walked around it to the bank of three floor-to-ceiling windows it sat near and propped on the top while he drank his coffee and watched the sun bring the city into focus. This morning it held his gear.

Guns, knives, an oversized backpack, first aid supplies, boots, a wool blanket, and various camping tools lay scattered across the smooth wood top. Though he didn't dare put more on the table, save for the two sheets of paper. The narrow metal legs likely couldn't hold much more. Would the thing hold Carmen with his weight on top and the power of his body thrusting inside her?

He tossed the pages onto the table, ignoring his burgeoning erection. But really, what guy could look away from his Johnson when it saluted? Not him. He shook his head at the damn fool, who obviously had no sense of self-preservation. The gnarled red skin at his middle caught his eye. Slowly the sex-starved appendage followed logic and, despite the cold, hung low and long between his legs.

Vail ran his hand over the puckered skin, appreciating that it hadn't harbored an infection. Unlike two of the five scars scattering his torso. If this shot had been one foot in the grave, those had been body in, lid shut, but for some ridiculous reason the dirt hadn't piled on top. So, like an idiot set on provoking his own demise, he headed to his bedroom to finish packing, shower, and drive to Kentucky.

* * *

It shamed Vail that his own world-class, elite operatives were so easily given the slip. Then again, he went to great lengths to keep the sleek Audi he'd driven out the back gate and right past the agent a secret. They also worked at a disadvantage since they were on alert for people trying to break into the building, not him trying to escape. Add to the fact that no one knew he lived here in the first place and they all thought he was dead, they worked at an extreme disadvantage.

Glasses and a hat helped conceal his face, but everyone knew his obnoxious truck by sight and sound. The thing gave him away a mile or more down the road with its rumbling engine. Its burnt red paint made it pretty hard to miss too. If training didn't keep his hand eye coordination on point, parking that thing on a busy street without using the cars around him as speed bumps did. It fit in the city about as well as a straw of buckwheat between the First Lady's lips. He loved the damn thing and would drive it until the day he died. Judging by the way things were going, that could be any day now.

The low-slung S5 whispered through the fallen leaves at the roadside and hugged the curves as asphalt hooked through the foothills nearly five hundred miles from his safety detail. He didn't understand why Khani put them on him in the first place. Neither of them expected Carmen to come finish the job, not that Khani knew it was Carmen

Félix-Ruez who'd shot him. She still dug for her
own answers and prodded him for information
nearly every day, not that she expected to gain anything from him. Yet, if the roles were reversed he'd
take the same precautions and hunt for answers
just as doggedly.

East of Morehead, Vail turned south into
Daniel Boone National Forest. The road dipped between a valley of matchstick trees. Their thick,
supple vegetation had long since changed from
green to eye-popping yellows and reds, and covered
the ground in a brittle brown blanket. At the top of
a low ridge the sparse winter foliage allowed him to
see the clear lake to his right. The cabin sat only a
mile from the expansive reservoir near the end of
one of its near stagnant tentacles.

Vail hooked left at the next two-lane highway
and passed the gravel road that eventually forked
and turned to a narrow dirt path leading to Carlos's
newest piece of real estate. With no obvious nooks
or side trails to hide his shiny black car where it
wouldn't be spotted a mile away, he continued on
toward a convenience store he'd spotted on the
satellite feed he studied late last night.

He'd been ready to leave the city before dawn,
but had waited until the commuters trickled out of
his building so he wouldn't draw unwanted attention. It put him arriving a little later than he'd like
with the sun already yawning at the horizon. The
late February weather threatened snow, filling the
air with hazy gray clouds and dimming the daylight
that much more.

Rounding one more bend, a clearing opened
in the trees. Light stone gravel that complemented
the muted sky filled the lot, save for a slab of neat
concrete beneath the building's awning. Where
once gasoline pumps sat, a chunk of raised cement

anchored two metal support posts, more rust than white paint coating the surface. A wall of surprisingly clear glass revealed what looked to be an office. Less convenience and more service station, the place hosted two bays with large glass-front doors buttoned low.

By the time Vail reached the storefront, parked, and straightened from the car, a young man—boy, really—stood, his face nearly smashed against the window, gawking. His side hurt less each day and didn't cause him pain after sitting for so many hours in a row, but tightness held him stiff as a two-by-four. With the kid's eyes on him he didn't try to work out the rigidity. He just tried not to look like a toy soldier when he walked.

"Can I help you?" the boy—John, by the name embroidered on his coveralls—asked. His light blue eyes never left the sports car. Puffs of steam floated from his gaping mouth and his greasy hand shoved at the spiky blond hair above his forehead.

"You have an open bay. I'd like to rent it for a couple of nights. A thousand bucks up front and another thousand if it's here when I get back."

That swiveled the kid's head. His gaze rose to Vail's. "Two grand? Is something wrong with it? Cause we can fix it. We may seem backwoods, and we are, but I've got a computer for diagnostics. I guarantee I could have her purring in no time a'tal'." His hand left his hair and burrowed into his pocket. A shiver wracked his lanky frame.

"I'm headed into the woods and want to keep her out of the weather."

"Oh, uh...sure. My gramps won't mind. It's his place. But...I know we wouldn't make that much in a week with both bays open. Business just isn't that steady. These days everybody's drivin' a new car." He rocked on his heels and then hopped, like only a rubber-jointed kid could, toward the building. "I'll lift the door and you can pull'er on in."

"No you won't," a worn, yet strong, voice came from the far side of the building.

The kid stalled mid-step and squinted at the old man barreling around the corner with a tire iron clenched in his sun-leathered grip. "But Grandpa, this guy said—"

"Get inside and lock the door, John," his grandfather interrupted.

A scowl as deep as the San Andreas trenched the man's brow. His shoulders, wide enough to have done considerable damage in his prime, swayed in Vail's direction. With the metal weapon, he expected the guy could still bring the hurt to a vast majority of the population. White hair shorn in a military issue high-and-tight gave him an air of authority.

John squeaked out a confounded, "But..." while he hustled to the door.

"We don't need your tainted money. Now, take your car and go."

Vail relaxed his stance as much as his body would allow, in an effort to appear non-threatening. As a muscled guy of six-three he'd never succeeded blending in out in the open. "I don't mean to offend you. I'd be paying for a service. Just like any other customer."

"Kids these days can't see danger when it's staring them in the face. He's smart in every other respect, but I bet my grandson would pet a cobra, if it bobbed its head in front of him. Society's made them all soft. But I know a threat when I see one. We want no part of what you and your friends are up to."

"My friends?" Vail asked.

"I may be old, but I'm not stupid. Nobody in their right mind would set out to camp in the face of a snow storm. The only place in three square miles of here is Hank Higgin's old place. Wads o' cash and flashy cars have no cause in these woods. Damn you dealers. If y'all are cookin' meth up at Hig's old place, I don't want to know. So long as you stay off my property and away from my family. We don't want any trouble. But, if you're lookin' for it, I'll give it to you."

"Oh, I'm looking for trouble. But not from you, sir."

The man cocked his head and his murky blue eyes studied Vail from top to bottom. He let the iron hang by his side. "You're not a cop."

"No, sir."

"Could be a fed. I'm betting you're ex-military, though I've never seen a jarhead make out quite so well."

"No jars here, leatherneck. I earned my trident every day. Still do, in a different way."

"You a merc?"

"No. We'll say I'm sanctioned and leave it at that."

"You here to take out the trash?"

"I am."

"There's at least six of 'em."

"How many cars did you see?"

"Two. Three got outta' one car. Two outta' the second, but the way their eyes kept darting back to the thing, I suspect there was more in there."

"You have people meeting you, huh?"

"No, sir."

"Damn. I mean, SEALS are good, but not invincible."

"I'll manage."

The old man chewed his cheek. His gaze narrowed. "Somethin' tells me you will." He waved his grandson from the building. The kid's hand hadn't left the lock and his gaze had been riveted the entire time, bouncing between him and his grandfather. John flipped the lock and took a hesitant step out. "Raise the door. Seems Mr...."

"Tucker," Vail supplied.

"Mr. Tucker isn't quite what I thought he was."

"Yes, sir." The kid moved to do as the man asked, but the pep of his earlier steps had disappeared.

"Bring your car in and I'll tell you what I know about Hig's place. It's a lot. We've been friends since the day we were born."

"I'm sorry he had to go into a home."

"Age." The man chased Vail's words away with a swat of his hand. "No one escapes it, until they die."

* * *

Vail nodded to Gunnery Sergeant John Batten and his grandson and then headed across the street for the overgrown path the sergeant took to Hig's house as a young boy. As promised, in the time he'd spent reminiscing about the good ole' days and talking details, the temperature had dropped a good ten degrees, settling it between uncomfortable and freeze-your-nuts solid, depending on the wind. The brisk pace he set and the rising grade of the passage heated him enough he didn't worry with gloves. His T-shirt, wool sweater, and light jacket were adequate until he bedded down for the night.

He shivered at the thought of propping against a half-frozen tree for even a minute. Cold had never bothered him. Not one bit. He was a

SEAL for fuck's sake. On assignment he'd taken a polar bear plunge in Russia. In training he'd treaded water for more than twelve hours in the middle of the Atlantic during the dead of winter. But after lying on the concrete in a pool of his own blood, the chill clung like it had seeped into his marrow and turned the stuff to ice.

The stiffness melted away, replaced by the sure tingle of a thousand needle pricks. At least the burning had faded. An ache still lingered, dull and unobtrusive, but always there. He walked on the edge of the trail instead of weaving through the crop of saplings flourishing in the sergeant's absence.

Never mind the trees didn't have leaves on their branches, the width of their trunks and spread of their limbs blocked out what little sunlight made it through the cloud. The longer he walked the less and less light peeked through the forest. The thinner the light, the thinner his blood apparently. Blue tinted the well of his fingernails and his lips had taken to quivering twenty minutes back.

Was this it? What losing a step looked like? How it felt to see everything you've spent your life working to achieve slip from your grasp? Sure, he wasn't in the field anymore. Not much. But was this the beginning of the slow and steady decline to doomsday? If the physical faltered, how soon before the mental? Jesus, he was only forty-fucking-two. But that was only eighteen years till sixty, and then what? Covert. High-stakes. Life-or-death. That's what he knew. He didn't know how to do life. Not anymore.

This weakness stirred an emotion he hadn't tangled with in quite a while. It bubbled at a simmer for a minute, but quickly turned to an all-out boil. The urge to roar and snarl like a feral beast overwhelmed him. Only years and experience kept the rage inside. If he gave in to the baser instincts, he'd alert the mob to his recon.

After a while Vail arrived at "the kicker," as the old man had called it. "You'll know it when you see it," he'd said.

Yeah, no kidding.

A thirty-foot wall of sculpted rock protruded from the earth like one day it had gotten ambitious and leaped for the sky. It didn't make it all the way, but it gave commendable, as well as irritating, effort. Vail stepped up to the watercolor wall of tan, grabbed hold with his numb fingers, found a foothold, and poured his anger into the rock.

Damn Carmen. If she hadn't shot him, he wouldn't be here, freezing his sack off and realizing he was closer to the end of his life than he was to the beginning, and that he didn't have much of a life to speak of anyway.

Sweat trickled down his back. Mid-way up perspiration slicked his palms, endangering his grip. Between each hand hold or finger hold, whichever he could find, he rubbed his free hand down the leg of his charcoal-colored cargo pants. It cost him more time and energy. When he reached *fall-and-you-could-die-or-just-lay-incapacitated-until-the-coyotes-or-black-bears-maul-you-to-death* height his grip slipped from the tiny two-finger hollow he'd chosen out of necessity to be able to place his big boots against a wide ridge. As his weight swung with the pendulum of his position, jagged rocks scraped like a combination of sandpaper and knives across his left wrist.

The earth seemed to lunge toward him. No. He lurched toward it.

His chin grazed the rough outcropping and his shoulder tackled like a lineman. He'd been one, once upon a time, and had never hit anything so immovable. Not even Marv, the three-hundred-ten-pound guard of the Blue Ridge Bobcats. Impact forced the air from his lungs, but that he could live through. As long as he could get his muscles to co-operate. He shoved hard, digging into the solid footing he'd found on the previous position and rammed his shoulder even harder against the rock. Vail Tucker, the human plank. It would be funny. One day. If he made it past today.

Every bit of fibrous tissue in his body strained against the awkward arrangement. Molecule by precious molecule, air migrated back into his lungs. He used it to fuel his strength. Amazing how he didn't feel his mending wound at all right now. Adrenaline, what an amazing thing.

With great care, Vail wedged the heel of his left palm against the sheer rock below his nearly horizontal position. It wasn't much in the way of security. His blood seeped from the cuts, staining the limestone. It allowed him enough leverage to search for a hold with his right hand.

A drop of sweat plunged to the ground. He couldn't see it or the next few that followed, but he knew that wasn't the only bodily fluid he'd likely leave down there. Finally his fingers found purchase on a jug-sized outcropping. He collected every ounce of bravery he possessed and went for it. In one swift motion his hands joined on the large rough stone and he spread his legs wide, jamming them on either side of the trench.

No way in hell did the old man climb this trail three years ago. If he did, then Vail had zero qualms about getting older. Seven more feet of carefully placed holds saw him to the top. He wanted to slump back and take a rest on his ruck, not so much from physical exertion as mental. But he pressed on, proving he could take it all and ask for more.

Fifteen feet from the sheer drop he'd climbed he ran into the trail again. His gaze followed the path that swung in a thirty-foot arc of smooth-footed dirt that pressed against the edge of the cliff and provided a safe, simple way around the deathtrap of a wall.

"You sorry son of a bitch," Vail whispered. Despite his sure anger at the sneaky old man who'd led him up the side of a cliff, the corner of his mouth quirked.

A quarter mile from the cabin, dusk crept to night. Vail struggled to control his trembling body. The T-shirt he'd worn as a layer of protection from the scratchy wool sopped with sweat from his efforts climbing. Now that his blood had stopped churning and his muscles had quit working overtime, the shirt had become a siphon, draining his skin of any heat with its frozen touch.

Vail took cover behind a wide hardwood trunk. Around him the forest stilled in that lull between the daylight roamers' bedding and the nocturnal critters' rise. The bugs sang a repeating chorus, but he blocked it from his mind. His attention focused on seeking out other sounds. Footsteps. The *snick* of a gun being switched from safety. The chatter of men. A phone or television. None of them registered.

Light filtered through the trees dim and distant, but showed exactly where the cabin sat among the trees. His quarter mile estimate had been spot on. With the barest hint of sound, Vail slipped the pack from his shoulders. The right one would bruise like a mother, but there wasn't anything to do about it. He unzipped the brown leather bomber-jacket one tooth at a time, even though he'd oiled the metal last night. He dragged a fortifying breath, and then he shucked the jacket. Next came the military issue wool sweater and the cotton that turned his skin to gooseflesh. Using the upper corners of the shirt, he soaked up the remaining moisture from his skin. Then he practically dove back into the itchy shirt and jacket, and rolled his eyes at the pansy he'd become.

Keeping the tree between him and the cabin, Vail took a knee and opened the rucksack. His fingers easily found the holster in the blackness. He strapped the drop-rig through his belt loops and around his right upper thigh. The nylon snug beneath his groin, he slid the CZ P Duty into place cocked and locked. A ten-inch fixed blade came next. He glided the tip into its sheath. The knife snugged to his leg just in front of the barrel. He shoved the wet shirt into the pack, hunkered down against the tree, and waited.

Chapter Ten

Sophia lay on the tiny mattress in the tiny room in the tiny cabin in the middle of a big forest. If only she knew where the heck it was, she could sneak a phone and make plans to get out of here. They weren't careful with many things, but their location hadn't slipped, yet. It would. Eventually. She could get a phone without even trying. Manny lost his at least twice a day, leaving it on the back of the disgusting toilet or on the lumpy cushions of the plaid sofa and forgetting about it for a few hours at a time. Her legs stretched up the wall. Her hair hung over the opposite side of the bed. She relaxed her feet, letting them fall to the side, and then she pulled them back together. The motion allowed her to play peek-a-boo with the mountain lion in the painting above the bed.

"Now you get 'em. Now you don't. Now you get 'em. Now you don't."

Feet together, her light orange Converses hid the snarling cat, its lean lunging body, and ready claws. In that brief moment the white horse was beautiful, his head held high as he galloped across a meadow. Then she moved her low-tops and the poor thing became breakfast. Sophia's gaze shot to the dark window. She could open the thing, drop onto the awning below, slip off the edge, and be gone in a minute. Their sentry skills sucked. They'd fall asleep or watch whatever Manny did through the window. Sometimes they'd go in for a pee break and never come back out. But she didn't have a clue about which way to go and she sure as heck didn't want to be breakfast for a hungry beast.

She'd grown up outside. This outside had bigger carnivores than hers. Yep, she'd had to contend with scorpions and rattle snakes, but they couldn't rip your arm from your body while you were still alive to feel it. She'd take her chance with the snakes she knew. And know them, she did.

They had—when her mother wasn't around to vehemently object—given her piggy-back-rides as a little girl, twirled her around in wide whirring circles when she'd gotten bigger, and stared down boys in the streets when she'd gotten even bigger. And yet, maybe she didn't know them at all.

That terrible morning they'd dragged her from sleep, from her bed, while she fought and screamed. The dark still scared her. Because of them. They'd nearly suffocated her with a black bag over her head, knotted tight on her neck. They'd tied her hands and legs after she broke Ricky's nose with her heel and tossed her into the trunk for two long, hot days. She'd been soaked in her own sweat and urine. Curse them all to the devil. They'd laughed.

Tears stung her eyes, but she hadn't given them the satisfaction of her tears then. She shouldn't now. That horrid experience seemed a lifetime ago, but had really only been six weeks, if she'd counted correctly. She flipped to her stomach and grabbed the hard-covered book from beneath the bed. The inside cover showed six rows of seven tick marks, plus one row of four. Sophie grabbed the pencil and added a slash across the four straight lines.

She replaced the writing utensil for tomorrow and flipped to her marker toward the back of the thickly piled pages. Father in heaven knew she was bored, if she read a book. To her surprise though, this one was remarkably fitting and had cemented her sanity throughout the long days. Heck, Fernand Mondego in his captivity had given her the idea of tracking the days. His lost hope had mirrored hers on the first sad and scary days, and now, his renewed hope bolstered hers.

The blows on the bedroom door came hard and fast. "Sophia!"

"I'm not hungry." She stuffed the fright deep inside and was glad to hear it didn't reveal itself in her voice.

"Open the door or I'm breaking it down," Manny bellowed.

Sophia shoved the book under the bed and stomped to the door. He hadn't called for dinner. They usually called from the stairs or, when she refused to come down, left a tray by her door. Her shoes didn't make quite the ruckus she'd hoped for, so she yanked the door hard and tried to snarl like the lion to show her anger.

Manny's gun was out of his holster and in his meaty fist. She reeled from the shock and lunged for the window, but his other hand came down hard before she'd completed a step. It bit into her collarbone. He hauled her into the hallway. Her feet went out from under her and she landed butt first on the grimy floor.

"Get up," he barked.

His boot shoved at her back and she sprawled forward, catching herself on hands and knees. Manny's hand stayed knotted in her curls.

Pain ripped through her neck and skull and she was on her feet. He used it like a horse's mane, guiding her down the steps. She reached toward the railing for balance, but he maneuvered her like a puppet.

The thought enraged Sophia. Her mother would never allow them to toss her about like yesterday's garbage, and neither would she. Halfway down she reared back, ramming her head toward his face. She hit something hard—really hard from the *gong* ringing inside her head. His hold on her hair loosened. A heel to his instep set her free. With a firm grip on the railing and two leaps she cleared the remaining stairs, only to find two stares locked on her in wide-eyed bewilderment.

Ricky and Pat both had really big guns in their hands and were cuddled up against the two large window frames in the living room. Whether Manny tackled her on purpose or fell onto her she wasn't sure. And it didn't matter when someone that boasted three or four times your body weight landed on top of you. What mattered? Air.

Sophia inhaled, but a vacuum sealed her lungs, refusing to let anything in or out. She lay on the floor, watching the men alternately run from the front to the back, but not seeing them. All she saw were her lungs flat as a sheet from The Count of Monte Cristo.

Two *booms* drew her attention from her panic. Sweet air—dusty air, but sweet all the same— filled her lungs only to lodge in her throat on the exhale. Ricky and Pat joined her on the ground. Unlike her they didn't fight for air. They no longer fought for anything. In an instant they shifted from living to dead. A bullet, she guessed from the noise and size and shape of the hole in their heads, went from a barrel through their skulls. The end.

Before Sophia could wrap her mind around the jarring concept, a hefty arm snaked around her throat. Again the floor dangled beneath her feet for a moment. And again pain spread through her neck and drummed in her skull.

"Let her go." A calm, deep voice issued the command.

Though Manny wrenched her head so high it might snap off, she could see the entire room. Two dead men fallen among the cola cans, plastic wrappers, and chip bags they and the others had accumulated over the last two months. Yet, she didn't see the man who would decide her and Manny's fates. She knew it and, judging by the way the fat arm smashing her windpipe shook, Manny did too.

"I'll kill her, if you don't leave, now. And then I'll kill you," Manny screeched. The end of his gun swung from the fractured glass to her temple.

Her entire body seized, as if the tightening of muscles could block out a bullet. She imagined a tiny red circle on her head and the bloody damage it would do flying out the left side of her face. "No." She meant to scream the word, to heave the breath from the bottom of her toes and roar like a big cat. It came as a strangled whisper, a pitiful cry.

She hadn't even kissed a boy. She couldn't die. The metal pressing into her skin said otherwise. Fear paralyzed her synapses. Every self-defense move her mom had taught her froze in mid-fire, rendering her and the skills useless. Her mother would surely die of a broken heart. All because she was too small and weak to defend herself.

While Sophia reeled at her inadequacies and the coming end to her short life, she didn't notice that the voice remained silent. Not until the bite of Manny's gun eased its sinking teeth from her skin. Her gaze darted from window to window, but saw nothing through the cracked black glass. Both relief and soul-deep sadness buckled her knees. The crushing weight of Manny's arm doubled as she sagged. Maybe, if the guy was gone, her uncle's thug wouldn't shoot her. But...she'd remain a prisoner.

The man, the voice gave her no reason to think he was any better than Carlos's gang. Proof of his deadliness lay lifeless before her eyes. She'd only heard the tales of the AFO's and her family's apparent penchant for power and violence. Yet, something in his menacing voice said peace. It flared with no south of the border accent, and she guessed it wasn't another cartel coming to steal her away. Perhaps it was her wild imagination conjuring a rescue from a deranged man's attack.

"Stand up, damn you. He could still be here." His arm loosened and his hand dipped below her right pit.

She could breathe. Instead of celebrating, her esophagus convulsed. She wheezed and hacked, her middle nearly jack-knifing from the tantrum.

"Quiet," Manny growled.

But there was nothing she could do. Just as she no longer had control over her life, she possessed even less over her body at the moment.

Manny still held her in front of him, a human shield for his vital organs. "Callate. Callate." The force with which he spoke jostled her, but did nothing to stop the coughing. He aimed at the nearest window, stepped forward, and dragged her along. He smashed the barrel into the softness of her neck. "Callate," he whispered.

Her body responded to the greatest threat, forfeiting the struggle for air. Funny how as soon as it quit fighting the breaths came. Pained and labored, they came.

"You hear me, fucker? I'll kill her unless you go," Manny blustered.

"I heard you." The voice and its quiet, razor sharp menace whispered in their ears. A *crack* of bone followed, and then she was free, stumbling forward. "Go to your room, lock the door, and wait for me." Somehow she heard his quiet words over Manny's howl and the deafening *snap* of another bone.

Sophia's stomach lurched. She'd broken her arm as a little girl and remembered the sounds and pain too well. Despite it all, her hands braced against the couch's back. She used it as a crutch, towing her shaky frame in the direction of the stairs. The set of ninety-degree angles rose like a mountain before her. One wobbly step at a time she hauled her puny weight higher.

When she reached the last step that would give her a view of the living room she tightened her grip of the rail and turned. Manny and the man were gone. Her gaze swept the room, found two bodies, but they didn't count. She studied the door. It gaped, revealing the porch and a hint of the dirt and grass that made up the front yard.

Assuming all the other men were scattered corpses around the cabin, she didn't dare go outside, even if she had the strength to run. Instead she mounted the remaining stairs, walked past her door, and slipped into Manny's room. With the hallway light burning, Sophia could easily see the cedar chest at the foot of the unmade bed. She swallowed past her sour throat and apprehension, and stepped to the sloped top box.

She heaved the lid and nearly wept. "Not so helpless now," she said and hardly recognized the voice that breezed through her lips. The pistol was too big for her hand, much larger than the one her mom taught her to shoot, but it would do the job. She hurried to her room, forgetting the lid. Inside, she locked the door and sank onto the bed. She waited. And waited. Eventually, she eased back against the wall, drew her legs up, and rested the gun on her knees.

As her heart settled and her brain caught up with her actions, Sophia stared at the hulking gun in her small hands. She hadn't even checked to see if it was loaded, she'd just assumed it was. She hadn't checked the safety or to see if there was a bullet in the chamber.

Lord above.

Sophia pointed the barrel at the floor, wrapped her left hand around the slide, and pulled. Nothing happened. She repositioned her grip, gritted her teeth, and strained with everything she had. The thing budged a quarter of an inch. Nowhere near far enough to do her any good. She flipped on the safety, not that it would matter unless there was a round already in the chamber. But she didn't want to accidentally shoot herself.

She didn't want to shoot anyone.

Why was this her life? Self-defense training, firearms safety, target shooting, cataloging her surroundings, checking for concealed weapons, watching people's hands, meticulous planning for life on the run, imprisonment. Why couldn't she be normal? Talk on the phone, listen to loud music, hang out with her friends, romanticize about her first kiss.

The first tear fell hot on her cheek, stunning her. She hadn't cried yet. She couldn't cry. She had to be ready, prepared for anything. But it was normal to cry, and if she was about to cry, damn it, she wanted to do something normal for a change. With that simple permission her body took over once more, breaking her soul on unyielding fear, sadness, and anger.

Chapter Eleven

Vail braced his forehead against the tree and pulled a breath. His billowed exhale caught in the porch light's dull glow, curling like smoke as it lifted and dissipated, shoved on by the sharp breeze. The cold had driven him to move far sooner than he should have. If he'd waited until the dim morning hours, she'd have been asleep, tucked safely in the bed and out of harm's way. He held no delusions that the man wouldn't have just as easily snatched her from sleep to cower, like the worthless wretch he was, behind the innocent girl. But later in the night the bastard would have been sleeping too, and wouldn't have had the opportunity.

He pushed off the smooth bark. Crimson on his hands caught his attention. The dried crusty stuff on the left one was his. The slick fresh blood coating the right was not. Turning to the small shed, he shoved the arm dangling out of the narrow wood frame inside with his foot and shut the door. When the latch caught the thing flapped like a sheet of paper in the wind. He shook his head and headed up the hill to wash off. With any luck the door would hold until his team could get here and deal with the pile of bodies inside.

None of the men, the few he'd left alive for the briefest of moments, had been able to tell him much he didn't already know. Carlos had learned Carmen planned to leave the family, ordered her daughter—his niece—kidnapped and held until further notice.

"No harm! No harm to her! Senior!" Manuel Dominguez's pathetic cries still rang in his ears.

How could they not see that taking a child from everything she knew and holding her captive for weeks on end wouldn't harm her? He plainly saw that his actions, killing two men before her pure eyes, had hurt her. That thread combined with the others in his head, forming the world's largest ball of yarn inside his skull.

Why did she have to be a little girl? A woman he could handle. But he wasn't equipped to handle a child of any gender, most especially a girl.

Vail made his moves through the house deliberate, letting her track his progress. His earlier comings and goings he'd kept quiet. She didn't need to see him hauling dead men, cleaning up their blood—or the filth of their existence. The place made a pigsty seem inviting, and it had taken twice as many loads to clear out the trash as it had the burly bastards. He'd also stayed quiet to give her privacy. When he cried, which wasn't often these days, he didn't want an audience. She probably didn't either.

No. That wasn't quite true. She probably wanted her mother there. He imagined Carmen's swollen curves in a whole new light, as a mother, pulling her daughter to her bosom. She'd hold Sophia with her entire body wrapped around the girl. Like the physical barrier could block out the bad. Like she'd protect her with her life.

She would. He'd seen it in Carmen's eyes the moment she'd dropped into his office. He just hadn't realized it. Vail liked to think his mother would have done the same for him. But she'd never been pushed to it. Ellie... Ellie had thrown her arms across her middle in a desperate attempt to keep the bullets from her baby.

Moisture that had nothing to do with the water pouring from the sink's spout plopped onto his bare forearms. The fat tears spread across his skin and pooled in a muscled groove before sliding down to meet the water trapped in the basin.

"Damn it."

He rinsed off the remaining soap and wiped the tears on the shoulders of his shirt. Set on holding his emotions in check and coaxing Sophia out of her room, he turned away from the dark window and darker thoughts. Slowly he ascended the stairs, giving Sophia time to adjust to the idea of him. She had to be scared out of her mind. At twelve he'd have shit himself if he'd witnessed what she had. And he had military parents who talked *Guns and Ammo* articles over the dinner table, war tactics while they went about the cleaning.

Knuckles at the door, he stilled. She had that kind of mother. They wouldn't talk guns at the table, but ten to one odds Carmen had taught her daughter the slick moves she'd used on the steps. Never underestimate an opponent or a person frightened out of their wits. He'd learned the hard way in the beginning of his career and had a small scar on his bicep to prove it. Sidestepping, he placed the log wall between them, instead of the hollow door. Then he knocked.

Light footsteps shuffled across the floor, and then the lock *snicked*. One eye leveled about his sternum peered through a slit in the door. A wide circle, dark as semi-sweet chocolate, brimmed with lashes and nurtured a degree of sadness that shot him right in the heart. That gaze looked so much like her mother's.

God, what a softie.

The door swung wide and she walked to the bed. Not backward exactly. Not forward facing either. No, both her eyes stayed planted on him. So he stayed put, watching her sneakers shuffle. Her gray sweatshirt with white polka dots kicked to the side. Its wide-cut neck revealed a red striped tank and a bit of her puny collarbone. Slim fitting dark jeans punctuated just how narrow she really was. When she came down the steps he hadn't seen it. Her nerve and sneer had masked her fragility.

The gun snagged his attention the moment she opened the door, but he didn't worry. If she'd wanted him dead she'd have shot through the door or as soon as she'd cracked it.

"Are you going to shoot me?" he queried.

"No." She sat on the edge of the bed and catalogued him from head to foot. The muscles in her face didn't move much, like they too were as exhausted as the set of her shoulders said she was. "Are you going to shoot me?"

"No."

"Kidnap me?"

"No. I think you've had one too many kidnappings already."

"Molest me?"

"God!" Vail's head jerked back as though the little girl boasted a left hook Henry Cooper would envy. "No." And boy did she. Direct. Watchful. Tiny. "Hell no," he added for good measure. Too late he thought better of the curse and gnawed the inside of his cheek.

"Okay." She nodded toward a small wooden chair just inside the doorway. The top of her curly ponytail flashed black in the room's fluorescent light, but shaded brighter at the ends in natural highlights.

Vail stepped into the room and took the chair, leaving its back against the wall.

"You're bigger than I expected," she said.

"What do you mean?"

"You were so quiet. When you snuck up on us...before, I thought you had to be small and skinny to move that way. Not that you're fat or anything."

He folded his hands in his lap and—trying to make her more comfortable—lowered his eyes. The gun and red-tinged knife handle sat snug in the holster and sheath.

Son of a bitch.

He'd cussed more in his head and aloud in the last day than he had in the last year. It never occurred to him. Just like it never occurred to him to remove the holster before talking to a frightened child.

"I'm...sorry. I...should have removed my sidearm. I didn't mean for you to see what you saw. I'm sorry for scaring you then and now. That was never my intent."

Her little fingers shoved beneath her lap on either side as she nodded. "What is your intent?"

"To return you to your mother."

Her hands flew to her mouth and her head bobbed like his grandfather's cork, frequent and unceasing. Tears welled. The breaths expanding her slight chest came faster and faster.

Vail's instinct to run from the room as though it were on fire churned the blood in his veins. He shifted in the chair and, unaware, turned his feet toward the door.

"I'm sorry," she cried.

"It's okay," he lied. Realizing his unease must be adding to her own, he settled. "Have you eaten? Could you eat anything, if I cooked it? I swear on my grampa's prized pig it wouldn't be poisoned."

Her brow furrowed. She shook her ponytail. "If I ate, I'd probably hurl and make you that much more uncomfortable."

Well, she was sharp. "Fair enough. I've cleaned the place up. So, you don't have to worry about seeing anything."

"That's what took forever," she said with a tremulous laugh. "I thought you'd left, but I knew you hadn't because you said to wait for you. For some reason, I knew you weren't lying."

"I'll never lie to you. The truth hurts some-times, but at least it's honest."

"Yeah." She swiped the backs of her hands under her eyes.

"I know you've been here for a while, but we're going to stay a few more days. Until I figure a few things out, this is the safest place for you. Can you handle that?"

"What's a few more days in this dump," she shrugged.

"Okay." He shifted to stand. Sophia's eyes bugged and Vail was shocked they could get any bigger. The poor girl was obviously uncomfortable. He eased back into the chair. "It's late and I have to make a phone call," he said by way of explanation.

She blinked and shivered. Those big brown eyes darted this way and that while she thought. "I'd like to hear whatever call you have to make. You know, if you're not going to lie about anything, you can talk in front of me."

"True enough." Vail pulled a small phone from his cargo pocket. Satellite phones sure had shrunk since his active duty days. He stared at the keypad for a minute trying to remember the number he never dialed because he was always on the other end of the phone. After a beat his fingers took over, pounding out the long series of digits. A chime rang and he spoke. "Whiskey. Oscar. Lima. Foxtrot. Mike. Alfa. November. Two. Zero. Zero. Two." After a couple more beeps silence stretched so long every hair on the back of his neck stood on end. "Hello?"

A quavering female voice answered, "Commander?"

Shit.

He should've thought about this sooner. His poor secretary probably suspected he was calling from beyond the grave to remind her to file the bi-annual reports to the UN's Audit Operations Committee. Everyone at the Base Branch office, except for Khani, thought he was compost. They'd had his funeral, buried him next to Ellie and Deanna. They didn't know he'd been there for almost thirteen years already.

"Yes," he said. He realized how terribly un-eventful the single word was, but Sophia's fastidious gaze unnerved him. At twelve years old, she had the eyes of a trained operative. She'd have to, living with the likes of Carlos Ruez and his men. He promised to tell the truth. Yet, he found the need to protect her from the ugliness of the world took precedence. He wouldn't lie, but he wouldn't give her more to deal with tonight than the maelstrom she'd already witnessed.

"Y... You're alive? How? Oh my god," Rhonda whispered, "I need to get Lieut—"

"Rhonda, you're not new to this job. You've seen and heard the crazy stuff that happens every day. I'm just fine, but no one can know that yet. No one."

"Oh...yes, sir. But you're okay? I mean, I saw all the blood. I put a rose on your..." she broke off and gave a sniffle.

Great, he'd made two women cry today. Since he could rely on Khani to cuss a longshoreman into a belly-up position and not ever think about crying on him, he spoke quickly. "I need to speak with Lt. Slaughter. She already knows. She's the only one besides you, now."

"Yes, sir. I'm glad you're all right, sir." The line went quiet.

Vail chanced a look at Sophia. Her shoes lay askew at the side of the bed. The knobby ends of her knees pointed to either side of the room. Ankles knotted, she clutched a pillow in the X of her folded arms. A crease ridged the skin between her brows as she continued to study him.

"What the hell are you doing calling here? I thought you were smarter than that. Shit, I thought you were the smartest man I knew. And that's saying something because the lot of you are hardly one step removed from apes to my way of thinking," Khani rambled.

"I hate to drop the average down a notch, but I need clean up on aisle five," he said.

"That's not funny," Khani growled. "If you're bored, play solitaire. But you're not getting out until I get some answers. And since you won't let me question Ruez, I'm stuck going the long way around."

"I am out," he said simply.

A moment of silence hung in the quiet phone static while she tried to work things out. "Were you attacked?"

"I found a lead. I followed it," he said by way of answer.

"By yourself? In your condition? Without getting my input or at least giving me a heads up?" Each question grew in volume.

Sophia's brows rose with each raised pitch. "Are you in trouble?" she mouthed.

He thought about that for a moment, and then shook his head.

Her baby fat cheeks rounded as her mouth thinned in a look that said, *Yeah, sure you aren't.*

"Hello," Khani shouted, her irritation bringing the word straight from the top of Big Ben. "This is my job right now. Your only job was to heal."

"I couldn't just let it go," he huffed. "Take a moment and put yourself in my shoes. Could you let it go?"

"Hell no," she said with more than a hint of irritation. "Then you really do need clean up."

"Yes," he agreed.

"How many bodies? And do you want a team to stay with you?"

"Six and no. I may need one later, but not yet."

"Why am I surprised?" Khani muttered to herself.

"I'll send you the coordinates and be in touch."

"Give us a ring, if you change your mind about back-up."

"Will do." He depressed the end button, sent a secure message with their location, and then slipped the phone into his pocket.

"Where are we?" Sophia had scooted back to the wall. Her small shoulders and the crown of her head rested on the dark wood. And still she surveyed him from the corner of her eyes.

"Northeast Kentucky."

"Huh," she muttered. "Even though my mom and I have dual citizenship, I'd never been out of Mexico. I don't think she has either. She's probably ripping the country apart looking for me, but she'd never think to look across the border. She'd never find me, if not for you." She straightened her head from the wall. "Did she hire you?"

"Not exactly."   She opened her mouth to speak, but he spoke first. "I'll tell you everything tomorrow. You've been through enough tonight. Sleep." He stood and stepped to the doorway.

Sophia bolted from the wall. "Where are you going?"

"I'll keep watch downstairs."

"But..." She picked at the pillow's seam. "I..." Her cheeks puffed on a breath and she slumped back against the wall.

Vail sat back in the chair. "What is it? Truth goes both ways here, all right?"

"The truth hurts sometimes, but at least it's honest. That's what you said. It does hurt. I don't want you to know I'm scared, but I am." Moisture welled in her eyes.

"Of me?" Vail asked.

"No. Maybe I should be, but my gut tells me you're a good guy."

"You have smart guts, Sophia. Listen to them always. They're smarter than your brain, which doesn't seem too shabby either."

She nodded at that and gave a half-masted smile. "Could you stay, for just a little bit longer?"

"You got it."

Chapter Twelve

Carmen's right arm reached high. Her back arched as she rose onto tiptoes. Like a rubber band set free, she snapped down with the force of her muscles. *Whack!* The racket connected with the tennis ball, deforming it for a split second before it sailed over the net and smacked high into the box-wood hedge.

"You're destroying the bushes," Carlos Her-sio-Ruez's rapid-fire Spanish chastised from the narrow opening behind her.

She didn't turn. Didn't speak to her father. She honed the hatred eating her alive from the inside, gripped the leather handle tighter, and repeated the process of impaling the shrubbery. What more could she do? The question had kept her up more hours in the last three weeks than should be humanly possible. At some point she expected sleep to claim her for more than twenty minutes at a time. Yet, it never did. It came in exhausted intervals, always interrupted by one of two recurring dreams.

"Your brother will not be pleased," her father pushed.

Only one of the two dreams had a right to her thoughts. She would wake, pillow soaked through with tears, imagining her daughter huddled in a ball at the far corner of a dark glass room she could see into, but never enter. She would wake screaming her daughter's name with her arm outstretched, trying to reach her.

Whack! She pummeled another ball.

"Carmen Félix-Ruez, stop right now, or I'll call Manny and have him slice sweet Sophia's cheek."

Carmen hated the name, but even more she hated the power her father, brother, and their minions held over her head like a guillotine. They toyed with the line, letting it loose a few inches, then a foot before hauling it back to the top to repeat the process. He wouldn't hurt Sophia because they needed her daughter alive as leverage to keep her here. Christ knew it was the only reason she'd returned, the only reason she'd stayed as long as she had.

Though she knew it would cost her, Carmen pivoted and backhanded the ball as hard as she could, using her anger for fuel.

Whack!

The yellow sphere's impact left a red misshapen circle on her father's cheek. His wide hand flew to the painful stain. "You stupid bitch! Men!"

She smiled. He wouldn't try to take her alone. He'd learned over the years that the weapon he'd painstakingly crafted had a will of her own. She'd enjoyed teaching him and his men with their every bloody cut and broken bone. For a long time she'd been obedient. It upset Sophia to see bruises on her hands and face from the fights. But they'd taken her baby from her. The incentive to play nice had vanished with her daughter.

The ache of loss doubled her, but she hid the pain, morphing into a crouched athletic stance. One. Two. Three. Four. They skidded around the corner. "I see you remember," she whispered. "One on one just isn't fair for your boys, now is it?" She spoke English. She always spoke English to her father, brother, and the goons. It pissed them off because most couldn't speak or understand a lick of what she said. It also separated her from them. Their atrocities. Their greed. Their family business. Their sins. And her. Her greed. And her sins.

Freeing her daughter from the people who shared her blood and spilled that of others took precedence over everything else. The space in her brain wouldn't allow concern for all the other people the AFO hurt, as long as it wasn't her daughter. Failure threatened her singular task. So how was she supposed to save all of Mexico from her family, a group she couldn't even stop from hurting her and Sophia? If that made her greedy, then greedy she was. Unapologetically so. Hence, her sins and the other dream that disrupted her sleep. Her wake too.

"You stupid little whore. Why can't you just follow directions? Be good for a change?" Her father shook his finger. "Raf and Saul, get her and lock her in the room. For three days, this time."

Go home and run the business, Carlos had said. Right. More like go home and be ordered around by idiots. She didn't want any part of the business, but being a prisoner in the place she'd grown up was getting old. Her poor father didn't seem to recognize his flimsy grip on power. The men rubbing their fists for a chance at her took orders from her brother, even when locked behind yards of metal and concrete. Her old man was destined for a bullet from his son's barrel. He just didn't know it yet.

Perhaps, like her father, she didn't see her own demise yet. Soon Carlos would grow tired of her disloyalty, decide the trouble outweighed the effort, and have her eliminated. If only her mother hadn't died. How different things would be.

Thoomp. Thoomp. The automatic ball feeder continued to serve, buzzing fuzzy yellow balls past her face. One large step toward the men brought her out of harm's way. Or closer, depending on how you looked at it.

The two young men broke off from the group, moving wide to attack from the sides. Any person in their right mind would fear these two. It wasn't that ink scrawled over their faces, dipped below the hem of their wife-beaters, and encased their arms. It was what the black doodles depicted. Faces, numbers, and acts of death polluted their brown skin. Heads severed from bodies. Bullets busting into a forehead. The skulls of Santa Muerte.

Carmen wasn't in her right mind. High on sorrow and rage, she winked at Raf and simultaneously launched the racket at Saul's head. The *crunch* and subsequent howl proved her aim true. Love game for Saul. Raf barreled in quick and heavy, fury rippling the ink imbedded around his mouth and forehead. At the last moment, she bent at the knees and waist, guided his momentum over her shoulder, and then stood, helping him flip.

The other men gave her no time to gloat, which was bad sportsmanship anyway. Though, integrity had no place in this life. Obviously it didn't. She'd shot an unarmed man in the belly. Yeah, he'd been armed with his capable hands. Hands that, given the chance, would have inflicted serious damage. Why was she going over this again, when other men with less precision and more malice crowded her space?

They circled like starved coyotes on a wounded animal. Her heart bled, but her body craved a good fight. The man in front of her, with a tattooed one and zero split between his sunken cheeks, flipped a knife from his jean's pocket. His capped teeth greeted her in a smile.

"Don't kill her, for Christ's sake," her father yelled from far off.

"I'll kill you for Santa Muerte," Ten whispered.

Not unless I kill you first.

He lunged fast, aiming for her belly, but would have needed a sword to sink flesh. The man behind her backed off, giving them the dance floor. Not a fan of this particular tune, she stood her ground. He ran in this time, using quick choppy steps, and stabbed higher. The blade glittered in the early morning sun less than a foot from her face.

Carmen blocked hard with both forearms. The knife flew from his impotent grip. While his eyes followed the knife as it skittered over the slab, she plowed the back of her fist into his face. Bone snapped under the weight of the assault. His eyes shut and he fell to the ground, clutching his ten.

He'd threatened to kill her, in front of his friends. And he couldn't get away with that. She should turn and guard her back, but she wouldn't. If she left him unpunished, she'd leave herself and Sophia more vulnerable in the future. Choking him was neat and tidy. So, she raised her foot high and stomped. Once. Twice. Three times before a body rammed into hers.

The damage had been done. His cheek deflated into a pile of blood and teeth. He wouldn't die, but he'd never talk right again. A bold statement for a bold threat.

Looking back at her ugly triumph twisted her body so that her shoulders took the brunt of the tackle. Great for her lungs. Not so great for her brain. The horizon and all the gorillas on it blurred a wash of white that smeared to black.

The whine in her ears built to a full-fledged ring. A chorus of church bells played, refusing her the peace of unconsciousness. Rough hands dug into her armpits and the bite of rock and earth scraped her left knee. Carmen fought with her legs, willing them to kick or at the very least shuffle along and save her skin. The din of voices, muffled and loud, and the damn ringing muted her order. Her body hung in the in-between.

Someone yelled. Her head jerked. Warm blood pooled in her mouth. She tried to catch it before it slipped over her lip and onto her tennis whites. Her lips moved and the trickle became a stream. It tickled her cheek, rolled down her neck.

"Grab her legs and get her into the room before she comes to. Get him to the clinic and clean up the blood before it stains." Her father's words aired through a cave, echoing and bouncing a hundred times before registering.

What a thoughtful man.

Arms hooked her knees and spread her legs. Hot cotton-covered skin slipped between them. Carmen's heart plummeted into her bowels. Energy surged. She screamed. Bucked. She demanded freedom. In her head. Outwardly all she could manage was a slit of blinding sun, wavy in the sea of moisture collected in her eyes.

She swayed in their hold. As helpless as Sophia had been when they'd stolen her. As helpless as Vail Tucker had been when she launched a bullet into his stomach. In her altered state, her mind rushed to him as it did anytime she let her guard slip in the slightest. His face woke her literally, but figuratively too. And she hadn't realized she'd been asleep. His features possessed her in a way she couldn't grasp. Without a doubt his drawing, intelligent brown eyes would haunt her until the day she died.

Though the man was hot enough to melt the panties off a nun, the dream had nothing to do with sex. Raw and painful longing, yes. In time the dreams would surely multiply and devolve into a sick fantasy where she rode the man she'd shot and maybe killed. Damn it. She didn't even know if he'd survived.

For now he just stood there, inches away. His plain white button down opened at the neck and cuffed at the sleeves as it had been that night. Bright red stained the middle, though he didn't seem to notice. His eyes stayed locked on her, mapping her features. The perfect square of his jaw stayed set as well as his narrow mouth. His thin pink lips parted just a hint like he would say something. He never did, only swallowed the sentiment down his wide muscled neck. His Adam's apple would bob. She'd catch herself staring and her gaze would jump to the thick brows that hooded his eyes. Then she'd map the frame of his close-cropped hair. The dark strands lay flat against his head, pointing down on his forehead, but fading and shining into vibrant silver at his temples.

They would stare for hours, it seemed. And she would only wake when the desire, the overbearing need to touch his face, to stem the tide of his blood grew to impossible proportions. She'd wake crying, wishing she could see him. Explain things. Help him more than scribbling an insignificant note. Go back in time. Change things so that Carlos hadn't found out she planned to leave.

Carmen never expected his touch, in the dream or reality. But somehow he'd already touched her. He hadn't said, "Okay, shoot me." But the look he gave her expressed understanding she could never fully comprehend. Where hatred and anger should have been plain, there was calm.

"Just drop her here," the man near her head spat.

"On the bed," the other countered.

"The floor's easier."

"Not for what I'm gonna do." The man between her knees slipped deeper, pressing his weight between her legs.

Lightning flashed in Carmen's eyes as again she tried to open them. Her head pounded as though a group of Jarabe dancers stomped, whirled, and flung their colorful skirts about her skull.

The hands beneath her arms released their grip and circulation stung its way back up her arm. She expected to meet the hardwood of her bedroom—not that she could do anything to stop the crash—yet the cool downy of her comforter pillowed her short fall.

"I'm not a part of this. If you want to get your head cut off over some fancy pussy, that's your business." Steps sounded one man's retreat.

"Ah, I'm just gonna have a little fun," the asshole between her legs called after him. The door clicked into its latch. "I didn't want to share anyway."

His hands coasted up the backs of her thighs, levering her wide open. The ridge of his crotch met her bloomers. The pounding in her head receded to a dull hum, but still her arms and legs were useless. She'd been knocked for a loop too many times to count and sometimes full function took time to return. Time she didn't have, based on the progress of his hands.

He searched for the top of her panties, shifting and tugging her limp body. Thank God they were attached at the waist of her shirt and she wore actual panties beneath her tennis whites. Though, what would that accomplish, prolonging the inevitable? No one would save her. No one here cared enough to try. Carlos might be pissed, if he ever found out, which he would because she'd slice the son of a bitch into a thousand pieces and dance in his blood. If she could ever open her eyes enough to see the face of the man about to violate her.

Carmen braced herself for the hell pressing upon her. She could survive this. She had to, for Sophia. Tears wet her cheek. Though Sophia's absence ate her heart one nibble at a time, she was thankful her daughter wasn't here to see this, or by the devil, experience this. God, what if she had? No, Carlos's men wouldn't hurt her. She had to believe that. But there were eventualities you couldn't plan for. Like the fingers pulling at the waistband on her skirt.

Her eyes, lubricated by tears, popped open. Gordon's baby face sneered as he wrestled with the difficult clothing. She tried to lift her hand, but it was like lifting a mountain. Impossible. His light hazel eyes narrowed on her face and he stilled.

Using every ounce of will, thought, and motor skills she possessed at the moment, she spoke, barely above a whisper. "I see you, Gordon. Take your pleasure, if you dare. But know, I will take mine in return. Then you'll wish every day for the rest of your life that I had killed you the night I snuck into your room, tied you to your bed, cut off your penis one millimeter at a time, and shoved it down your throat."

He spoke no English, but maybe he understood. His hands fell away from her skin. He straightened and she could no longer see his baby face—much too young for the life he led. The heat from his thighs left hers and they drooped over the edge of the bed. The door opened and clicked shut again. Carmen clamped her mouth shut again, the sob threatening to rupture her delicate grip on sanity.

It came anyway. The force jackknifed her middle and she rolled onto her side. White fabric bunched around the widest part of her hips, revealing the top curve of her butt. She curled into a ball, fighting for control as her torso heaved. Her shaking fingers clamped over her mouth to mute the raging emotions. They poured out of her eyes.

Just when she thought she'd die from the helplessness of missing Sophia, Vail stepped into the forefront of her mind. His stern, steady face eased the death grip sorrow held on her heart. And for that, she was both grateful and ashamed. Sophia should dominate her every thought. Not this man. Not those eyes. Not that chin. Not that mouth. But, unbidden, they did.

Chapter Thirteen

Sophia walked down the stairs a few hours after dawn as though she hadn't seen two men murdered before her young eyes the night before. The clothes she had on the previous day hung wrinkled and askew on her slight frame. She stopped on the bottom step, gave a hesitant smile and quick wrist-flick wave. That same hand rushed to smooth the fly-aways from her forehead.

"So..." she rocked back on her heels, "what should I call you?"

"My name is Vail Tucker. You can call me Vail." He gestured at the cup of coffee between his hands. "Do you drink coffee?"

The purse of her mouth told him *hell no* before she shook her head vehemently.

"Why don't you go get dressed and we'll head into town, have breakfast someplace, and get some groceries? Judging by the food in the pantry and refrigerator—the term food being a loose generalization—you haven't had a decent meal in over a month."

Her mouth dropped open and her eyes swelled. "You're letting me out of here?"

"Let's get one thing very clear," he said, abandoning the stale drink. "You are not my prisoner. I'm here to protect you, find your mom, get some answers, and send you two on about your lives, preferably outside of your uncle's realm of influence."

"I didn't really mean it like that... You told me as much last night. I just... I haven't even been outside, much less in town. I haven't seen people other than the ones who kept me prisoner in so long. I'm just excited."

"You might not be after," he warned. "We have a bit of a hike to my car."

"I don't mind, as long as a mountain lion doesn't eat us."

He smiled and it felt odd on his face, but then Sophia grinned too and he forgot all about his own awkwardness. Her smile lit up the state with its simplicity and sweetness. "The picture in your room got to you, huh?"

"Yeah. I'll go get dressed," she beamed. An athletic hustle brought her halfway up the stairs before she stopped and turned. "Are you going to change? The scratch on your face isn't too bad, but the blood on your clothes might get us arrested. I'd rather this place than metal bars. Especially now." Her gaze swept the living area and open kitchen. "It looks like a whole different place with the curtains open and the trash gone. Both kinds."

"I have clothes at my car."

"Okay," she all but yipped and left him to the terrible coffee.

Vail's dealings with women were limited to operatives who could get battle ready in the blink of an eye. When he'd said get dressed, he imagined Sophia might take fifteen minutes to change. That proved his astuteness lacking. Extremely lacking. She hopped down the stairs an hour later. Fresh spirals and full-bodied curls bounced around her shoulders. A new outfit, still very similar to the one she wore before, covered her slim frame.

Outside, the chill covered the ground in iced dew, but the threatening snow hadn't fallen. Not yet, at least. Sophia tilted her face to the sun and spread her arms wide. She inhaled and exhaled the clean air, and then shivered.

"Have my jacket." He hadn't put it on, suspecting she'd need more layers between her and the cold. His nipples were hard enough to cut glass, but he could handle it.

"It's huge on me," she laughed. Her handless arms flapped.

"Be still." He rolled each sleeve before finding the tips of her fingers. "That should do. You can get to your fingers, if you need them. But keep them tucked inside otherwise."

"Yes, sir."

He smiled again. "Let's go."

They started out at an easy pace, but the girl had a competitive streak edged in stubborn independence wider and fiercer than the Grand Canyon. He held out a hand to help her over the rocks. She skipped across them on tiptoes. He went first down the steep walkway beside the rock-face he'd missed on the trek up. She skirted him, running wide open down the lofty slope. By the time they reached the highway they cackled and sucked wind.

"Not too bad, Sophie."

Palms planted on her knees, head lolled between her shoulders, she kicked her head to the side and lifted an eyebrow.

"What?" he asked between laughs.

"Nobody's ever...called me that. It's always Sophia. Same amount of letters, but so formal. My mom says, 'It's lovely and dignified.'"

"It's beautiful and a little stuffy."

"Thank you! Finally, someone understands."

"Come on, Sophia," he said, dragging out her name. "The car's this way."

They headed across the road and gravel parking lot. Both bay doors were shut tight to keep out the weather, which gusted pretty stoutly every now and again. Through the glass a truck sat in the right slot, its hood up. His car on the other side hid under a tight clean cover. He would've smiled, but one already shaped his mouth. Odd. He hadn't smiled or laughed this much in a while.

"And," Sophie said, "if I'd known the way, I'd have won. Cutting across that last curve would've saved a hundred yards."

Youth.

"You'd have ended up at the top of that rock face," John called from the door.

Vail had heard the door whisper open and the kid step out from the shop. Heck, he'd seen him bound from around the truck, skirt the precious car, and bolt for the door. Sophie, as attentive as she was, had been navigating the dips and pots in the shale. Her head snapped to attention. She stopped mid-step and her prim mouth fell open. He didn't know why. The kid wasn't a threat. But he had called her out.

"It was a good thought though," Vail offered.

"Oh, yeah." Her gaze flew to him, as though she'd just remembered he stood beside her. She smiled and slipped her hands from the jacket pockets. Hurriedly, she smoothed her wind-whipped mane and looked back at John.

"Yeah, he's right," the kid agreed, "you couldn't have known about the drop." John's eyes shifted over and up. "Your car is perfect. I checked the oil, coolant, water, air in your tires. You take real good care of it, sir."

"Thanks. Is your gramps around? I want to settle up," Vail said.

"He's at a doctor's appointment. Nothing major. Just a check-up. But he said if you came around, to tell you..."

They neared and John offered them inside, holding the door for them, just shy of awkward. As soon as they were through the door, Sophie shed the coat and held it in her small hands. Then she chaffed her arms.

Girls.

John looked from him to Sophie and back again.

"Tell me what?" he reminded.

"Tell you?" John squinted. "Right, to tell you to keep your money. He ordered me to burn it in front of you, if you gave it over anyway."

"Could you burn it?"

The kid shrugged. "Sure. He told me to. It's just paper anyway, right?"

Vail decided to put the promised money and a little more into a scholarship for the boy. He may well work in this shop all his life, but it'd do him good to learn accounting and business. "Right."

"Is this your daughter, sir?" He slipped the question in before Vail could lead in to the next topic.

"Yes. Can you get her some water, while I go change?" To Sophie's credit she didn't start at his answer or call him a bald-faced liar. They looked enough alike with their dark hair—dark, graying hair—and eyes, their ages were such that people would assume they were father and daughter. If they denied it, they'd have to explain their relationship. People were automatically wary of older men and young girls when they weren't related. In Vail's opinion, they should be always wary and watchful of older men with young girls, related or not. Men were bastards. Girls were impressionable.

"Yes, sir. The bathroom's through the shop door to the left," John directed.

Vail headed for the door, but once through it his stomach flipped at the thought of leaving Sophie alone with the kid. Sure, he'd been respectful at every turn, but he was a boy. Boys were horny. John drove—in all likelihood illegally—so they were only three or four years apart at the most.

He removed the cover and popped the trunk, all the while watching the two fumble about for a cup of water. Sophie was a beautiful girl. She took after her mother. Vail switched his ruck for the duffle and walked toward the bathroom. Almost even with the door he poked his head inside the office. "I told you she's my daughter, the most precious thing in the world to me, right, John?"

Wise beyond his years, John stepped around the bar dividing the two-chair waiting area and the desk, files, and computer, putting the wood and Formica between himself and Vail's "daughter." "Yes, sir."

Sophie rolled her eyes. Vail smiled.

* * *

"So," Sophie dragged the word out to three syllables.

"So?"

"Anything you want to tell me?" She shifted in the seat next to him and groaned. "I ate too much."

"You did pack it away. Made me look bad."

"The waitress didn't care about you losing an eating contest. All she cared about was you batting your lashes at her."

"I do not bat my lashes," he scoffed.

"Maybe not, but you pour it on thick."

"She was nice. I was nice. What?"

"Vomit."

"Yeah," he said mimicking her teenage girl whine of the word. "Well, the way you and John fumbled over each other made me want to hurl."

"We're getting way off track here," she huffed.

"Agreed. No, there's not anything specifically that I want to tell you. So, maybe you could be more specific."

"Were you telling the truth when you answered John's question? Are you my father?"

Wow. That was specific all right. He cleared his throat. Twice. "No and no."

"I just thought..." She turned away and stared out the windshield at the highway, leading them slowly back toward the cabin.

"Thought...I might be your father," he finished.

"Yeah." Her muted tone gave the word a whole new meaning. "I thought maybe you two had a torrid affair, and then you disappeared."

There were so many different ways he could go with this. First, she shouldn't know a damn thing about torrid affairs. Second, if he had an affair with Carmen Ruez there would be no end to the sheet melting sex. Third, if he had a daughter nothing could make him turn his back on her. Nothing.

"Sophie, you are a wonderful girl. Any man would be honored to call you his daughter."

"Not any," she said, swiping her hand across her cheek.

The girl didn't know who her father was. That brought a whole new level of crap to a kid's table. He hadn't died or run out on her. For her, a father only existed as a concept, not a flesh and blood person. Certainly her mother knew. She'd have had to have at least caught a first name in the exchange. Right? Now Vail had yet another reason to find Carmen Ruez.

"I've only met your mother once. Our encounter was strained, to put it mildly."

"What do you mean?" She turned back, as though glad to have a different topic of conversation.

"She shot me."

The sadness in her eyes doubled and the perk of her shoulders withered with the news. "What did you do to her?"

"Nothing, she's fine."

"I meant, what did you do to her to make her shoot you?"

"Nothing. She didn't want to shoot me, but your uncle used you, your wellbeing, as leverage over your mother. He didn't give her much choice."

"She's not a bad person," Sophie defended.

"She was protecting you. So, no. She's not a bad person. She's in a bad situation."

Sophie's chin rose. "We have been for a long time. She's tried to change that a lot of times, but my uncle always found out. This time he stole me to keep her there."

"He used your secret location as leverage to get your mom to go back to the compound on San Carlos. Your uncle is in custody, in a very safe prison no one except your mother has even attempted to infiltrate. He's under watch around the clock, but I fear something he's already set in motion will hurt a lot of people. Your mother may have information about the event. I need to find her to get the information I need and return you to her."

She studied him for a minute with eyes much older than her twelve years. "Are you going to hurt my mom?"

"No."

"She shot you."

"I've been shot before."

"And what did you do to the person who shot you before?" Her skinny arms locked over her chest and her head tilted in that all too knowing way.

"I killed every one of them."

"So, why not my mother?"

"Because she didn't shoot my wife and daughter."

Both sat quietly as the car wound through the naked trees. Bits of ice hit the windshield and melted on contact. Later, as the temperature dropped, slick roads would be an issue. Especially with the steep incline heading to the cabin. His Southern boy roots itched for his truck, but there wasn't anything to be done about it now.

They made it to the cabin without incident and both hauled up armloads of groceries from the trunk. On the would-be lawn, tire tracks and foot-prints decorated the dirt, but he didn't worry. They marked a path to the shed and back, and he knew it was his clean-up crew. Here and gone with barely a notice.

Inside, Sophie settled her bags onto the counter, turned to him, and held out her hand. "Give me your phone. I can contact her." His skepticism must have shown. She propped her other hand on her hip. "We've made contingency plans. She has a hidden cellphone and checks it daily for my call. I didn't call earlier because I didn't know where I was and it wasn't worth the risk of getting caught, just to say hi."

"Do you think she can get away from the compound?"

She smiled, though not nearly as brightly as she had that morning. "She got the drop on you, didn't she? She'll get away and she'll come for me."

Vail counted on it.

Chapter Fourteen

"Enough brooding. Come on." His big jacket landed in her lap, sliding smoothly between her arms, the cup of orange juice she'd been staring into, and the table.

"I am not brooding," she huffed. "And you could've spilled my drink."

"Nah, I've got mad skills."

Mad skills? He did, no doubt, but did he have to say it like that?

"Besides, that OJ would do about as much good on the floor as it has been swirling around your mug for the last forty minutes. Let's go." The last he said with a drill sergeant's burr. Crazily enough, it worked. She set the cup on the table, stood, and slipped inside his jacket before she even realized her compliance.

"Bring your plate," he said from the door. "We'll feed some critters."

"I might be hungry later. Right now, I just can't think about food."

"Then I'll cook you something later. Who the hel...heck wants cold eggs, soggy toast, and burnt bacon. Sorry about that, by the way." He held the doorknob, but didn't open the door. Like he expected her to bolt to the bedroom as she had after sending the message to her mother.

She didn't dash away, figuring this time he'd break the door off its hinges and force her to face the day. When she made it to the door, his left hand —big enough to palm her head—came forward. She expected him to lift the plate from her grasp, but it moved higher. Warmth and solid strength settled onto her shoulder. It should have weighed her down. Instead, it lifted her from the murky sadness that cast itself over a day with such promise.

Yesterday, when Vail said they'd shot his wife and daughter she didn't have to ask whether or not they'd lived. In the last two days, she'd seen him kill methodically, laugh with the most obnoxious roar, and run around like a teenager, whizzing past pitted holes of rotted out roots and flipping over fallen logs. In every moment she'd recognized his soul deep sadness, maybe because it had mirrored her own.

No, she hadn't lost a spouse or a child. But she was a child who'd lost her mother. Hope lived, wild and ferocious, that she would get her mom back. Yet, it was only hope. More easily her mother could be murdered, tossed into a ditch, and Sophia would never see her again. She'd never have a grave to visit. The world would become her place to mourn.

"You've been so careful not to touch me." She spoke the thought aloud.

"I didn't want you to think I was trying to molest you."

A breathy, nearly silent laugh shook her. The smile on Vail's face told her he was about to join it, but before he could, her laugh distorted into a sob. His hand shifted, though not away as she thought her tears would drive him. He grabbed her shoulder more fully and it was all the invitation she needed. Whether an invitation or not, she didn't much care.

Her face buried in the itchy wool of his green sweater. Not the blood-stained black one, thank goodness. She laughed at that thought, then cried harder still.

Vail took the plate from her hand. Free, she threw both arms around his waist. His arm coiled round, enveloping her. The morning sun and the pitiful cabin lights disappeared in the harbor of his arm.

"I'm...sorry...about...your...family—"

His right hand smoothed over her hair. He must have dropped the plate or something because it wasn't in his hand. "*Shhh*," he soothed.

So, she quit trying to form words and spewed snot and fat tears on his shirt. After so long she feared her face had pruned, Sophia turned her head, dragged a ragged breath, and another. His mouth pressed into a narrow line and he squinted, as though trying to read her thoughts.

"I'm sorry about your family. I'm sorry my mom shot you. I'm sorry I'm crying on you because I'm desperate to see my mom, to know she's okay. I'm—"

"No more sorrys. I'd like for you to tell me why you're upset, but don't be sorry. You've done nothing wrong."

She waited a beat. "I'm," she started. He glared. So she rearranged her sentence and began again. "I'm pissed at my uncle for taking me away from her. I'm pissed that I don't know who my father is, much less where he is, or if he ever wanted me or even knows about me. I'm sad and scared and mad."

"Scream," Vail said.

"What?"

"Scream as long and as loudly as you can."

"I don't think—"

He pulled her arms from around his middle. She forced her hands to release their lock on his sweater. He stepped back and roared. Even though she saw it coming, her body reacted, jerking from the sound, but more so the raw emotion laid bare for the world to hear. Or, in this case, her to hear. His mouth stretched taut over his straight white teeth. If she were taller, she could probably peer inside his mouth and see all the way down to his stomach.

After more than half a minute it died an abrupt death and his strained neck relaxed. "Don't think. Feel it, all your anger, confusion, hurt, and release it."

She inhaled, held it, and abruptly deflated. "I can't."

"Bull shit. A girl who can nearly run circles around a former Navy SEAL, has the guts to find a gun to defend herself, and who speaks her thoughts and names her emotions can do anything she wants. Do you want to be trapped forever by your pain?"

"No," she hollered.

"Do you want your insides to slowly rot until you're an old maid with nothing and no one?"

"No," she screamed.

"Why are you angry?"

"Because I have no one," she yelled so hard her torso lunged forward.

"Let it out," he hollered.

And she did. It swirled in her toes and shot from her body, deep and wrenching. A noise she never knew her small body could make. It rumbled and shrilled. It released the pressure threatening to crush her heart. It purged the weight from her shoulders.

Too soon her breath and overflowing rage vanished. She panted as though she'd run five miles. Immediately the spent energy recycled itself, renewing her spirit. Vail waited until she straightened before he grabbed the plate from a homemade sideboard, and then he opened the door. With a nod of his head and a satisfied smile on his face they stepped into the forest to greet a new day.

He didn't say anything as cliché as, "You have me," or "You're not alone. I'm here." Part of her wished he would, but then he wouldn't be Vail. Honest to a fault. Read your thoughts before you think them. Simple. Logical. Vail. That somehow would be more tragic than her perceived solitude.

Worrying wouldn't do her or her mother any good. They couldn't reasonably expect her until tomorrow. That was assuming she'd gotten away the night of Sophia's message and she'd traveled through the pitch-black hours. She decided to enjoy this time with a person so unlike any she'd met before.

"So, what do you want to do?" she asked.

She followed beside him in the opposite direction than the one they'd taken yesterday. He swished his lips this way and that in thought. The food he chunked to the side near a bush and sat the plate at the corner of a small shed they reached.

"I was thinking fish for diner. Let's go catch some." He stretched wide, hands over his head, and groaned like a sleepy bear.

"I've never been fishing."

His head snapped around, interrupting his yawn. "Say what?"

She shrugged.

"You lived on the Pacific ocean. That's fantasy fishing area."

"Sorry. We can do something else or you can fish. I'll go read." But she didn't want to hole up in the room, even though she'd found on her fourth read through of *The Count of Monte Cristo* she enjoyed the journey and safe adventure of a book.

"Oh, no. We're gonna rustle up some worms and you're gonna learn how to fish." He opened the shed and removed a plastic box and two fishing poles. "Tackle box," he said, holding the rectangular box. "Fishing rods. Reels." He pointed to the spool of clear line.

"I'm not touching a worm." She raised her palms and shook her head.

"I'll give you a reprieve today. You can see how to find 'em and hook 'em. But tomorrow it's all you."

"Hook them?" Her voice went reedy. "Disgusting."

Vail threw his head back and laughed as heartily as his roar had been. They made their way through the woods in silence, except for his chuckling. Several yards into the thick set of trees, he handed her the poles and box. When he stopped, dropped to a knee on the ground and scooted rotten leaves out of the way until he reached dirt, she broke.

"It's not funny," she protested. "They're barf city."

His laughter picked up again. She shoved him with a knee.

"Where are you from, anyway? I've never in my life heard anyone say, 'critters,' and, 'rustle up.'"

"I'm an Army brat, from all over. But those little jewels come by way of Dale, Alabama. My parents were stationed at Fort Rucker when I was a kid."

"So, you're military?"

"My parents were Army. I was Navy."

"And now?" she prodded.

"And now, I'm not." He dug a bit deeper. "Ah, look at this beauty."

Wet dirt clung to his fingers. Pinched between them hung the most disgusting creature in all the world. It wiggled and squirmed in his grasp. Her skin crawled with gooseflesh.

"Eew. I can't imagine anything wanting to eat that."

"Lots of things eat worms. Birds. Moles. Lizards. Snakes."

"Please," she said waving a hand, "stop talking. Or talk about something else. Anything."

"You don't want me to demonstrate how to hook your worm?" he asked with an evil smirk.

She shoved her finger toward her mouth and gagged.

"Eew," he grimaced, "you're way too good at that sound. How do you do it?"

"You're such a boy."

"No denying it," he agreed while digging for more creepy crawlies. "We age, but only mature so far." He added several tiny wigglers to his pile, stood, and swiped his free hand on his pants leg. "Ready?"

"I don't think so, but whatever. They're not very big. Don't you want fat worms, so you can catch fat fish?"

"Being winter, the fish are lethargic with a low appetite. We want them to think this is a quick, easy meal, worth the effort to give a bite. A big worm will shy most of them away this time of year."

They reached the water's edge and Sophia watched as Vail tied fresh hooks to the lines. He placed fake bait on each line and cast them on the shore several times. Satisfied, the plastic worms came off and a real one went on.

"That poor thing." It wriggled and squirmed, trying to escape the pain.

"Wouldn't have pictured you such a softie, the way you socked the guy on the steps."

"He wasn't innocent."

Vail *zipped* the line way off shore. The water rippled as the worm disappeared beneath the surface. "Casting is all in the wrist and timing. This is a spincast reel. It's easy to learn on. You just hold down this button, rear back, fling forward, and release when you want your line to cast. Give it a go. On the shore," he pointed. "Can't have you chasing our dinner away."

Was he baiting her competitive side? Probably. He was too smart for her own good. Sophia picked up the rod, pressed the button, and the fake worm plunked to the ground. She crinkled her lips at him.

"I didn't say it wouldn't take practice."

She puffed out a breath and turned her back on him. The cranking was easy, like rolling up the window in mom's secret—and really old—car. She thought that until the metal *clink*. The hook jammed into the circle at the tip of her pole. Irritated, she pressed the release button, but it refused to let her bait go. Over her shoulder, Vail flicked his wrist, reeled once, and waited, flicked, reeled, waited.

Sophia mashed her lips together, studied the line, and thought. She pressed the button again and tugged the line from the reel's metal case. The worm slipped from the metal circle and hit the ground again.

What had he said? Hold the button down, rear back, fling forward, release where you want it.

Miracle of miracles, she cast the thing a good fifteen feet. "Ha! I'm ready to catch my first fish."

"No, you're not."

"I am," she corrected. "Look. I casted the line."

Intent on the water, he didn't even spare her a glance. "Pick a spot twenty feet from you. Aim for it. When your worm lands there three times I'll give you a real one."

"Yes, sir."

What seemed like an hour passed with her muttering, failing, and trying again. She'd landed two. One by width of the lure's tail, but she'd take it. Water sloshed behind her. She turned. Vail's reel bowed like the curve of a J and a smile stretched his face. Slowly he worked the fish toward the bank, tugging and reeling.

"Oh my gosh." She squealed and rushed to his side. "It's huge."

"Decent for sure."

He snagged the line in his hand, ran it down to the end, and hooked his finger in an exceptionally large mouth.

"Won't he bite your finger off?"

"He's not a shark. Has teeth, but they're nothing to worry about. Take a look."

"Whoa, what is it?"

"Largemouth bass."

"They got that right."

He chuckled and reached his hand into the wide-open mouth.

"What are you doing?"

"Taking the hook out. Aaah!" His body jerked along with his cry.

Sophia's heart lurched and for a split second she'd thought he'd pull his arm free only to find his hand had been gnawed off. Then her brain caught up. She shoved him with both hands, nearly stabbing him in the eye with her fishing pole.

He doubled over laughing.

"Jerk," she laughed.

"That was bad. I just couldn't help myself. Come here," he managed between breaths. He offered her the wet wiggling fish.

"What do you want me to do, beat you with it?"

"No, we're going to release him."

"After all that time and casting, you're just going to let it go?"

"It's not good eating. We'll move up the shore a little. See if we can find some bream."

"How do you hold a fish without sticking your fingers in its mouth? Because that's not going to happen."

"Cup your hands around its belly and hang on tight." She did as he instructed. Good thing too. The fish's body was pure muscle, jostling her upper body with the force of its thrashing. "Good. Now, when you get to the water, lower it gently, and wait for it to swim from your fingers."

Afraid the thing would flop out of her hands, she walked carefully to the water's edge and crouched. "Ready to go home, big guy," she whispered. Vail stood silent behind her, monitoring the progress. She eased the slimy green fish into the water and he took off like a champion swimmer. "That was neat." Hands already in the water she scrubbed them together, riding herself of the goop. "And this water is freezing."

"Your turn."

She shot from the ground. "I still have one cast to nail."

"It wasn't about the number. It was about practice. You're ready."

He baited both their lines and handed her a rod. "We'll split the bank. You go about twenty feet that way and I'll go this way." Seeing the widening of her eyes, he added, "I'll be able to see you and get to you in seconds. If you need something, signal. If you really need something, holler."

"'Kay."

She turned to go her way, thankful for the trusted space and a little sad to be away from Vail and his stalwart comfort.

"Hey, first things first." He pulled two knit caps from his back pocket. The first he hid his two-toned hair with. The second he fluffed up and opened wide. Stepping forward, he pulled the soft knots low around her ears.

"Thanks." She smiled.

His smile brightened, and then his mouth narrowed. "Sophie, I know tough ladies. I work with a few of them, and your mom is the toughest I've seen. If anyone can make it back to you, it's her. No one is more determined."

Chapter Fifteen

No one is more determined.

Vail played the words over in his head again. Maybe he had lied to her. Unintentionally though. The realization came gradually over the long day spent freezing and fishing, the dinner they shared, the quiet night, and the morning expended teaching Sophie how to chop down a tree and split it into firewood. The more time he spent in her presence the more his sanity went too.

Because there wasn't a single thing he wouldn't do to protect Sophia. His condition rivaled that of Carmen Ruez.

For so long he'd been living on Novocain. And now he felt everything. Finally the sadness was bearable. Joy lifted its smashing weight from his chest and he breathed deeply, mountain air filled his lungs, laughter sang in his ears.

"Come on," Sophie yelled. She ran from the shed, tackle box and rods in hand. "I bet I'll catch more than you today."

He tossed the hunk of wood onto the stack on the narrow porch by the front door and hollered over his shoulder. "You're baiting, remember."

"I know," she said, quirking her nose. "You made me dig these boogers up. How could I forget. I'm still going to win."

"Haven't you ever heard the saying, 'It's the journey. Not the destination.'"

"Nope." She smiled. "They're tickling my hand. Let's go. The wood will be here when we get back."

"Yeah, and you can help me stack it too."

"I promise," she shrilled in excitement. Not about wood stacking, but fishing. She'd taken to it quickly, making him work to keep up.

He tossed one last log on top, bound off the deck, and zipped past her. "Who's slowing progress now?"

"I can't run with all this stuff in my hands."

She did resemble a pack mule. Rods stuffed beneath her armpit, tackle box in one hand and worms in the other. Softie he'd become, he stopped and turned. They met in the middle, each giving a few strides. "Hand it over. But you keep the worms."

Sophie did and her smile bloomed, her round cheeks reddened by the cool air. "Sucker!" She leaped past him and gathered speed, aiming at the lake.

"Little sneak."

He ran after her, a bit awkwardly, but he'd carried worse things at a dead run. They made it in a quarter of the time it had taken yesterday, her trailing by thirty yards. Vail set the fishing gear on the ground and turned, noticing the first tug of the wound he hadn't thought about since he arrived. Having officially lost, some would have slowed down, coasted in the last several yards. Not Sophie. She pushed harder, stretching her legs to the limit as though if she ran fast enough she could turn back time and claim victory. And hadn't she? Like casting was all in the wrist and timing, success was in the attitude and preparation. He couldn't be more proud of her effort, if it was his own.

They smiled two big, dumb grins as they caught their breath. She hadn't said any more about her mother. Last night as he'd fried up the fish they'd caught and this morning her mood had been upbeat. Her smile fueled a life high he hadn't experienced in ages. The thought of losing it hovered overhead, but he didn't look up. He pulled the hooks from the rod eyes and handed one over.

"Where'd the dead bodies go?" Sophie asked, while he spoke at the same time, "Why don't you have an accent?"

"I don't work alone. My team collected them and will properly dispose of the waste."

"Like body fairies," she said, widening her eyes and flashing an exaggerated frowny face.

"Heck of a way to look at it."

She deposited the worms onto a dish they'd found yesterday inside the tackle box. "Take your pick. I've got big ones, skinny ones, short ones. And every one of them is gross." Her hands chaffed the legs of her jeans. "Hat please."

He handed it over. She stuffed it onto her head. Her big curls poofed around the rim. "No more stalling. Grab a worm and get to baiting." The gag and eye-roll appeared and it flipped his gut. Of all the horrible sounds in his life and that one grated his teeth to the root. "You're killing me with that."

"I know," she giggled. "I don't have an accent because my mom always spoke English to me and made me speak it in return. Of course, I picked Spanish up from the people around the estate, but if she caught me speaking it, ooh-we."

"Wonder why?" He mused to himself, mostly, not expecting an answer.

"It separates her from them."

"Them?"

"Her family."

"Aren't they your family too?"

"She doesn't even claim them. They do terrible things," she shrugged. "But you know that."

He mussed her hair, shaking the top of her hat with one hand. "If you can pick up Spanish. I suppose you can pick up a worm and put it on your hook."

Of the entire fishing process, she'd done it all yesterday, except put worms on her hook. She'd weaseled him this way and that, but he'd assured her today he wouldn't be bamboozled. Honest on her word, she scooped the fattest sucker from the pile with only a few groans, and set about finagling it onto her hook.

"So, John seems nice."

The comment stunned him like a heavy fist to the jaw. Sophie wasn't his daughter, but the protective instincts of a father steamed to life. "John?" he practically shouted.

Her responding cry, sharp and strident, pierced his soul. He hadn't intended to hurt her. Her interest in a boy and his inclination to defend her honor had just surprised him. He dropped the rod with its bait sitting on the bottom of the lake and turned, apology on his lips. The sight of crimson on her skin chilled his blood. For a moment he was on the street, helpless and terrified, watching someone he loved being stripped from his life.

But he wasn't helpless. He surged forward, looking for an injury when tactically he should have been looking for the person who inflicted it. No leaves had rustled. No shoes scuffed the ground in approach. No gunshot had exploded before she screamed.

"What is it? Where are you hurt?" His tone was higher than ever. Panicked. He didn't panic. He was cool. In control. Always.

"Oh shit," she said, thrusting her thumb toward him and dancing side to side. "I'm not supposed to cuss, but shit."

The barbed end of the shiny metal fishing hook protruded through the nail, while the curve of the J lodged inside her flesh. "Jesus Christ," Vail all but sighed. "Don't ever scare me like that again."

"I have a hook jammed in my finger and you sound relieved?" Her uninjured hand flagged the air.

"I thought you were shot."

"Not shot. Just thumbless. Oh God! Are they going to cut it off? That thing can only go one way. Look at that pokey thing. I can't believe we do this to fish."

"Are they who going to cut what off?"

"Doctors," she said impatiently. "My thumb," she shouted.

Vail scooped her up in the crook of his arms and ran up the slope toward the cabin. "I'm sure it hurts, but as injuries go it's minor. I'll take care of you. I'll have to cut the barbed end off and pull it out. There are some tin snips in the shed."

"Minor? This?" She shook her hand in front of his face. Actually, she just held it up and his rapid strides did the rest.

"Yes, that."

"You know what to do? I thought you were more into the," she pulled her other hand from around his neck and made a slicing motion across her own, "business."

"I'm in the business of keeping the peace, no matter what it takes. I've definitely taken more lives, but I've saved a handful." Not the ones that really counted, for him. The other lives counted for the people still walking around, to their families, and friends. It was something. Not enough on most days.

"It wasn't your fault," she whispered.

"What isn't?" The lump in his throat barely let the words pass.

"Your family."

"You can't know that."

"Sure I can. Yeah, I've just met you, but already I know this." Her tiny cold hand rested over his heart. Through her sparse tears and pain, she smiled. "You're carrying me up to the cabin, running as though I'd been shot over this." Again with the thumb. "I know terrible things happen. I know you've had to make terrible enemies, doing the type of work you do. I know you would have done anything to save your family." She grimaced. "Now run faster, it's starting to hurt."

He shook his head and furled a brow at her, and he ran faster. His boots thundered through the dirt and splotchy grass in front of the old house. At the shed he stopped and set Sophie on her feet. "Don't you pass out on me, hear?"

"Yes, sir. Wouldn't think of it, sir."

"Smart ass."

Vail burst into the dim shack of an outbuilding, the door slamming wide onto the exterior. The interior shuddered, but he didn't much care. He'd already snagged the tool he need and leaped from the shed. Before he skidded to a halt in front of her, he reeled himself in. Calm. Slow. Steady.

She stood exactly where he'd left her, back to the shed, facing the lake path, catty-corner to the house. He walked up to her as if his heart weren't in his throat at the prospect of causing her more discomfort. "The less you think about it, the less it will hurt. So, give me your hand and tell me exactly how you feel about John Batten III."

A smile curved her mouth and she tried to squash it. It didn't work. He pillowed her hand in his and positioned the snips about ten thousandth of a millimeter below the barb. "Your smile says it all and I don't like it one bit. You're twelve. Boys have cooties, remember?"

"Maybe when I was seven, but some girls have boyfriends already."

"And some have babies. Babies are a huge responsibility."

"Gross. I'm not talking about—"

He snipped, pulled the hook from her finger. A good half second later, when the blood really started to pour, she howled.

"Get your hands off her." The voice was feminine, but night to the day from Sophie's. Where the girl's was soft, and sarcastic at times, this one held all the rasping displeasure of an injured grizzly. One separated from her cub.

Seeing exactly how this looked to Carmen's perspective and seeing a flash forward preview of how badly this all could go down, Vail tried to diffuse the situation. His right hand, tool and all, slipped from her elbow, while his left released her wrist. Both hands went up slow and steady. Sophie's face contorted in a cartoon strip of emotions. Agony. Surprise. Confusion. Elation.

"Stay behind me until she puts the gun away," he said to Sophie in an almost silent whisper.

"Gun?" she breathed. The valley above her cute nose wrinkled.

"Lace your fingers behind your head and turn around," Carmen snarled.

How had he allowed her to get the drop on him twice? He hadn't expected her at all the first time. This time he expected her in about five hours, at the earliest. She must have left the Mexican peninsula immediately, put the pedal on the floor, and hardly stopped for gas.

He turned one inch at a time. Vail looked past the gun barrel—most likely, the one that had already shot him once—to the woman who'd laid him up for days on end. More than her bullet had, her beauty assaulted him.

Unbound by a mask, her hair hung loose around her shoulders. The wind flirted with the ends, kicking them up and tickling her face before laying them down. Fury crinkled the corner of her red lips as impatience flexed her jaw. Her bound-less eyes poured forth every emotion that had played across Sophie's face and more. His gaze slipped south, roaming the contours of her snug jeans and white tank partially hidden by a smokin' leather jacket.

"Mom!" Sophie used the word as a repri-mand. She dipped around him on those agile little feet and stood as though she were twenty feet tall in front of him. Her arms spread wide. "You can't hurt him!"

Simultaneously, Vail's heart swelled and crumbled. His fingers bore down on the backs of his hands to keep from hustling her behind him. Any sudden move would more likely get her injured.

"If he's laid a finger on you I'll finish the job I started last month," Carmen said. Her keen gaze never leaving him, she immediately dropped the gun to her side, far away from Sophie.

"He was getting a hook out of my finger. He's the one who saved me. He's the one who helped me contact you." Sophie didn't yell, but it was close.

Carmen's head tilted as though trying to figure out a puzzle, but she slipped the gun into the waist of her pants at the small of her back.

"Never put yourself in the line of fire, ever," Vail said in the calmest voice he could muster.

"You save me. I save you," Sophie answered over her shoulder. Her stricken expression melted into a tiny smile.

Then Vail watched happiness slip from his grasp. Sophie sprinted to her mother. They enveloped each other in a crushing hug and smattering of kisses. All the while Carmen's eyes remained locked on him. He had his questions to ask, but then they'd go. And then what? Back to the empty condo and all-consuming job. He held the grip on the back of his head tighter still. At least he loved his job. There was always that.

Only now he knew it wouldn't be enough.

"Come, chula. Let's go." Carmen grabbed Sophie's hand and tugged as she stepped farther into the tree line.

But Sophie widened her stance and planted her feet. "I'm not leaving."

He and Carmen both went fisheyed at that, only hers also held contempt, which she flung in his direction. Stunned, he couldn't move to shrug or say, "Hey, news to me too."

"He needs our help and we need his," Sophie explained.

"No we don't," Carmen said, a palm cupping her daughter's cheek. "We're free. Let's go, Sophia."

"And run forever?" Sophie asked.

Chapter Sixteen

He taught her daughter how to fish. The evidence of it sat grilled on the plate in front of her beside steamed broccoli and a mixture of brown rice, mushrooms, and English peas. A million thoughts collided into one another. Of course the most ridiculous rose to the top, but the mother in her never rested. No way in hell would Sophia eat the mushroom rice she shoveled with her fork, and—oh my lord—slipped into her mouth.

Had the man completely brainwashed her? And, if so, was there any way he'd show her the technique? For ten long years Carmen had picked out and scooped up mushrooms from her daughter's plate because she couldn't stand the texture of the things, cooked or otherwise.

"Mom," Sophia said, leaning over and grabbing her hand, "try it. It's delicious."

The little witch. If she weren't so over the moon to see her daughter alive and well, happy even, she'd pinch a rib. Sophia disliked mushrooms about as much as Carmen hated the slimy things.

In the vein of peace, Carmen smiled at her daughter and scooped some rice onto her fork that held a small piece of mushroom. She chewed, swallowed, and grabbed her glass of water.

"Great, right?" Sophia asked.

"It's very good," she lied. The flavor was exceptional, but the mushroom's gooey slide down her throat knocked the dish to unacceptable in her book.

Her daughter's smile brightened and Carmen felt as though the roof had been removed from the structure and the sun warmed her face. Sophia leaned toward Vail—who Carmen had managed to avoid eye contact with for the last few hours—and giggled. "She hates mushrooms."

Carmen zeroed in on them both. Vail clamped his lips between his teeth, holding back a smile. Though she'd tried to avoid looking at him altogether, she'd caught the shocking glimpse of his ripe and ready smile. It seemed Sophia could pull it out of him at every turn. Carmen had thought his mouth small and narrow. When he smiled as he did now his entire face transformed. Big white teeth peeked from behind a truly wide pair of silky lips.

"You don't have to eat it. It won't hurt my feelings," he said...to her.

She had to rip her gaze from his mouth to meet his eyes. Heat pooled in her cheeks. He'd caught her. His eyes said so. Yet, he didn't hold it over her head. It appeared as though he didn't hold anything overhead. But appearances were rarely what they seemed. How could he not hate her for shooting him?

He looked no worse for wear with his snug sweater and cargo pants that hugged his high, tight ass. To her horror, his loose-hipped swagger was sure intact. She couldn't speak to respond, so she gave a weak smile.

"I've been spoiled over the last couple of days," Sophia beamed. "Vail is as good of a cook as you, Mom."

Flattery upon flattery for Vail had gushed from her daughter's mouth since she set foot inside the cozy home. The notion she'd clued into earlier all but solidified in her mind. Sophia was match-making. At first, Carmen had thought the idea ludicrous as her daughter regaled her with the story of her rescue. But the more Sophia talked, the longer they sat at the intimate round table together, the more tension mounted like a fog rolling in, the more convinced she became of her daughter's temerity.

To corner that thought dead in its tracks she looked to Vail. "I'm surprised you haven't killed me yet or slapped handcuffs on me, considering I shot you in the stomach."

"It was the large intestine actually." Plate empty, he lounged back in his chair, one arm draped over the back with his wrist resting in the curve of the wooden chair back. A smirk toyed with his mouth.

"He understands you were just trying to protect me," Sophia offered.

"I broke the law, Sophia. My reasoning doesn't matter. Wait. You know I shot him?" Carmen asked, incredulity thick in her tone.

"Yeah," she shrugged.

Carmen looked from one canary to another, wondering what exactly the two of them had planned and why it irritated her so much that they shared a bond that excluded her.

Chapter Seventeen

Try as he might, Vail couldn't figure out Carmen, or himself for that matter. He'd been strategically hiding his wayward hard-ons from both females, while mentally berating himself for their very existence. She shot him. Carmen shot him. And, gave him wood apparently. It wasn't a wonder. She would swivel heads everywhere she went. He knew it as sure as he knew if he continued down this path he'd be stuck at the dinner table until after the girls retired for the night.

Time to change tactics, since brooding silence had gotten him nowhere.

"How old were you when you found out about your family's dealings?" He didn't have to say her name. She'd been staring at him like he might sprout another head. He certainly hoped not. His pants couldn't handle it.

"Twenty-two," she said softly.

Her jacket hung over the back of the chair, which was one of the reasons he had so much difficulty. Her breasts sat full and high on her chest, held up by the straps of a soft pink bra. He'd caught glimpse of it beneath the edges of her tank. She folded her arms and he wondered if it was a tactical or defensive move. He had to strain his normally agile brain cells to follow the conversation he'd started.

"Were you that naive?" His voice held no accusation.

"Maybe," she bristled. "My father sheltered us. Except for my mother's death, we had a good upbringing, fairytale to most."

When he didn't speak she continued.

"Our father was attentive, playing with us, teaching us to defend ourselves and use weapons. His reasons were altruistic—or so they seemed. He wanted us to be able to protect each other, me and Carlos, from the bad people in the world." She heaved a sigh and fell silent. They all honored it with their own silence.

"I often wonder what things would have been like," she breathed, "if my mother had survived."

Worse.

Vail's immediate thought flashed like a neon sign in Vegas, threatening to slip between his lips. He clamped them shut. No one wanted their mother disparaged. Even if that mother had commanded brutal executions, the corruption of a police force, and the ruination of thousands of lives.

The hard lines of Carmen's face softened at the mention of her mother. She turned to Sophia, smiled and reached over, tracking a thumb over the girl's cheek.

His nape prickled.

Carmen turned to him. "She'd never have stood for his murderous ways. She'd have left him. Taken us. Run away and never gone back."

Vail nearly choked as the realization dawned. Carmen had no clue about her mother's involvement in the Arellano-Félix Organization. She only knew Ángela Arellano-Félix-Ruez as Mom.

"You taught me the same things Grandpa taught you," Sophie chimed.

Carmen's gaze shifted from his face and for the first time he was grateful. Her almost-black curls shook. "Yes, but in our case I wasn't the bad person from which you needed protecting."

"What happened at twenty-two to shatter your ideals?" Vail asked in search of solid ground.

As though she were as restless as he, Carmen straightened. She looked at him, then to Sophie, and back again. "My father rented out a club in Ensenada for my twenty-second birthday. I don't know why. The noise and alcohol entertained his business associates, not me. I walked into the back room to find some peace for just a minute. Instead I walked in on him executing my fiancé."

"I'm sorry. We don't need to talk about this now." He glanced at Sophie.

"I already know about it." Her chest puffed. "I'm not a child. She didn't even love the guy. Grandpa arranged the marriage."

"Sophia!" Carmen chided.

"You didn't," Sophie shrugged.

"You make it sound as though I was pleased," her mother continued.

"You didn't want to marry the creep," Sophie rebutted.

"No, but I didn't want to see him murdered either." Carmen's eyes flared wide.

Vail marveled at the girls' rapid-fire exchange. They spoke loudly, but neither seemed particularly angry with the other. In his house growing up, if a back and forth lasted this long or heated in the slightest it meant no life for a week at minimum. Sophie inhaled to speak again. He decided to intervene.

"Why would your father murder the man he chose for you to marry?" Both of them snapped their heads in his direction.

"Grandpa caught him stealing," Sophie spouted. Carmen shot her a withering look and the girl's hands went up. "Okay. Okay." She wiped her mouth and stood. "I'm going to enjoy my newfound freedom and quit saying the wrong things."

"I think that's a good idea," Carmen nodded, "but no calling friends or Oscar. We're laying low, remember?"

"I remember," Sophie agreed.

"Who's Oscar?" Vail pinned Sophia with his gaze as he spoke overtop her.

"Not your business," Carmen barked, while Sophia went palms-up again and said, "Just a friend from school."

Not your business.

She was right. Sophie wasn't his problem. So why did the sudden comprehension feel like someone syphoned the life right out of him? Luckily anger shored the dam. Vail took his rage, once again the only thing inside his scarred body, and headed for the door.

Chapter Eighteen

The door slammed behind Vail's immense frame and her body jerked. Out of the corner of her eye, Carmen saw her daughter flinch too. But she couldn't tear her gaze from the door. Shock froze her in place.

"He cares about me," Sophia's tiny voice warbled. "You may not care about that, but I do."

By the time she turned, caught in the quicksand of yet another surprise, only the heels of her daughter's receding tennis shoes were visible at the top of the staircase. When the *bash* of the bedroom door echoed down the wall Carmen succumbed to the morass of a situation too confounding and monumental to tackle. She shoved the plate to the side, laid her forehead on the table, and closed her eyes.

It had been more than twenty-four hours since she'd slept. And nearly a month since she'd slept well. Exhaustion, only partially due to lack of sleep, clawed at her. Though her eyes were closed, she could never sleep, not with his expression and her daughter's words on loop in her head.

If she kicked a kitten she couldn't sink any lower. Who could have guessed a fierce warrior was capable of such a wounded affect? He'd grimaced more when she'd informed him Sophie was not his concern than he had when she'd physically injured him.

Deny it all she wanted before, there was no denying Sophia's desperate and growing need for a father figure. Carmen had been overjoyed that she hadn't clung to her grandfather or uncle throughout the years. Now she cared about Vail Tucker. She couldn't have picked a more honorable man, but she sure as hell could have clung to a less perplexing one.

When she set a course for herself she never deviated. It may take almost ten years to see it through, but faltering wasn't an option for her or Sophia's sake. Vail's unsettling stare and delectable body terrified her because he could make her stray from the solitary path she'd set.

Carmen ignored the thoughts of temptation and peeled herself from the table. The stairs creaked only once as she snuck up. She placed her ear against the door to the tiny room Sophia showed her around earlier. Silence greeted her. It was better than tears, worse than an open door and arms. Her daughter couldn't possibly have guessed that though Sophia needed the hugs before dinner, Carmen needed the reassurance Sophia was okay even more. The thought of never seeing her daughter again had plagued her so. By God, she wouldn't lose her now that she'd just gotten her back. She'd go after Vail, for Sophia, for absolution she didn't deserve, and for irrational curiosity.

The roar of the engine hadn't started after he'd left. So, he couldn't have gone far. Carmen grabbed her jacket off the chair, slipped it on, and headed into the cold. It took less than a step from the door to find him half-naked in light cast from the porch.

Her lips parted to speak, but her jaw hung there uselessly. Back to her, his grip spread wide on a low branch. He lifted his own weight, raising his chin above the bark in a quick pull-up. His muscles bulged to the point of exploding. Shadows etched in the grooves of his lats, the hollow of his swollen shoulders, the dips of his ass above the waist of his pants. Vail lowered himself and then dropped to the ground in a plank. He eased his bulk to the dirt, pushed-up, bound from the ground, grabbed the tree, and repeated the process.

Despite the ice clinging to the puddle's edge where she'd rinsed Sophia's finger with the hose earlier, sweat slid over his taut skin. Steam rose from his body and his exerted pants. She shivered. Vail seemed immune to the chill. Then again, her quake wasn't exactly due to the weather.

She thought to turn around and go back inside. Damn her boots, but they froze to the wooden deck. She'd never seen a man shirtless. Her brother didn't count. They were related and he looked nothing like the specimen before her. She wasn't a prude, but his bare flesh seemed too intimate, too much for her to bear without leering.

The water turned on in the bathroom upstairs. The *whoosh* of its flow through the pipes stopped him cold and he turned, coming up short at the sight of her.

She showed him her empty hands. His sweaty head shook. Droplets of his effort slung gently from his hair. "How is it you sneak up on me? Three times now. No one sneaks up on me. They try." He heaved a breath and every slab of muscle flexed and never seemed to relax. It took a full minute of silence for her to realize he wasn't holding his breath or holding himself at full tilt for battle. Those blessed grooves that lined a perfect—

Santa María, was that eight—eight pack jammed between obliques worth drooling over.

"What is it, Carmen?"

Her name on his lips nearly toppled her down the three small steps in spite of the agitation suppressed in his tone. She grabbed the railing and made her way to the dirt, struggling to remember why exactly she'd come out in the first place.

Sophia.

At least some part of her fuzz-filled brain operated properly.

"I'm sorry," she blurted.

"For what exactly?"

Her mouth moved to answer, but he walked forward, short-circuiting her synapses. Closer and closer he came until his chest nearly collided with her shoulder. She caught a gasp between her lips, just barely, as he reached around her to the shirt she hadn't seen on the opposite railing. He dragged the cotton over his face and chest and then arched a brow, which she missed for a while, staring at the spray of nearly white scars and one vibrant pink ruck of angry skin.

She swallowed. "I'm so sorry for shooting you."

"I don't blame you." He stared at her and blotted at the sweat on his arms.

"How is that possible?" The slenderness of her voice translated her disbelief.

"I'd have shot you to save my family."

"You have a family?" She didn't know why the thought surprised her. He was a very desirable man. Handsome as red-hot sin. Kind as the Pope. Able as anyone she'd ever seen.

"Had," he corrected.

Carmen's heart stuttered and she rubbed at the ache. "I'm sor—"

He stopped her with the smallest shake of his head. He didn't want her sympathy. Tough. He had it all the same. Though she'd had nightmares about it daily for the last few weeks, she couldn't fathom losing Sophia, much less a family. She wondered what happened to them, but wouldn't ask. It explained the hint of sadness she'd seen in his eyes the moment he'd turned on her in the office.

"About earlier. I didn't mean to rip your head off and eat it for dinner."

"No?" he asked, with a shifty brow and the barest hint of a smile.

"It's just... No one has ever shown protectiveness nor possessiveness over Sophia. I'm not used to people helping me or looking out for her." He reached around her again, grabbed the sweater he had on earlier, and pulled it over his head. Carmen stuck her hands in the pockets of her jacket and looked for stars to keep from staring. "It's always been the two of us. I love her, care for her, protect her. No one else. I'm greedy. I've never had to share her affection."

"So, you're not married?"

Her jaw slacked again. "How is that relevant?"

"If you're married it's quite relevant."

"How?"

He stepped closer and his breaths, now slow and easy, tickled her neck. "You're a smart, capable, devastatingly beautiful woman, Carmen. Figure it out."

Chapter Nineteen

Carmen's mouth opened and closed so many times she resembled a fish. The most beautiful one he'd ever seen. She mumbled something about having a jaw wired shut and he wondered if his gentle overture had been too much. He'd never gotten a busted jaw from coming onto a woman, but Carmen was so dynamic he could see it happening. Damn, he shouldn't proposition her at all. But he couldn't stop the kinetic bursts her presence, or even the thought of her, provoked. Not one little bit. The one always in control watched it evaporate as though it never existed for only the second time in his life.

"How can you think of me without unadulterated hatred? I shot you. My name is Carmen Félix-Ruez." She ticked off the offenses on her fingers and then held them up. "That's only two, but they should count as ten apiece. No foul balls. No pass balls. No interference or walks. Just swinging-at-the-air strikes. This is America. Three strikes and you're out."

"You know baseball."

"Of course," she said, cocking her head and cutting her gaze. "Doesn't everybody?"

He smiled.

"Stop that," Carmen ordered.

"Stop what?" he asked with an even bigger grin.

"Smiling at me. I don't deserve them." Her head shook so vehemently that a thick, gentle curl fell forward over her shoulder.

"You're an interesting woman, Carmen."

"And you're confounding, Mr. Tucker."

"Call me Vail."

"We'll see."

She had this way of looking at him with a mixture of surprise, disbelief, and hope that cut him deep and flayed him wide.

"I don't hold your family against you," he whispered.

"I do."

"Maybe you should stop."

Her chin tilted to the stars, glistening high against the black of night. A long swirl of steam curled from her lips. Vail banked the urge to take her chin in his grip, turn it to him, and kiss her crazy, crazy as he felt.

"Maybe one day I'll try. After I get Sophia away from them for good. After we start over. Maybe soon. Finally." Her chin dropped and her gaze met his. "I am married, have been since before Sophia was born. But...the union has never been con-summated."

Now Vail was the one left looking like a fish. Three failed attempts later, his voice cooperated with his mouth. "So, you're telling me you're the next Virgin Mary?"

"Hardly." Her eyes rolled toward the heavens and her mouth spread wide. Peals of laughter slipped between her red lips. He watched the heat turn the cold damp air to smoke, yet still didn't be-lieve his ears.

Except for beaming at her daughter, Vail had only seen fear, sadness, and mistrust in her features. Her laugh was infectious, but he held his own awed chuckle back, afraid it would interrupt hers.

"The look on your face is priceless," she continued giggling. Too quickly though she sobered. "I get the feeling you laugh about as often as I do."

"It's infrequent." He dragged his hand over his mouth, scraping it across the stubble collected on his face.

"Sophia brings it out in you." A prideful smile lit her eyes.

"And you too," he offered.

"Ah, most of the time we fight like cocks in a cage."

As if called upon, his dick stirred. Vail held the balled, sweaty T-shirt with both hands in front of his waist. He cleared his throat. "Nah, I wouldn't worry about that. It's the parents who don't fight for their kids, which often means fighting with them, that worry me."

"I hope you're right."

"So, you're not the next Virgin Mary and you are married, but you've never had sex with your husband and you have a daughter. By birth?"

"Yes." Her voice rose near to a yell. "Twenty-three hours of labor and stretch marks prove it."

"It was just a question, Carmen, not an accusation. I'm not trying to take Sophie away from you."

"Her name is Sophia. Not Sophie. Sophia!" She slapped at a lone tear on her cheek.

"You're accustomed to people trying to take her from you." He ignored her outburst and simply stated what he knew to be true. It went a long way to explaining her overbearing nature with Sophie.

"My family…" She didn't bother to finish the thought. She didn't need to. Her bitter sneer said it all.

"You are not your family."

Carmen barked a dour laugh. "I've done horrible things." Her gaze dropped to his torso.

"So have I, but reasoning makes all the difference."

"Not to the people you hurt." The barely audible rasp reached his ears an instant before her hands slipped from the pockets of her jacket and clutched the edge of his sweater.

Vail held his breath. Inch by inch the chilly breeze met his skin. Higher and higher Carmen lifted the fabric until it crowded his chest. Her fingers grazed the freshest scar on his middle. His eyes closed and he swallowed as the touch slowly circled the healed wound.

"Does it hurt?" she whispered.

"Yes and no."

Her touch left his side and the sweater slipped down, blocking the chill he'd happily endure for her feather-light caress. As if she read his mind, one of her hands cupped his wrist and lifted, while her other skimmed his chin. Vail's eyes popped open at the intimate contact. A hint of lilac tickled his nose. With not a flower in sight he guessed the scent came from Carmen. Before he could commit the essence to memory it flitted away on the wind.

"What happened to your chin and wrist?" A frown grooved her siren's face.

Only then did he notice the blood and lipstick-caked split on her lower lip. "What the hell happened to your lip?"

"It's nothing." Her warm fingers slipped from his chin, but her grip shifted on his wrist and tightened on his forearm. Almost absentmindedly, she clung to him while she hid her mouth and blinked back moisture. "You really should have cleaned these wounds better. Come in and I'll help." Carmen moved to turn. Realizing she clutched his arm, she pulled her hand back. "I didn't mean to—"

He snatched the cold, leather covered arm and turned her back. Vail tamped his flaring temper. At least, he tried. Counting to ten in the five languages he knew didn't help much. "Tell me what happened," he insisted, without yelling.

"It's nothing. As I said before."

"You boil my temper." Lord, what happened to his icy detachment? It suited him better. The itch that lay just under his skin irritated him like a mattress full of bedbugs.

"I was so enraged and helpless to save Sophia... I provoked them. It's not a big deal. I took out my frustration on a few of my brother's men. The ones left standing took theirs out of me."

"How many were there?" he bit.

"A few," she lied.

"At least now I know your tell. When you lie you stare at my chest and your nose twitches."

"What?"

"Yep, almost like Samantha on Bewitched, but not quite."

"Who's that?"

"Jesus," his rage ebbed replaced by disbelief. "I'm not that much older than you."

She smiled and her tongue flicked out, swiping over her busted lip. Her smile fell. "I didn't want Sophia to notice. I only wore lipstick to conceal the cut. She has enough to worry about. Please, don't mention it around her." Big and soft, her gaze implored.

"All right."

He tugged closer until her boots butted his own. With little thought he slipped his hand beneath her chin and tilted. Her gaze, which had bounced between his chest and forehead, settled on his. The whites of her eyes grew along with the black of her pupils. As before her mouth fell open. Vail slid the pad of his thumb over her full lower lip, taking care with the abused flesh.

"You didn't tell me about your wrist or chin." Her murmured breath warmed his thumb.

Vail's heart thundered in his ears, but he didn't shy from the spike in his adrenaline. He bent his head. Licked his lips. Inhaled delicious lilac and clean woman. Carmen relaxed into his touch and he closed the gap.

"Oh, man! Sorry," Sophie begged.

He jerked his lips from Carmen's sweet mouth. Both their heads swung around to find the young girl wide-eyed in the frame of the front door. A smirk quirked one corner of her mouth and red stained her cheeks. Carmen's too. The red cheeks, not the shy smile. If he thought the woman's eyes were wide before, he apparently hadn't seen anything yet. They looked close to popping from their sockets. Sophie eased behind the door.

"Sophie, are you okay? What's the matter?" His questions stopped her before the door reached the latch.

"I'm fine." She peered from the safety of the shelter, biting the side of her mouth. She held out her hand. In it his phone's screen lit. "Someone called. I figured it might be important."

"You did great, Sophia. Thank you." Carmen slipped from his grasp in more ways than one and hurried to her daughter's side.

Chapter Twenty

By the time Vail reached Sophie the screen had turned black. Her little lips pressed together so tightly a dimple formed on one cheek. When he reached out for the phone her reserve broke and she whimpered.

"I figured it was important," Sophie said, looking at a spot somewhere above his head.

"I'm sure it is. Thank you." The last social call had been months ago. His mother had phoned to wish him a happy birthday.

Vail entered his obscenely long security code, saw the encrypted number for the Base Branch office, and hit redial. While he leaped through the hoops to gain access, his gaze veered over Carmen. His blood had cooled to a simmer, but one look at her and it rolled. Desire as he had not experienced in so very long clawed at his neat restraint.

Her hands hid in her pockets once again. The gesture most often hinted at a lack of self-confidence. In others it alluded to deceit. Carmen had taken charge after breaking into the Base Branch's Washington Headquarters. With her weep-worthy curves, stunning agility, and the seductive beauty of her face she had to know most men would kneel at her feet, if she only gave the order. Vail didn't figure her lacking self-confidence. He'd found her tell and it most certainly wasn't hands in pockets.

So, what did it say? That he overanalyzed her, himself, and this entire situation? Probably. The way her gaze flitted about like a mayfly, though the hidden hands spoke of avoidance. And he was what she looked to dodge.

Not a chance.

"Bloody hell," Khani blurted.

"What happened to, 'Hey, how are you?'" Vail asked.

"Smart ass, answer your phone. You almost had the team you don't want shining a light up your keister."

"It was one minute, Khani. Hardly anything to get worked up over."

"You think. I know better. It's going like a bomb around here." Good thing he'd worked with her for more than a year and knew that last bit was Brit speak for, 'Shit's going down fast.'

"What's happened?" he demanded, hating being in the dark when his people needed him. Then he looked at Sophia and Carmen. Other people needed him too. For now, at least.

"Radio chatter is abuzz. A bomb took out Sinaloa facilities in Caborca. We have three teams en route. One to collect evidence and survey the sites. Another is headed to the Sinaloa's hold in Puerto Peñasco; it's a tourist town. The last is headed to Hermosillo. The word is at least four more bombs are set to blow. But none of this is confirmed." Khani huffed, impatient of the wait.

"Jesus," Vail breathed. "Do you have any idea of the death toll? We didn't take those facilities in February because of their proximity to civilians."

"It doesn't look good," Khani stated.

"Who?" Vail asked, though he had his guess.

"Some say Zetas, but my money is on Carlos Ruez and his AFO. The pudgy bastard is behind bars, has been beat to hell and back thanks to your shooter, but the look on his face is smug. Triumphant."

"I'd put my money there too."

Vail pinched the bridge of his nose. His people could do more than most. Still, they weren't miracle workers. They could maybe stop one bomb, but what about the others? With radio chatter, second hand, and after the fact intelligence was as reliable as a million marbles, bouncing and rolling across a tile floor. The information changed direction, tripped you up. He needed information from the source, or as close to it as he could get.

"What you said about Carlos's promise to get out puts me on edge. I would have thought it impossible to infiltrate the office, but if your assailant can, it leaves us exposed. Damn it to hell," Khani added, giving voice to her irritation.

"Double security, especially at her entry points, and—"

"Her, who?" Khani demanded. "Look, I've given you time and too much space. You have to give me something."

"She's not a threat," he skirted.

"She shot you. Almost killed you. Carlos's leverage over her or not, I bathed in your blood," Khani rebuffed.

"If someone held your brother captive," Vail whispered, "is there anything you wouldn't do to get him back safely?"

The line was quiet for a weighted minute. "Fine," Khani relented. "Maybe she's not. I still want to know."

"I'll tell you. Just not yet." He depressed the end button before she could protest and stared at Carmen.

Chapter Twenty-one

Was his stare accusing or were her guilty conscience and his intense stare wreaking havoc on her brain function again? Carmen couldn't be sure. Curiosity gnashed at her heels, but self-preservation won out, as it always did. She slipped one hand out of her coat pocket and grabbed Sophia's hand.

"Sophia, it's time for bed." Carmen tugged and her daughter followed, dragging her sneaker covered feet. Her other hand left the comfort of her cozy pocket and reached for the doorknob. Vail's fingers encircled her wrist before she touched brass.

A tight smile sat upon his face, but finally his intense eyes didn't study her. "Sophie, I need a moment alone with your mother."

Carmen's stomach *zinged*. It had little to do with their name war she'd grown to appreciate.

"Sure," her daughter smiled, "take all the time you need." She wiggled her brows.

"Sophia Ruez." Carmen could have died on the spot. "It's not like that."

"Speak for yourself," Vail chimed.

Sophia wriggled free of her grasp, skirted through the door before anyone could blink, snickering all the while. Shock again held Carmen's mouth agape. Her tongue had been exposed to the elements so much, it was a wonder it hadn't frozen solid.

Vail planted himself between her and the door. His hot touch seared her skin through the leather as it slid to her shoulder. He bracketed her other arm in his grip and poured the full force of his gaze onto her. Indignation at his brazen touch should have strengthened her spine. Instead, her insides softened at the harbor he provided from the frigid wind and simultaneously melted like liquefied steel at the provocative slant of his brows.

"You might want to close your mouth. It's awful tempting."

"Tempting?" Why had she asked that of all the questions floating around her head?

"Mmm." He slipped closer. "All it would take is a slide of my hand." His fingers caressed their way up her neck. Her cheek nestled in the warmth of his palm. "A tilt of your head." He urged her head back with his thumb. "And I could lick the heat flickering in your eyes to an all out inferno."

Lord, she shouldn't want this. He should want it even less. Yet, her heart shimmied and her breaths came in heavy pants. Longing electrified every nerve ending, making his light touches exquisitely acute.

"But," he continued, only an inch from her mouth, "Sophie is watching through the window and I don't know if I could bring myself to stop kissing you, touching you, once I started."

Carmen should care about her daughter watching, but her body submitted to his spell. She pressed into his hand at her neck. Filled her lungs with his heady scent. Sweat and the promise of sex. An animalistic self-indulgence that quaked her knees at the mere image it scorched into her mind.

"Tonight, when you're lying in bed, I want you to think about...your willingness to help stop your brother. He detonated one bomb in Sinaloa territory dense with civilians and has more planned."

She stiffened. The trance lifted. Reality slapped her cheeks, both sides. Here she was expecting to hear him, the Base Branch Commander beguile her with thoughts of him moving between her thighs. Shame and anger heated her cheeks. All he wanted from her was Carlos's keys to power.

Did she want to stop her brother? Hell yes. Nothing would give her greater peace than to never worry about that psychopath and his goons again. But foremost, over anything else—even her withered but sprouting libido—she had Sophia to think of. Carmen possessed the will, yet lacked the ability to charge into battle against her family. If anything happened to her, Sophia would be alone, completely unprotected in this world. Getting Sophia to safety remained priority one, regardless of her brother's actions.

Sadness over her greed plopped onto her back, a relentless burden she'd lived with for eleven years. For the first time, the will to change that flickered in her soul.

Vail donned the mask of cool detachment she had not seen since their first encounter. Just as well. The price for a sexy fling with this man was greater than she could afford. She withdrew from his heat and the cold embraced her, a cold she'd likely carry for the rest of her life. When she turned to the door footsteps scuttled across the interior floor.

"Carmen." His gruff voice pulled her like a gaping vortex, but she couldn't turn. "While you're in bed, think about our kiss too. About how it will feel roaming every bit of your flesh."

Chapter Twenty-two

Vail had the lion's share of long nights during his career. The longest weren't the ones spent laid-up in the hospital nor the ones perched securely in the nest of an enemy camp awaiting the quietest dark morning hours to make his move. Time all but ground to a halt his first day back in the home he'd shared with Ellie and, strangely enough, this night. The moon swung across the muted night. The sun brightened the sky one degree at a time. The windows frosted and collected the easy snow that fell all the while.

At one point he turned the water in the kitchen and bathroom to drip to keep the pipes from freezing. Walking past her bedroom door he'd paused, not knowing exactly what made him stop, until the rustle of sheets caught his attention. Sleep evaded her too. The urge to go to her sent him one step in the direction of her door. He needed to better explain what he didn't understand himself. His desire to protect her and Sophie. His need to possess her as perhaps he'd never possessed anyone before.

A primal surge sent him forward another step and another. Soon he stood inches from the flimsy wooden entryway. His hand hovered over the knob. One hushed sniffle halted his advance and nearly knocked him on his butt. When she'd hurried from the porch hours ago sadness and indecision had marbled her eyes, and still he'd never imagined Carmen Ruez crying. The one tear he'd seen slip from her lashes seemed all she'd been capable of producing. A deep inner strength allowed her to deal with the hell of her life, so she could enjoy Sophie. Resolve like that also set her apart from the rest of the world, an untouchable force even he couldn't reckon with. Then again, maybe not so untouchable. Regardless, he'd slunk back down the stairs, lay with his hands behind his head, and watched the minutes crawl past.

When Vail could no longer stare at the sun's arduous climb into the sky he hurried upstairs and rushed a shower. He ignored his jutting cock. The hard flesh and harder desire refused dissuasion, swelling thicker under the hot beat of the water. Vail turned the hot water off altogether. He braced against the icy water, while he eradicated the day's and rough night's grime from his body.

It did the trick. His pants buttoned and zipped without crushing his manhood.

Small favors and all.

After a full seven hours awake with no food, Vail's stomach turned against him like a rabid dog. He hurried downstairs, failing in his effort to ignore the light shining from beneath Carmen's bedroom door. After raiding the fridge for the essentials, Vail set about preparing breakfast. His stomach snarled as the salty richness of pan-seared bacon wafted up his nose.

Not one minute later, Sophie bustled down the steps while wrestling her hair into a messy blob atop her head. Her molars gleamed in her oversized smile.

"Morning Sunshine." He saluted with the spatula.

"Good morning." She placed a hand on his shoulder, launched her dainty frame into the air, and *smacked* a kiss on his cheek.

Vail spread the sizzling meat onto the napkin-covered plate he'd fixed earlier and hoped she didn't desire conversation. True enough, that insignificant peck rendered him dumb. Sophie bebopped to the refrigerator as though the world hadn't just flipped poles. She pulled the jug of orange juice from the recesses then grabbed three glasses from the cabinet.

"You want juice or milk? Or coffee?" she asked.

For the life of him, his lips refused to move.

She sidled up to him, jug in hand and now a silly grin on her face. "Hey, you in there? Or are you daydreaming?" Her stomach must have tormented her too, because her gaze zeroed on the scalding bacon and her hand followed.

"Sophia!" From the steps, Carmen's voice spiked with panic.

The girl's delicate fingers hovered just over the still cooking meat. Vail snatched Sophie's hand away and pulled it protectively to his chest.

"What?" she whined. The wispy fly-aways framing her face flittered in the breeze of her swiveling head.

"You could have burned yourself." He intended to speak normally, but the words hardly broke the hum of the refrigerator's compressor.

"I'm hungry."

"Me too," he said with a little more gusto.

"Sophia Ruez, remember your manners," her mother admonished.

"It's okay. It seems I've also misplaced mine." He pinched a piece of bacon between his thumb and forefinger, tossed it into the air, and bobbled it between his hands until the heat dissipated. Then he broke the length in two and handed one to Sophie. "I'd like juice, please."

"Mom, what do you want? Juice? Milk? Water?"

"Water, please." Carmen's voice grew nearer.

Sophie hopped off to fill their orders. Her mother took up the post her daughter vacated, allowing more space between them. Unlike her daughter, Carmen didn't give him a smile. Her mouth pursed and her brows snuggled in the middle of her forehead.

"What?" he whispered.

"You're making me the bad guy," she huffed.

"What?" he said again. He truly had no idea what she referred to. Maybe the Base Branch. Maybe her brother.

"Sophia." She managed to yell in a whisper. "You can't just give her what she wants. It does her no good in the long run. Life isn't like that. Ask and receive."

"No, it's not." He placed several more slices into the pan. "Will you push down the toaster?" he asked without looking up. She sidestepped and depressed the lever, sending the bread to tan. When she settled her hip back again the bar he found her gaze and smiled. "But sometimes it can be."

Carmen buried her face in her hands and shook her head. Her dark curls danced about her chest. Then, little by little, in the small separation of her hands a smile stretched her lips. Her hands dropped and slipped into her tight jeans pockets. The move shifted her already up-right posture, thrusting her cotton-covered breasts at him. He shifted the bacon to keep from panting like a hound-dog.

"You're impossible," she laughed.

I'm way too possible.

He barricaded the word inside his mouth. Any more prodding from him and she'd scoop Sophie into her arms and go to ground.

"So, Mom?" Sophie's words questioned without asking anything at all.

"Yes, Sophia." Carmen turned her wattage on her daughter.

"Me and Vail planned to—"

"Vail and I," he and Carmen corrected in unison.

"You're ganging up on me." Sophie wrinkled her nose. "Ugh!"

Carmen's gaze cut toward him. "It's all for the good of your grammar. Now, what did you plan?"

"Vail and I," she elongated the *I* as only a petulant child could, "planned to fish this morning. You wanna... Do you want to come with us, Mother dearest?"

"You might want to take a peek outside, Sophie." Vail warned.

He pulled the last of the bacon off the flame, yanked the final two pieces of toast from the machine, and constructed their BLT's.

"Aw, man. Wow." Sophie muttered from the front window. He turned at her bedazzled exclamation. Laughter would have plagued him. Her nose nearly smashed against the glass at the winter wonderland. However, the one duck-taped pane whiplashed his humor with utter solemnity.

The gravity of their situation choked him, until Carmen assumed the task. Next to him, she leaned closer to peer out of the kitchen window. His head snapped around as the heat from her jutting breasts whispered over his arm, curling need deep in his belly.

"We can go," he choked, "but we probably won't catch anything."

"But a cold," Carmen corrected. One corner of her mouth quirked in amusement.

"There is that possibility," he agreed.

Carmen's head pivoted, huddling them eye to chest. Her cheer expired the moment their gazes locked and the proximity of their bodies registered. Those likable red lips parted on a silent gasp. His fingers itched to cradle her nape in his palm, pull her forward those few inches, and fuse their mouths together.

"Let's go for a little while, please," Sophie begged.

For Carmen the trance broke with her daughter's voice. She eased away. He let her retreat and turned to Sophie's bright and hopeful eyes. Whether about the near kiss or the snow, he couldn't be too sure. Either way, he couldn't deny that face. Not him. He nodded. Carmen's nod came after a suspended delay, entering his periphery. But it did come.

He and Sophie scarfed down the sandwiches. With some prodding from her daughter, Carmen ate faster than she had last night. When she finished, she stood, collected Sophie's plate and glass, and then tried to get his.

"I can clean up. You don't need to do that," Vail said, guarding his plate.

"You cooked. I'll clean." She scooted his hand from in front of the dishes. The contact, casual and insignificant, ignited their gazes. They locked and held for several seconds.

"Thank you," he conceded.

Sophie had the gear ready and Carmen had the kitchen cleaned in no time. They stood at the door. When he hustled downstairs Sophie shifted back and forth on her heels in a comical dance of impatience. "Jackets off," he ordered. Carmen's eyes inflated, while Sophie's narrowed. Both females' cheeks reddened, though Vail guessed for very different reasons. He waved the sweaters in his hand. "Put these on underneath. It's too cold out there for your puny layers."

Realizing what he meant to do, Sophie dropped the gear and shucked her jacket in seconds. She held up a hand. "Are those yours? Because I'd rather freeze to death than wear anything that belonged to those scumbags."

"They're mine. They'll be a little big, but we'll fold up the sleeves," he explained.

Sophie grabbed eagerly for hers. Carmen looked loath to touch the one he offered, like its insulating layer was elementary school cooties. The young girl wormed her way into the cocoon. She stared down at herself. "Gah, it's huge." The bottom hem hit her mid-thigh and her hands hid a good five inches up the sleeves.

"Come here," he instructed. She shuffled forward and presented the drooping fabric. He knelt and maneuvered the extra up her arm. By the time he finished she had nearly two layers of wool covering her arms. She hopped to the door, retrieving the gear. His gaze lifted to Carmen.

"You need help?" he asked.

"I've got it," she insisted, even as she wrestled with the excess fabric.

She pinned the end she struggled to fold back against her breasts and attempted to flip it with the other hand. Time and again, she shoved the wool up her opposite arm and twice the stiff material straightened over her fingers, thwarting her efforts.

"Here. Let me help." He stayed on one knee and offered his hand.

After a last useless push, she stepped in front of him, but remained far enough back that she didn't enter the part of his thighs. He grabbed the edge of the sweater. The muscles in her sleek neck worked on a large gulp. Pleasure coursed through him. He flipped both without touching her, and then stood, closing the distance between them.

"Thank you," she croaked.

"No problem." Slowly he slid both hands on either side of her neck, reveling in the smooth, warm skin under his touch. Again she swallowed, but this time her muscles danced beneath his hand. When he almost completely encircled her tender flesh he lifted his hands, tugging her trapped hair from between the sweater and tank. Her lashes rested on her cheeks and her chin arched slightly. He settled her flowing locks around her shoulders. "All right?"

"Yes," she breathed and opened her eyes.

The softness of her upper lip tempted him. So, he stepped around her and hurried to open the door for Sophie. Progress to the lake was slow as they dodged ice slicks and felt their way along the hidden trail. Finally the ice-glassed surface came into view. On either side of him, the females stalled.

"Whoa," Carmen gasped. "It's frozen over."

"Oh my gosh," Sophie squealed, dropping the tackle and tugging his arm. "I've never been ice skating."

"And one day you will, but not today." Vail squelched both girls' excitement with that statement. Carmen's wide eyes narrowed and Sophie's everything drooped like a wilted flower. "It may look frozen from here, but this isn't Michigan. It's probably only paper-thin ice toward the middle. And I'm sorry to break it to you, but we're not fishing in it either."

"But can we go closer?" Sophie prodded.

"Sure," he agreed.

Growing up in Mexico, they'd probably never seen snow or a frozen lake. Sophie forgot the fishing equipment in the powder. She grabbed Carmen's hand and they ran to the water's edge. Vail hung back, giving them distance, and also working diligently to stuff the well of emotion into the neat and tightly sealed travel case where he usually toted them. The desire to pack these two into his car and drive north until they found a proper ice staking rink overwhelmed him, along with the knowledge that something so familial and carefree would never happen with the girls or anyone else.

"You've got to come see this," Sophie hollered back. At him.

The knot in his throat looped and cinched so tight it would do any sailor proud. He coughed, and then strained for simple words. None came. So, he nodded, ran a hand over his growing scruff, and put one foot in front of the other.

"Look." Sophie eased one foot onto the crystalline ice and settled her weight more heavily on the frosty surface.

Vail shook his head. When he reached her side he tugged her back onto solid ground. He leaned down and picked up a rocked half the size of his palm. "Hold out your hand." She did and he placed the stone in her bowled palm. Carmen sidled next to him, but he paid her no attention. He couldn't right now, not when desperation pushed him toward ridiculous notions. "How much do you think it weighs?"

"Less than a pound." She shrugged. "I don't know. Twelve ounces."

"That's a good guess." He took the chunk of earth back and tossed it a few inches into the air a couple of times. "How much do you weigh?"

She grinned and swiped at her nose. "It's a good thing you didn't ask my mom that question. You'd never get an answer."

"I weight one-hundred thirty-five, or so, pounds, thank you," Carmen scoffed.

A chuckle lightened his burden. He clung to the temporary high. "And you?"

"Ninety pounds at my last doctor's appointment." Sophie smiled.

"Look." He used the word she'd said only a moment ago to drive the message home. Then he slung the rock across the ice. It slid and ramped the small seams where the water sealed together. It stopped about forty feet off the shore and sat at the water's surface as though suspended by magic.

"See," the girl beamed. She leaped into the air and turned to face him. "It's safe."

With a hand on her shoulder he pivoted her back to the water.

"What. Where'd it g... Oh, man," she whined, staring at the black hole punctured on the otherwise pristine ice.

"Not one foot on the ice, Sophie," he warned.

"Yes, sir." She huffed and shuffled away. Several feet down the shore, she picked up a rock from the bank and hurled it. The pitch was so steep it crashed through the ice into the lake. Seemingly pleased with the sound and splash, she repeated the cycle several times. Wandering and tossing.

Carmen stood staring at the winter wonderland. For a moment Vail catalogued her sways and dips, the way the wind caught tendrils of her obsidian locks, the strong set of her jaw that hosted lips plush enough to suck a man into a coma.

"Why do you call her Sophie?" The surprise of her voice kicked him in the nuts.

He huffed.

Way to go, Tucker. What an upstanding gentleman you are.

"She hasn't grown into Sophia, yet. It's a lovely name and she will, probably too soon, but for now she's just a kid." She broke her gaze from the lake and squared him with it. "Why do you call her Sophia?"

"No one's ever asked me that before." She covered her mouth with her fingers, and then let the hand rest at her side. "My father's great-aunt was a nun at a mission in Ensenada." For only the second time he heard the accent thick on her tongue. The first had been when she used Sophie's full name, reprimanding the girl as only a mother could. "Her name was Sophia and she was the only good person I could find in all of our bloodline. I hope for her the wisdom of her name's meaning and the grace from her name's sake."

"What about the wisdom and grace from her mother?" he asked.

"Ha, there is good in me. Just not enough. I'm tainted."

"Most of us are," Vail countered. "But I think you sell yourself short."

"Or maybe I'm just honest with myself." She ducked around him, heading in the opposite direction of Sophie.

Vail hooked his index finger around hers. Their arms outstretched, facing away from each other, he found an obscene amount of comfort in the simplicity of their touch. Her cold finger tightened around his and the edge of her thumb brushed his skin. Breath wedged in his throat. He squeezed in return.

"Maybe you sell yourself short too," she whispered.

Maybe he—

A large splash severed his thought. Immediately he searched out Sophie. Her sunken footsteps meandered in the snow to a fallen tree protruding from the woods and gradually sinking below the surface twenty feet from the bank. He and Carmen released each other at the same time and bolted toward the last place they'd seen Sophie. Carmen faded into the background as he surged forward, terror lending him speed. It took too long to clear the distance.

The tree's mossy bark boasted a scuff mere feet from the submerged end. The closer he drew the blacker the hole in the ice on the far side of the tree grew.

Fucking no. Christ, no.

Not a ripple broke the water.

Vail pushed harder. Perpendicular to the chasm, he launched himself belly first onto the ice. He skidded. The sharp, uneven terrain clawed at his chest for what seemed like miles. At last the murky water centered his aim, he drew one full breath, and plunged into the depths.

Fear already shocked the heat from his body. So the freezing water didn't sting. He forced his eyes wide, whirling in a circle as his body righted itself. In the distance a tornado of bubbles danced. He kicked hard, bearing down on the little girl who clawed and beat the frozen surface. Her need for air overwhelmed all other urges. Vail knew this from his training. He'd been pushed to the edge, where Sophie hung, and further.

Training dictated he wait until she sank into unconsciousness and then revive her at the surface. He refused to wait and watch. Instead, he elongated his strokes, cupped his hands, and kicked from the hip to his rubber soles.

Vail's hand fisted in Sophie's jacket. He turned her to him. Desperation gnarled her pretty face. She clawed at his. Her body took over, panic and the anxiety to live usurping all else. He kicked to keep them from sinking deeper and pulled her closer still. One arm banded her in an unrelenting hug. They lurched and thrashed through her struggle.

He held tight, managing to pinch his thumb and forefinger over her nose. With all his might, he wrenched her face to his, sealed his mouth over hers, and blew gently. Once her body caught on, she sucked the air from his lungs. His pipes burned for air. He snuggled to the sensation, refusing panic, the normal human reaction.

With unceasing kicks Vail turned them toward the dim light shining through the hole and propelled them forward. He looped one arm around her torso and used the other to power forward. The nearer the light grew the more tunneled his vision became.

He shoved Sophie at the hole. She burst thought the surface. Sweet air filled her lungs. And for that he'd be ever grateful. As he fought for consciousness and the strength not to inhale, he drifted, at peace with the sacrifice he'd made.

Chapter Twenty-three

Carmen stared into hell. It had been more than a minute since the splash and her hope turned as colorless as the water. The slick surface refused to crest with life. She gripped the ice. Tears pooled onto the tiny glacier. A scream ripped from her throat, echoing across the barren wilderness.

Not her baby. Not after she'd just gotten her back. Not after they'd just gotten away. If Sophia never surfaced, Carmen would end her misery in the murky water. She'd slip beneath the surface and bury herself with her daughter.

And, Vail.

Her stomach lurched at the loss of something not hers to lose.

"Please, God. If you're there. Please." Her sobs were but a feather in the heart of a typhoon. Weak. Doomed.

The *whoosh* of water startled her cry. It broke under her nose. Sophia was practically thrust into her arms. Her daughter's eyes were wide. Her heaving mouth cleaved wider as she sucked for breath. Sophia's hair slid across her face, sending a shiver to Carmen's toes.

Wild, failing arms tipped Carmen off balance, but hope imbued her with strength. She locked one arm around Sophia's waist, braced the other on the ice and wrenched her daughter from its grip.

Sophia choked. Her little lips, as blue as the clear sky, sputtered. But she breathed.

How was that possible? She'd been under for far too long. There was no way Sophia could have held her breath that long. Even she would have been hard pressed to stave off an inhalation of lake water.

Realization crackled like lightning behind her eyes.

Vail!

Bless it all, but she turned away from her daughter. Turned her back on the most precious thing in the world to her. Carmen crawled on hands and knees back to the hole. Without hesitation, she looped one leg around the tree trunk to her right and dunked the top half of her body into the water.

Electrocution had to be kinder than the icy water. It flash-froze her brain, rendering her useless. She hung there for what seemed like an hour, as her body screamed for relief.

Vail.

Determination, so deeply engrained, refused to give up without a fight. She willed her fingers and arms to move, and they did. Twisting and thrashing about, she stretched lower into the water, searching for the man who'd saved her daughter, the man she didn't have, but still didn't want to lose.

The need for breath stung her lungs like a porcupine burrowed deep inside for the winter. She refused to give up. He hadn't given up on Sophia. Or her. He deserved no less.

There it was. A brush. Something warmer than the water. Carmen arched back. Stretched so much her boot gave way. Panic seized her. If she went in, she couldn't save Vail or Sophia.

A frigid mass caught her leg, draping over both, and soaking her jeans through.

Sophia. My girl.

Pride renewed her efforts. Another swipe brought direct contact with flesh. She grabbed hold and yanked hard. Like an angler, she let her line loose—her line being her body—grabbed lower and reeled fast. His hand. His arm. His torso. She looped her arms under his. Using Sophia's weight as leverage and every muscle she possessed, Carmen levered them both to the surface.

Sweet Jesus.

Like Sophia had a minute before, Carmen hacked and wheezed, and pulled at Vail, who coughed and gasped, his body convulsing in uncontrollable fits. She grabbed his belt and yanked one last time. His torso firmly on the ice, she collapsed to the side. Amazingly, he army-crawled his body the rest of the way out of the water. Then his gaze was on her, fierce and... What? She didn't know. Then he looked past her toward Sophia.

The concern in his gaze jackknifed her. Tired or not, she reached for Sophia. Her daughter smiled weakly, but the beautiful sight could not distract from the shivers that wracked her small body. Carmen's hands moved to the zipper of her jacket, but a large hand stopped her.

"No. Let me." Vail's voice sounded as though it had been stored for a millennium and never used until now. He hacked. "I have...more body heat. You...ll freeze."

He crawled past her to Sophia, unzipped his sopping jacket, and wrapped it around her legs. Carmen felt its weight on her own legs, and its heat. She nearly groaned. She hadn't noticed how cold she was. Then he peeled the wool sweater from his chest. Like manipulating a doll, he lifted Sophia to sit, draped the cloth over her head, and tied it around her chin and neck in a make-shift hood.

The only things standing between him and the sub-freezing temperature were soaked pants, socks, boots, and a white T-shirt. Too bad she didn't have time to appreciate the hands-down winner of every wet T-shirt contest in the history of mankind. His arms shook as he bore his weight and struggled to his knees.

Carmen rolled onto hers more easily. She stood and, giving the hole a wide birth, hurried to his side, her boots slipping on the wet ice. Yet, she didn't worry about falling through. The layers were thick close to the tree trunk. She had no idea how Sophia managed to make it through the solid sheet. Bracing her legs for balance, she offered Vail a hand. Shocking her for the tenth time in as many minutes, he rested his elbow in her palm and gripped her upper arm. He used her as a human crutch to lever upright.

"I want you," he rasped, "to go to shore." After a breath and a swallow, he continued. "I'm going to drag her across the ice. It's thick, but not thick enough to hold our combined weight, if I carry her off."

"You can hardly carry yourself," she pointed out gently.

He touched his finger to the tip of her nose. "Get that sweet tush movin'. We're wasting time."

She tried to speak, but her lungs refused to cooperate. So, she cooperated with him for all their sakes. From shore she watched him wrangle a smile from Sophia's pale lips and then drag her across the ice toward shore. Once there, he leaned down, scooped Sophia up like a babe, and held her to his chest.

In that moment something rigid cracked inside Carmen. A bit of her he-woman, *'I can do it all on my own, hear me roar,'* succumbed to Vail's fierce, yet gentle, protective nature. Sophia trusted him with her life. It was time Carmen started trusting him with hers. Because Vail might be the only person on the planet who could protect Sophia better than she could.

Chapter Twenty-four

Vail's boot hit the porch step. The sight and sound gave the only indication he'd left the snow. His feet tingled with numbness part-way up the trail. The tingles turned to shards of glass slicing his soles with each step for the next half. He pushed through the discomfort. Sophie's eyelids drooped lower and lower, despite the jostling from his awkward strides. Her exhaustion from the ordeal was plain. Hell knew he could sleep for days. But first, he needed her warm and alert before he'd allow her to doze.

"Hey," he said with a shake, "is that an icicle or a booger hanging from your nose?"

Her lashes fluttered then popped open. She struggled for the briefest of moments to free her hands from her jacket pockets where he had Carmen shove them before they left the lake. Unsuccessful in that venture, the girl used other resources. She turned into his chest and nuzzled her nose against his wet T-shirt.

"Eew," he croaked. "Good thing I was just kidding."

Her sweet brown gaze met his and once more she smiled.

"That's my girl," he praised. "We're here. A warm fire. Dry clothes. Hot coffee."

She wrinkled her nose.

"Okay, the coffee's for me, then."

"And me," Carmen chimed, skirting them to open the door.

Vail stepped into the cabin and wanted to weep in thanksgiving for central heat and air. The place was drafty and damp, but nothing compared to a frozen-over lake. Carmen shivered and chaffed her arms as she closed the door with her ample backside.

"Okay, Sophie, I'm going to put you down. I want you to do your best to stay upright. It'll be hard, but I know you can do it. For just one minute."

"I can do it." Her voice cracked for the first time since the fall.

"Carmen, I need you to help her get all these wet clothes off. Yours too, if you can manage it. I'm going to get towels and blankets, and then I'll make a fire."

Both girls nodded.

He ran, or at least tried to run, up the stairs. The movements more closely resembled a cartoon where the character's feet spin and spin and they go nowhere. Winded more than he'd ever care to admit, he reached the top of the stairs. He thought to grab them both fresh clothes too, but the thought of touching Sophie's panties made him a little bit squeamish. His original plan had all kinds of merit, but he did take a moment to grab a fresh pair of pants for himself. Not much good he'd do running around naked.

In the bathroom he stripped his paltry tee and draped a towel over his shoulders. Then he set about collecting the rest of the dry linens. With a pile of towels and an armload of bedding, Vail hurried downstairs. Taking pains to avert his gaze, he got a good look at some rafter cobwebs. When he heard both girls sigh he stilled. "What's wrong?" It almost killed him not to look, not to rush to their aid, no matter the cause of their anguish. But it would kill him to breach Sophie's privacy. Carmen's...not so much.

"I can't get her clothes off," Carmen sniffled.

"I can't help her," Sophie moaned. "My arms won't work."

"Hey, it's all right," he crooned. Able to lower his gaze, he found Sophie still in her pants and the double-sleeved sweater he'd put on her earlier. All Carmen's clothes remained plastered to her body. She held tight to the sweater she'd taken from Sophie's head, while the jacket, sopping socks, and shoes lay on the floor.

He walked to the couch, scooted the clunky monstrosity closer to the fireplace, and then he set all but two large towels atop it. They weren't bath-sheets, but neither were they hand-towels masquerading as bath-towels while revealing your goods to the world. When he reached Sophie he walked around to her back.

"Carmen, take this." He offered her one of the towels and draped the other over his shoulder. "Get in front of her." She did as he asked without question. "Sophie, I'm going to stay at your back and help get these wet clothes off you, okay?"

"Okay," she whispered.

The three of them wrestled and sweated to get her clothes off, and Vail did it all while looking at his toes, the wall, the ceiling. He wrapped the towel under Sophie's arms and around her body, while Carmen dried her hair with the other.

"Here, let's get her to the couch and you can finish that there. I'll start a fire." When Carmen stepped back, he scooped Sophie in his arms and hurried to the couch. He settled her upright and piled her with two blankets. Then Carmen was there mothering.

He hustled outside, hating to let in any of the chill. Even more, he hated the way the sharp wind stiffened his man nipples.

Son of a bitch!

He was some kind of cold. Now that the girls were safe, it seeped into his pores. He hauled two stacks of wood and set them just inside the door. The third he brought directly to the fireplace.

"It's a good thing we cut all that wood," Sophie said through the chattering of her teeth.

"Absolutely," he agreed.

"Hey, Vail?" Sophie continued. Earnestness steeled her tone and jaw.

"Yeah, sweetie?" He swiveled on shaky legs. Bracing both hands on the floor for support, he smiled up at her. She was bedraggled—and beautifully alive.

"You told me not to put a foot on the ice. So, I walked the log, thinking I was smart to get one over on you. You know, technicalities and all." She staved off threatening tears with a sniff. "I'm so sorry. I almost got myself killed, and you too." Her lips scrunched and anger lit her eyes. "You shouldn't have given your breath for me, your life for mine."

He let a moment tick by, breathed deeply, and shook his head. "I can't think of a better person to give my life for, Sophie."

Vail didn't wait for a response. He turned to the empty hearth and loaded it with wood. Thanks to years of practice, he prodded the fire to crackling in less than five minutes. He turned to the girls. "Good?"

"Heaven," Carmen said, while Sophie bobbed her head adamantly. Carmen sat on the floor in all her wet clothes, chaffing her daughter's feet with the towel meant for her.

"Up you go," he said, hauling her off the floor. "Clothes off now, and towel on, or I'll help you too." He lowered his head to her ear and whispered, "And I won't avert my gaze." She drew a shaky breath.

Hard as it was, he snagged his pants from the pile on the couch and retreated to the kitchen for that pot of coffee and a small kettle of tea for Sophie. While he waited for the water to boil, he scrubbed his head with the towel. His chest, back, and shoulders came next. Then he stared at his still-frozen bottom half. The cargo pants had to go, along with the shoes and socks. He should've grabbed fresh boxers too. But he'd been in a hurry. He considered running up the stairs and grabbing some, but who was he kidding. His arm shook where he propped himself up on the counter. His legs may as well have weighed a ton each. There was no way he'd make it up the stairs right now. All his adrenaline stores depleted, he crashed hard. There was also no way he could stand the cold cotton on his keister for one more minute. He shucked them, dried his goods, and pulled on his blessedly dry pants.

The kettle piped and he made tea, ignoring the gooseflesh covering his chest and his razor-sharp nipples.

Chapter Twenty-five

Carmen fidgeted with the top of the towel and fussed with the blankets covering her and Sophia.

"It's fine, Mom," her daughter whispered. "He's not a perv."

"I know that. Otherwise, I'd have picked you up and run the second I got here."

"Then why the squirming?"

"I'm not squirming," she protested.

"*Ooooh*," Sophia crowed in realization.

"*Shhh!*"

"You like him." The first signs of color rose in her daughter's cheeks. No matter the cause, Carmen smiled. Which only incited Sophia. "You do. See."

"Will you just *shush*?"

"If you admit it, I'll zip my lips."

"He saved your life. Of course I like him," she deflected.

"Lame."

"It's true." Carmen cupped Sophia's cheek. "Twice over." She leaned in and kissed her cheek. "I love you so much, baby."

"I love you too, Momma. But that's not going to get you out of this."

"Little bulldog."

"I get it from you," she shrugged.

"I suppose you do."

"So," she said with exaggerated brows, "give up already. I'm younger and more determined. And he'll be in here in a minute. I'm sure he'd be interested in the answer too."

"Vicious," she chided.

Her daughter only shrugged the layers of blanket in return.

"Fine, yes. I like him. What's not to like? He's honest, caring, and capable, loyal and hardworking."

"He's smokin' hot too. In an old man kind of way," Sophia supplied with a little nose wrinkle.

"There are no signs of age on that man's body," Carmen protested. "I've not seen a finer specimen in all my years. His hair may be silver, but it's sexy. He's sexier than—"

Sophia smiled like a clown.

"You goaded me."

"I knew it already," she inclined her head. "You just needed to admit it."

"You are some piece of work, child of mine. Some piece of work."

"I'll second that," Vail chimed in, walking around the corner from the kitchen with a steaming mug, with no shirt, and no towel this time to interrupt her gaze.

Were the gods sculpted as beautifully as this man? Carmen didn't think so. It wasn't just his body, but his face too. Artful lines, dips, and sways. That regal jaw and cute nose, serious mouth and soulful eyes. She relaxed back into the sofa, and may have swooned for the first time in her life.

He walked straight for her. Carmen's body responded in kind. Her heart galloped toward him. Her nipples followed, shamelessly stiffening. She barred her hips from rocking forward. She wasn't a whore. In fact, next to a nun, she was the furthest thing from one. But her body seemed to have contracted amnesia.

Those hooded, almost-black eyes never shied from her body. They did take the tour though. Twice, lingering at the barest hint of breasts at the top of her towel. When he stood in front of her his gaze lifted, somewhat reluctantly.

"As soon as this hits her stomach she'll want to sleep. But make sure she drinks at least half. Our coffee will be ready in a minute. How do you take it?"

Any way you want to give it to me.

For the sake of her daughter and her sanity, Carmen stuffed her first response into the recesses of her increasingly naughty mind. "Black." She said it while staring into his raven eyes, and wondered if he'd get the double meaning. But she wasn't good at flirting. She'd never done it.

He stared into her eyes—the same almost-onyx as his—and said, "I like mine black too."

Vail may have been talking strictly coffee, but her blood tripled its flow straight to her lady parts. The edge of his mouth twitched, and then he headed into the kitchen.

"Mom?"

Oh yes, she had a daughter. She had a daughter sitting right next to her while she sat in nothing more than a towel and blanket and lusted over a shirtless man.

Mother of the year. Not.

"Here you go, sweetie." Carmen snapped out of her stupor and handed her daughter the mug. She kept her hands around Sophia's and helped her steady the cup to her mouth.

"Mmm," Sophia sighed.

Mmm, indeed.

Sophia continued to sip. Sure enough her shoulders drooped and she rested back onto the cushion.

"Oh no you don't. Up, missy, and drink."

"I just want to sleep, Momma."

"Drink up. Or I'll be forced to pour it into your ear," Vail threatened.

The sleepy girl perked. "You wouldn't dare."

"Wouldn't I?" One brow arched.

Sophia took two large gulps.

"You're going to burn your tongue," Carmen warned.

"Nah," both the goofs agreed at the same time.

They all chuckled. That light laughter sheered the edge off the panic still prodding Carmen's mind. She took the mug Sophia offered, having surpassed the dictate from Vail, and she set it on the end table.

"Just in time for your own." He settled the piping mug in her hands then sat on the opposite side of Sophia. His huge bare foot propped on his opposite knee and his elbow rested on the arm of the sofa. He looked so at ease in his shirtless beauty. "How you feeling, kiddo?"

"Tired, but you and the other warden won't let me sleep."

Vail laughed outright. A sleepy, unguarded quality snuggled the sound. Carmen's lips curved in utter delight. Then she sipped the coffee. Contentment washed over her. This was all so difficult, but it could be easy. If she let it. If she believed in him. If she believed in herself.

"Give me your hand," he ordered.

Sophia obeyed with effort. Vail grimaced as he held her daughter's little hands and studied the jagged edges of her fingernails. "You're a fighter.

Just like your mom." He pressed at the base of her nail bed, held it for several seconds, and then released it. "Your color's good." He fluffed her hair, tangling the knotted mass all the more. "Snooze."

"Thank you, for everything." Sophia smiled.

"You already said that," he scolded.

"And I'll say it again, and again. Forever. You might as well get used to it." As if on cue, she yawned like a kitten. She leaned back into the cushion, but Carmen tugged her shoulders.

Sophia allowed Carmen to pillow her head in her lap. She stroked the hair a degree or two softer than her own, even littered with tiny bits of lake debris. Carmen leaned down and smoothed a kiss over her chilly skin. "I love you," she whispered.

"I love you too, Momma," she yawned.

Carmen sipped the warm liquid and coddled her daughter. Degree by slow degree Sophia's tense muscles relaxed. She stretched from her fetal ball, shoving her legs across Vail's thighs. He smiled, tucked the cover around her exposed feet, and drank from his mug.

By the time Sophia settled and her breaths came long and even, Carmen's cup sat half full—from her current way of thinking. She set it to the side with the other cup and cut her gaze to Vail. He stared into the fire. As she watched, his expression marbled from brooding to happy, and back again.

She shifted her legs toward him, Sophia not so much as stirring. Openly, she eyed him. Her heart jacked from her sternum to her throat. Once. Twice. She swallowed.

Time to go for broke.

"Do you want my help with Carlos or my body more?"

He took another swig from his mug and continued to stare. Maybe she hadn't said the words she'd intended. Maybe her brain intervened with what her body—and her heart—wanted, and hadn't let the right words escape. Because one way or another she expected a reaction from him.

Her cheeks had to be fire-engine red by the time he finally turned his head and accosted her with his gaze.

"Your help with Carlos..." her heart pitched "...should be my priority." She blinked and stared, transfixed by his flexing jaw. "But what I want more than reason is you, Carmen. Not just your body. All of you." Her mind obviously toyed with her, but she could have sworn his gaze dropped to Sophia. Before she knew it, those intense eyes were on her again. "Every last part of you."

Vail placed his coffee cup on the floor. The muscles in his back and arms toyed with her pitiful excuse for self-control. He sat back and eyed her. "So tell me, what is it you want, Carmen?"

"I want Sophia to be safe." He nodded. "And I don't think she could be safer than when she's with you." Carmen took a deep breath to continue, but he cut her off.

"I'll recommend you a top-notch body guard." Though his tone slashed with animosity, he cradled Sophia's feet like a newborn as he rose from the sofa. He settled her and stood.

"Wait," she begged.

"It's fine, Carmen. You have noble priorities. Other kids should be so lucky. I'm going to shower. Watch her for a while longer. I'm sure she's fine, but her wellbeing is the most important thing here," he said without malice. "I'll carry her to bed after I'm finished." Then, as if the coffee gave him super speed, he hurried to the stairs and took them two at a time.

Oh. Hell. No.

Chapter Twenty-six

"You didn't even let me finish," Carmen bellowed over the spray.

This woman had the ability to catch him with his pants around his ankles every damn time. "Well you hardly let me finish either," he muttered.

"What?"

Vail stepped under the steaming water. It sluiced over his head, shoulders, and chest, rinsing the soap and remnants of the brush with death from his body. He lifted his head from the raining droplets. His gaze locked with Carmen's through the dingy shower door. One hand slid across his chest, while the other gripped his still-throbbing shaft. Stroking his fully erect cock, he openly removed the sticky evidence of his lust for her and the too quick, too impersonal declaration of life he'd made with his fist and carnal images of her in his mind.

Her pretty mouth hung in an O. The flame red had returned full strength in her cheeks. How a stone-cold woman like Carmen could blush clear to her bones was yet another mystery he'd never solve. She held a sheet of paper in one hand and clutched the towel wrapped around her body in the other. In his fantasy, she'd dropped the towel and joined him, eagerly twining her legs around his waist and accepting every hard inch of him. The white of her knuckles said that was fiction written, edited, and published in his fantasies. Not reality.

"So, finish," he challenged.

Her lips all but curled into a knot. "All of me, huh? Seems you took only the physical to shower with you."

"You won't give me anything else. You won't give me anything at all."

"I had to know," she shouted. "I had to know whether all I was to you was a convenient source of information."

"Convenient?" Irritation raised his voice, something he rarely experienced. "Nothing about you is convenient. Seducing. Dangerous. En-thralling. Irritating. But not *convenient.*"

"Well, I'm sorry I can't just spread my legs for you like all the others. You may not think highly of me, but I'm not a whore."

Rage nearly lifted him off his feet. This woman got to him in ways that scared him piss-less. He'd never been angry with a woman. Upset, yes. But not roaring mad. He swiveled and flung the shower door wide so she wouldn't miss a word.

"There are no others. There is no one else. When my wife died she took my heart with her to the grave, and it's never stirred for anyone else. Un-til you. You, Goddammit."   He viced his head in his hands, and if his hair were longer he'd have pulled it out. "I deal with difficult shit every day. Life and death, and evil. I know good when I see it, Carmen, and I'm staring right at it. If you can't see that, fine. We all have our own demons to carry on our backs or slay. Do with yours what you will, but don't for one minute think I see you as anything other than what you are—devoted, and as beautiful on your walled-off inside as you are on the outside."

Her mouth did the gape and shut thing for several seconds, but not a word left her lips. He couldn't stand in front of her for another minute without ripping the towel from her grip, pinning her to the wall, and driving into her. And if he did, she'd come, and then hate him for treating her like an object only for pleasure. He yanked the towel from the rack and skirted her, heading for the door, not even taking the time to wrap it around his body.

"Shower's all yours. I'll get dressed and carry Sophia to her bed."

She didn't speak, but she thrust the paper into his hand. It crinkled under his furious grip. He charged through the door and down the hallway to the bedroom where he'd slept the last few nights. Managing not to rattle the door off its hinges took restraint that only came from a lifetime of training. He flung the towel and paper onto the neatly made bed and ground his fists against his forehead.

"Son-of-a-fucking-bitch," he growled at himself more than anyone. He was a big picture guy. A cool, collected planner. So, why the hell couldn't he see past Carmen and Sophie?

Because he'd never wanted anything since he'd failed Ellie. Guts in a ball, he collapsed onto the bed. Water beaded across his skin, pooled and dripped at random onto the sheets. The comforter was downstairs, warming Sophie. No matter his horny irritation with Carmen, and himself, he needed to go check on Sophie.

He lay there, seeking his steely calm. He found resignation, bitter and ashy in his mouth. A huff blew through his lips. Like any good soldier, he forged on, shoving from the bed. He yanked the towel so forcefully it *cracked* the air. The dry fabric

troubled his freshly shaven face. While he blotted
the rest of his body he glared at the crumpled ball
of white paper on the backdrop of ugly green flannel sheets. By the time he finished dressing he
could have been classified a gawker.

What the hell did she have to say that she
couldn't just say? Speak, as in words? He shoved
forward on bare feet, dropped the towel, and
snatched the note. Creases polluted every inch, but
the information on it was plain enough to see. On
one side, she'd diagramed the Ruez estate in Baja
California Sur and the facilities in Ensenada and
Hermosillo. She'd noted guard schedules, locations,
and cargo housed for each site. He flipped the paper and his jaw plummeted.

Bank accounts, maybe fifty, were listed in
tiny print. For each she'd scrawled the names of the
banks, amounts in each, routing, and account
numbers. Carlos's army roster took up the bottom
half of the page. Names, ranks, and posts were de-
tailed.

Jesus.

No wonder Carlos had been so desperate to
keep her. She held the keys to his empire in her
beautiful brain. And the rat bastard had extorted
her one weakness to gain her cooperation.

Carmen had given him everything he needed
to protect his people and take down Carlos Ruez.
But... She hadn't given him what he wanted most.

To keep from stewing and reigniting the anger
that shot through his veins like a drug, he laid the
page on the bed, snapped pictures of the front and
back, and sent it to Khani with a message. "Carmen
Ruez shot me, then saved me, and now she's saving
our asses. Get our people in and out. Double time,
before they blow."

She responded, "Well, fuck. Yes, sir."

He carried the smirk from Khani's colorfully blunt response down the stairs. When he reached Sophie's side and the covers rose and fell gently his mouth widened. With a bend and scoop he hugged her close. Those long lashes didn't even flutter. She weighed next to nothing now that his muscles weren't frozen to his bones. He toted her up the steps and settled her onto the twin bed where she'd sat days ago and had that frank and fearless conversation with him. She'd had every right to be afraid, but had shown the instincts of a seasoned warrior. He didn't wish that life for her. Her future should be filled with peace and love. Not battle.

"Don't scare me like that again, kiddo." He kissed her hair. His heart squeezed. Carlos was about to be a powerless schmuck and they were free to start anew. Without him.

Anger flared high and hideous in his chest. Icy impassivity used to keep him warm at night. He guessed rage would do from now on.

Quietly, he slunk from Sophie's room, past the open bathroom door, past Carmen's closed door, down the hall to his cubical. Because he was, in fact, at work. Nothing personal here.

But…there was something very personal on his bed.

Chapter Twenty-seven

"Vail," Carmen's voice quavered. She hated the way she shook. Not many things in the world scared her, but this... She tucked her legs beneath her in the middle of his bed. It hid more of her bare bottom and the small tuft of hair at the juncture of her thighs, but it didn't do anything to cover her heavy breasts or peaked nipples.

Anger clouded around him like a force field. He took one step into the room and closed the door, but his expression remained tight. Her heart quaked in her chest. She smashed her palms together and refused to believe this had been a mistake, though her stomach disagreed.

"What in the—"

She held up her hand, and, damn-it-all, her boobs jiggled. "No. You've talked over me twice tonight, and I have something to say."

His lips pursed and one brow slanted in a mean line.

"I want to give you everything...but I'm terrified. I've only ever presented myself in such a bold manner once in my life. Then it had nothing to do with the man, but the baby I desperately wanted."

His hard edges softened. "And now?"

"And now," she licked her lips, "it has everything to do with you. And the need you stir inside me."

He let loose a long breath, nearly a growl. His wide chest puffed and his hands fisted at his side. "What exactly are you here to give me, Carmen?"

"For now, my body." She couldn't tell him he'd already made gains on her heart. There was too much at stake for that.

She wanted him in return, but she didn't have the nerve to ask. She suspected she'd never get him. He held himself back. His joy and his anger were neat and tidy. Too ordered to be given freely. But she wanted whatever he would give.

And it seemed he wanted whatever she gave.

He stalked to the edge of the bed, the heat of his gaze smothering and raw. "Are you sure, Carmen?" His hand latched around her nape. Then he pulled her forward. She rose and scooted on her knees to the edge of the bed. The possessive action, and his mouth so close to her own, stole her self-consciousness. Her attention wrapped in the nuances of his features. "Once I claim your body, it'll be mine. You'll find it will no longer heed your commands. It will be waiting for mine."

"I don't follow easily," she whispered.

One hot finger coasted from her chin, down the side of her neck, and then over the mound of her breast. Her body leaned into the touch as if his finger were a magnet tugging her desire to the surface. She gasped. He slid it over her hip. Her breath quickened and her body came alive with tingling heat. A sensation all too new and overwhelming flamed in her folds. That sweet finger dipped between her legs, arching around her sensitive flesh, and then slipped down the inside of her thigh to her knee.

"No, you don't. And I don't issue orders. Not with my voice. Which will make this even sweeter." His lips skated over hers. The moisture of his breath clung to her mouth. The errant contact sparked the flame of her need.

"What?"

"Watching you crumble under my touch. Only to be built up stronger than ever by your reaction."

She expected his kiss, an assault on her mouth that would topple the awesomeness of the one they'd shared, or nearly shared. But he released his hold on her neck and dropped to his knees before her. His face reached near-perfect eye level with her crotch. Yet, he gave her no time to fret. Those large hands gripped the inside of her thighs and urged them wide.

Shamelessly, her body obliged, spreading wide and displaying her intimate flesh. His wide palms caressed her inner thigh in long, slow sweeps. They made their way to the tops of her legs, slid around back, and then he clamped her ample thigh. Her lips parted at the surprise contact.

He leaned in, placing his nose so close to her vagina it tickled the close cropped, almost nonexistent patch of hair between her legs. His chest expanded as he deliberately inhaled her scent. A groan rumbled. His eyes closed. His head arched. The view robbed her of breath. Her kneeling and him kneeling before her. He rolled his neck, spread his knees a bit, and lowered. Then he was back, his mouth dangerously close to her skin.

He tilted his head, opened his eyes, and caught her gaze, while his tongue extended toward her aching flesh. She should feel uncomfortable, but she only felt what he made her feel. Sexy. Needy. Yearning. Carmen moaned at the long, flat swipe. It slid across her lips and abraded her already-swollen clit.

"This body is already mine. It responds too easily to have ever belonged to another man."

There were words on her lips, but they fell away. His fingers sank into her skin, holding her in place while he shoved his face into her folds. Electricity tipped his tongue. Its lashing contact assaulted her receptive nub, charging her craving. Her breath came faster until she was panting. Her body flushed.

Solitude struck her square in the chest. She hadn't braced for the blindsiding punch of loneliness.

Carmen held her breath as Vail lapped expertly between her folds. She swiped at the tear that had no cause to fall down her cheek, though it did. Had she expected him to make love to her when love was not what crackled between them?

Foolishly, she had. And yet, the sensations driving her hard toward a wall she'd never crested, didn't cease. They compounded to an unbearable weight.

She wanted this. But she wanted it...differently. With emotion. With a connection. Not a means to an end.

His hands freed her legs. She should move away. Distance herself from the overwhelming phenomenon. But his hands slid around front, between her legs. He cupped her bottom, braced her thighs on his forearms, and stood. She was suspended in mid-air by his brute strength. The chiseled rock of his shoulders glistened with sweat. He took two quick steps with his lips firmly sealed around her clit. Cold wall met her back and she bowed, shoving her lady bits farther onto his ravenous mouth.

Cupping her ass, he held her up to his face as he ate. His fingers bit into her cheeks. He pierced her with his tongue. Carmen's head lolled back, hitting the wall with a quiet *thud*. She was trapped. Unable to escape the beautiful torment he wrought, she braced her hands on the ceiling and gave in. Her hips bucked. Every nerve ending in her body convulsed. And she cried in unbearable pleasure and inexplicable pain.

Where Vail's emotions were neatly pressed, his lust boasted total abandon. Which was almost too much to endure.

Chapter Twenty-eight

His imagination had done her a grave injustice. She tasted too sweet. So good that he'd lost himself between her legs. Her cry and the sweet cream it induced only aggravated his wild hunger. His cock pulsed with the need to be inside her.

He lapped at her one last time—for now—before sliding her to his hips. One hand on the button of his pants, he froze. She'd trapped her lips between her teeth and tears stained her beautiful face.

"Carmen, what's wrong? Did I hurt you? I... I'm sorry. I..."

Her damp curls wavered slightly with her denial. But her nose twitched and she hid her face in the crook of his neck. Her sadness punched him in the balls, making quick work of his raging need. He carried her to the bed with wholly different intentions than he'd had seconds earlier.

Vail sat on the edge of the firm mattress with her arms and legs coiling his torso, scooted to the headboard, and leaned back. "We're done, honey."

She jerked back at that, her brows narrowed.

"I'm not going to make you do anything you don't want to do. I'd never hurt you. Not intentionally." He moved the hair from her face. "I'll let you go, if that's what you want, but before you go I need to know what's wrong."

She bit back a sob that threatened to break his heart, and then mended it by tackling him in a fierce hug. He held her tightly against his chest. When she seemed content to stay there, he gathered her hair to one side and gently caressed the length of her back.

As driven as he'd been to pound himself into her, he was nearly as content to hold her. In a way, maybe even more so. Shared comfort lasted longer, went further than shared flesh.

"I ran away after I watched my father blow the brains out of the man I'd been assigned to marry. I took my inheritance, a bag of clothes, and made it as far as Mexico City before they caught me." She wiped the tears from her cheek and his chest. He closed his eyes, focusing on her touch and her words. "They told me I could never leave. We were family and family was loyal. Not to bother leaving because they would find me anywhere.

"They imprisoned me without bars, refusing my friends entrance to the house or me out without two escorts. When I ditched them at the market, they sent six with me from then on. I was so lost and lonely, surrounded by hatred and desperate for love. Someone to love. Someone to love me." Her head rocked beneath his chin.

"I was so naive, having been sheltered from boys my entire life. But I knew the mechanics of it. I also knew there was no man who'd come near me because of my father. Besides, what I'd seen of men and the way they treated women, I didn't want a man.

"I snuck out one night, found a forger who married me to an American man that doesn't really exist, so that when I left I could hide where they'd never find me...or my baby. The gardener was a kind man, nice looking. At first, he was too scared of my father to hear me out. I paid him twenty thousand dollars so he could move away after he got me pregnant. It was the most selfish thing I've ever done." She sat back, found his gaze, and added, "Aside from shooting you."

The warrior inside Vail wanted to strap up all by himself and go to war with Carmen's family. The primal man in him wanted to stay by her side for the rest of his days, stand between her and the world. He cupped her cheek and she leaned into his touch.

"I expected to get away before news of my pregnancy spread, but I was viciously sick from nearly the first day. Once my father realized I was carrying his grandchild he was both enraged and overjoyed. My guards doubled, and when Sophia was born they had all the leverage they needed to make me stay. I tried to find ways to leave, but I couldn't risk my daughter."

She placed her hand over his heart and it tried to leap into her hand. "All of that to say, I was a virgin when I began trying to get pregnant with Sophia. It only took two times, and I haven't..." She bit her lip.

"You haven't been with anyone since?" Vail asked. She gave a curt nod. "Jesus, Carmen. And I come at you like some sex-crazed maniac." He braced her face in his hands and lowered his forehead to hers. "I'm consumed with wanting you. I'm also a determinedly patient man. I'll wait as long as it takes."

"I don't want to wait. I want you," she smiled meekly, "but I want more than just your body. And if you still want more than just *my* body, I want to give it to you."

His cock stood at attention, but only succeeded in strangling itself against the front of his
pants. And it would remain there for some time.
Using the pads of his thumbs he smoothed away
her tears, then pulled her mouth to his.

The world spun backward while Vail truly
kissed Carmen for the first time. As slow as spring
in Alaska, his lips warmed against the silk of her
mouth. Her seductive pout breached the border of
his own lips with their full softness. He focused on
one at a time, taunting her top in easy strokes, and
then sucking her bottom gently from one side to the
other.

Her arms relaxed and slid up his nape. One
palm gripped his neck. The other explored his
close-shorn hair. He eased back to meld their gazes.

"I'm going to love you, Carmen." He'd meant
it in a purely physical manner, but no sooner was
the thought off his lips than he knew they were true
in deeper sentiment.

His heart burned. Rising on his knees, he
flipped her onto her back and covered her body.
Their chests met. Elbows under her arms, he continued to cup her face and graze her with his lips.
The embers floated away, reducing the discomfort.

The slight jut of her cheekbones pulled his
roaming mouth from hers. He coasted over her face,
across her stubborn chin, down her strong neck.
All the while, her eyes shimmered with desire and
the hint of tears. He nipped her clavicle. A rich
moan rose from her throat, sultry enough to make
a lesser man plunge himself to the hilt.

Vail straightened and released her head. Cool
air hit his chest. Wispy tendrils unwound from his
fingers. Sitting on his heels, he spread his pant-
covered thighs wide and settled her sweet bottom at
the juncture. Her legs draped exquisitely over his

lap. Leaning forward, he pressed his hands on either side of her arched throat, and then dragged
them down her body. His wide grip exerted sturdy
pressure as it prowled her breasts, abdomen, and
belly. When he reached the apex of her hips he lifted his palms, wedging them beneath her shoulders
and the bed before lifting slightly. He cosseted her
flesh, moving his hands back down. Her chest
arched toward the sky as he pulled. At her plush
ass his grip drifted the lengths of her thighs, across
her calves, to the tips of her toes.

He repeated the ritual until her body molded
in his palms like clay. When she was ready, and he
salivated with hunger, he bowed her chest. Leaning
forward he toyed at one nipple with the pad of his
tongue. Her arms stretched wide and she gasped.
The dusky brown tips engorged, shimmering in the
lamplight. Her chest flushed along with the large
circle of her areola.

"Sweet Jesus," he mumbled against her softness. He hadn't meant for the words to rumble from
his chest like a threat. But they did. He hadn't
meant to let Jr. participate. But his hips rocked
onto her globed cheeks at the center of his fly. His
cock rasped against her clitoris.

"More." Her head thrashed on the sheets
while she clenched them in her palm.

"In time," he said. As much for her as for
himself.

He moved to her other breast and suckled.

"Now." Levering her feet on his calves, she
met his shallow thrusts with ardor.

To maintain his grip on control, he closed his
eyes and continued to tug on her nipple. Maybe it
was an effort to keep himself from ripping his pants
off and burying himself in her silk, but he wondered if she'd nursed Sophie. Ridiculous as it was,

his dick throbbed to the point of bursting thinking of Carmen nurturing a baby. His baby.

He groaned, the sound long and painful.

"What?" Carmen asked.

He was about to issue his death warrant. Because if he didn't get inside of her, and soon, he'd keel over from the most acute case of blue-balls the world had ever seen. But he'd rather die than cause her pain.

"I don't have a condom," he panted, his forehead firmly planted in the valley of her lovely bosom. He could suffocate himself here and die in peace.

"Oh," she breathed.

It hadn't occurred to her. And why would it? She hadn't had sex in way too damn long, not that he could stand the thought of another man between her impeccable legs. He should have condoms, but it'd been a hell of a long time since he'd had sex. Not since Peggy, a lawyer who worked in the building. And he'd ended up throwing away most of the box. She hadn't liked being in the dark about his schedule, and she hadn't liked being eaten out. Both were deal-breakers.

He was a man who liked his job and pussy. At least his job had been steady throughout the years—credible women were not. Carmen and her pussy were sanctioned perfection. And he didn't have a condom.

"Vail, look at me," she whispered. He did and she grinned, dammit. Her smiled almost dictated he smile in return, but he didn't want to. "You look sadder now than when I shot you, for heaven's sake." She pulled his head to her mouth and kissed him right off the edge of sanity. Her hips pressed against his straining erection.

They broke away, gasping. Her harlot lashes batted. "I haven't been regular for a long time, so the chances aren't great that I'll get pregnant. But... there is a chance."

Stupidly, his chest swelled at the possibility, but then reality came crashing down. No way would she want his baby. Sophie was twelve. They were finally free.

"I'm willing to take it, if you are," she said. "I don't know what we would do, if I ended up pregnant. But I know the child couldn't be more loved than with us as her parents."

Vail's heart swelled so completely it threatened to break a rib.

"His parents," he corrected, a second before he sealed his lips to hers. She moaned, either in response to his crazy declaration or bearing his weight. He shoved his dick at her core time and again until she shoved at his shoulders. Instantly he stilled, thinking she'd had a crisis of conscience.

"I may not be an expert, but I know your pants are supposed to be off for this to work properly." She shimmied her breasts enticingly against his chest.

"Yes, ma'am," he growled.

With all the grace of an elephant in a mud hole, he fumbled with the buttons and zipper, and wanted to cry in relief when his cock sprang free. He shoved the pants to his knees and wiggled out of them without leaving the heat of Carmen's thighs. With hands at the crook of her knees, he tugged her high enough for her cheeks to kiss his heavy sack. He leaned over her, grabbed his thick shaft, and spread his beaded pre-cum through her slick folds. He paid her sensitive nub and tight entrance special attention.

Carmen used her heels, positioned herself square on his head, and shoved her hips forward. Boy, did he like a woman of action. The tip of his head pierced her

narrow opening. Their moans and cries mingled in a quiet symphony sweeter than Joseph Haydn's 104th at the Philharmonic.

He grabbed her in the protection of his arms and mapped her face. He thrust inside inch by maddening inch. Her hair spilled across the sheets in tousled heaps and frizzed all the more when they found their rhythm. In, just a bit. Out, to the tip. Then, back again. His muscles cramped with re-straint. The slippery wetness of her channel told him she was ready, but damn. The way she squeezed him, he wouldn't last long.

Vail breached the small distance between them. His tongue coaxed her mouth to open, and then slipped inside. She sucked on it, mimicking the fucking of their sex, only faster, greedier. Her moan vibrated his tongue as she pumped him near-ly mindless.

Her thumb played over his lower lip. She flicked his nipple with her other hand.

Dear Lord.

Surprise sat him back. It had never done anything to him before, but now it smashed his flimsy reserve of discipline into a thousand pieces. Arms anchoring her, he shoved deep.

"Ah, Vail." Her chin rose, exposing her neck. "Yes! Oh!"

Sliding a hand from her shoulders, he placed two fingers over her wet lips. "*Shhh*, honey. I've got you."

"No, I've got you." Hot breath slipped between his digits. She wrapped her legs around his waist. "And I'm not letting go."

He pulled completely from her heat, and then thrust back home. "Never," he growled. His balls smacked her soft bottom. Pleasure tingled up his spine, but he refused to give in to the sensation. He set a slow, steady pace that lasted all of thirty seconds before her moans and chaffing nipples against his chest drove his desperation to the brink. He plunged deeper. Recoiled faster, needing more.

Sweat sheened on their bodies as they scorched the chill in the air. He was so close to coming. Though he knew he'd gotten her there once already, and planned to do so many more times tonight, he wouldn't climax without her their first time making love.

Leaning back, he locked on to her gaze, slid his right hand around her nape and the other to her tailbone. He lifted her sweet ass and adjusted their angle, then sank to the root. Her mouth opened, but she banked the cry. Her hips undulated. The softness of her rosy breasts shimmied from his thrusts.

"Come with me," he demanded.

"You better...come...then," she panted.

A bark of laughter shook his chest, but the suffocating wave of orgasm locked down every muscle, nerve, and synapse. He tried to move, to keep from stealing her pleasure. His cheeks clenched. Rigidly he fastened their bodies together and filled her to brimming with his seed.

Chapter Twenty-nine

Vail coming was the most erotic sight in the history of mankind. Even caught in the maelstrom of her own breath-stalling orgasm, she marveled at the rippled cords of muscles bunching under his skin. The onslaught continued as his hips ground against her swollen flesh and his cum heated her belly. Through the storm neither tore their gaze away from the soul-detonating connection that flared between them.

He had to be as boneless as she, but he levered over her for a while. His hand slid from her nape. Those warm fingers stroked her cheek. Their bodies remained locked, the strength of his grip on her ass securing the union.

With shaky arms he finally collapsed onto her chest. The movement jarred his length, still deep inside her womb. Nerve endings sizzled and popped at the contact. He caged her with his strong arms. His lips danced over hers for the barest of moments before the room tilted and she straddled his hips.

"You are beautiful." He traced a finger across her collarbone, between her breasts. His hands hooked behind her knees and tugged. The motion shifted the angle with which she seated him. His full, hard dick speared her deeper. One hand coasted up her thigh and splayed across her belly. "Ride me, Carmen. I need to watch you come again."

Her core clenched as raw need stirred an uprising. She rolled and ground against his cock. Positioned as she was, the movements were small. His head brushed a sensitive spot with each circle that left her panting in seconds. Her face flushed as he stared unabashedly at her display. And she was on display. Her thighs parted, revealing her most intimate parts. Surely, he could see his wide shaft breaching her body. Her breasts jiggled, their stretch marks flashing like a neon sign. Carmen cupped her breasts to keep them still.

"Beautiful," he breathed. "Just...stunning."

Any vulnerability holding her back fell away with his adoration. The instant her fingers brushed her delicate nipples all thought evaporated. Her head lolled as she squeezed the overflowing handfuls. Vail's hand slid lower on her belly and his thumb brushed the tiny bundle of nerves between her slick folds. "Oh my God. Oh. Yes. Oh. Ahhh."

Oblivion pulled at her and she gave herself willingly. Pleasure grappled, pinned her to the ceiling, subduing her for a heavy moment before letting go. She drifted, euphoric. Totally blissed. And then she sagged onto his chest, exhausted.

"I could watch you come twenty times a day."

She smiled against his hard slabs of muscle. "Again," she murmured, "I'm no expert, but that seems a bit excessive."

"From where I'm lying, you're adept enough to keep me hard around the clock. And also, from where I'm lying, it doesn't seem near enough."

His lips brushed her cheek and he rolled them to their sides. He slipped from her body, groaning as though he hated to leave. She didn't care for the emptiness between her legs one bit. He grabbed the discarded towel and cleaned them both. When he settled with his head pillowed on one arm he tugged her closer.

"You're one dangerous woman," he said with a devilish smile.

"And you're no powder puff." She let her finger trace his scars, the lighter, slightly smaller ones that speckled his torso. They'd just shared a most intimate act, and yet she didn't know anything about him. Not true. She knew his nature and it was beyond reproach, but she wanted more. "Tell me about your family?"

His droopy lids widened and a frown carved his tan skin.

"Sorry, I didn't mean to pry." She put her fingers over his mouth. "That's not true, I did mean to pry, but I didn't mean to hurt you. Though how could it not?"

His lips kissed the underside of each knuckle, and then the tips. "I expected you to ask about my scars."

"I figured they were one in the same."

"And you're right." He entwined their fingers. "It hurts...still, but now it hurts in a way that reassures me I'm alive. For a long time, I didn't feel like I was. I didn't want to be." He drew a deep breath, his gaze warm and attentive on her face.

"My job is dangerous in that the decisions I make affect the missions, the lives of my people, and potentially thousands more on any given day. Before, I was in the Navy."

"You were a SEAL."

"Yep. Risky job. Never in one place very long. And I fell in love. Ellie and I got married two months after we met." The pain in his eyes lightened.

A prick caught Carmen's heart and she swallowed past the odd sensation. Jealousy. She'd had no reason to experience it before. And she had none now. She wouldn't begrudge Vail his happy memories. Not for anything. Hell, if she could resurrect the woman to make him happy...she'd think about it long and hard, and then do it for him alone.

"It was a whirlwind. Crazy really. I was on leave when we met. When I came back for a night a month later, I asked, she agreed, and we were married the next time I came home. It wasn't easy, but we managed to make the best of our time together." Absently, he brought her hand to his mouth and spread kisses along the side. "In two years of marriage, we were only in the same place for five total months, no more than two weeks at a time."

As if to comfort himself, he rubbed her hand over his cheek. "Enough time to make a baby. She would have been very near Sophie's age."

A tear slipped from her eyes before she could call it back. She didn't like where this was going. The thought of losing a child, even though she'd known he had... Her throat constricted.

"I had another two weeks about four months into the pregnancy. Since I'd shipped out the day after our wedding, I wanted to do something special for her. So, I booked a trip to Jamaica. A baby-moon, she called it."

Vail leaned in and kissed at the trail of her tears. "Don't cry."

"Impossible."

"I didn't think anything was impossible for you." His breath tickled her ear.

"There are a few things." And they all involved him and Sophia.

"There was a breach and my information was among that stolen. But the warning came too late.

The leader of a terrorist group my team had collapsed a few months earlier found us at a market on the island." His grip on her hand tightened.

"I was too far away." He laughed even though tears brimmed his eyes. "I was being stupid, holding fruit up to my chest and making boobs. The baby changed her body. Made her frame luscious and me ridiculously horny. Dumb."

"Not dumb. Happy and in love," she corrected.

"They opened up on her. She didn't see it coming. I didn't either. I should have been watching." A growl rumbled deep in his chest. His head shook. The muscles in his jaw threatened to snap from the tension. He broke. His face buried beneath her chin.

Carmen cradled his head and wrapped her arm around his shoulder. "*Shhh,* mi valiant hombre," she whispered, though he made not another sound. He raged, while her quiet tears soaked his hair.

She envisioned him, happy and vital, enjoying his wife in the brilliant light of day. Then the spray of bullets slicing through his world. No doubt he got his scars running full tilt toward his Ellie, not ducking for cover or waiting to find a tactical angle of attack. And God, their baby... Her mind walled the image, and for that she was ever grateful.

He burrowed lower, pressing his weight against her chest. His arms twined round her middle and he held her back as she rocked him, nice and easy. After only a few seconds, he shifted lower. The heat of his tongue licked her nipple before latching on and suckling. A gasp flew from her lips.

The desperation of grief. The finality of death. It drove people toward their own death or life. Vail chose to live in this moment. Here. With her.

When he rolled her onto her back and moved between her legs she didn't deny him. Without finesse or preamble he shoved to the root. His mouth covered her moan and melded it with one of his own.

He lifted her off the bed. Her arms and legs tightened around him, and their mouths acted out the torment they could not voice. Knees spread wide, he balanced their combined weight. His grip sank into the rounds of her ass. His hips retracted as he lifted, and their bodies separated for the briefest of seconds before he hammered them together.

The force slammed her clitoris onto the slight bulge of his lower abdomen. Her left hand gripped the whittled groove of his lat for leverage. She flared her pelvis, taking him deeper. That exquisite V of primal manliness and the dynamic aim of his cock catapulted her into orbit too soon.

Her breaths huffed hot and wet against his mouth. In a frantic effort to keep quiet, she viced her lip between her teeth. This was his deliverance. She'd be damned if she'd break his center.

A gap formed between them and her gaze flew to his. The intensity of his animalistic expression bowled her over. "You're strangling my dick, honey. You're coming. Let me hear it."

"Ahhh." The sweet relief of freedom reinvigorated her fulfillment. "Ah, Vail."

"Yes, fucking, yes. I'm here. I'm with you, Carmen. I'm pumping into you. And you're strangling me." His biceps bunched and his neck strained. "Oh, Go…" Climax seized him. Everything inside her tightened. She was trapped in the grip of

a mighty warrior and she never wanted to be released.

Chapter Thirty

Vail blinked into view the horrendous hunter-green sheet blocking half of his line of sight. It took a while. The sun streamed through the window, nearly blinding him. He flicked the fabric plagued with intersecting cream and red lines from his face. Stretching his arms straight over his head, he met the headboard and shoved. His muscles filled with the heavy syrup of a good night's sleep and a momentary shot of adrenaline that came with the short fit of exertion.

On a deep inhale he caught her scent and the fog of lethargy faded. His dick didn't need the jolt of sweaty women, a hint of flowers, and musky sex to get him going. The guy was fully erect and ready to go. Who could blame him?

He smiled and rolled over to an empty bed. And room.

Damn.

He'd come inside her for the second time, and then promptly smothered her with his weight and fallen into the most contented sleep he'd had in what seemed like decades. The bed creaked as he sat and listened for the slightest hint of sound. When he heard none his heart stuttered. He bound from the bed, to the door, cupped his sticky junk, and peeked out the door. Down the hallway Carmen's bedroom door stood open, but Sophie's remained closed. A breath rounded his cheeks and he blew it out.

Maybe she was just really quiet downstairs. The need to know for sure ate at him, but no way could he streak through the house to check, which was exactly what he wanted to do. Resigned, he retreated, pulled his last pair of clothes from his pack, and then darted for the bathroom, strategically covering himself just in case.

Water splashed and soap flung like he was in the pit of hell week with ten minutes to eat, clean, and nap. He dressed accordingly before skidding down the steps. His boots caught rubber with his sudden stop. Carmen snapped a hip to one side and propped a hand and the spatula in it on her hip.

"In a rush to get somewhere?" She batted lashes strong enough to blow him over.

He sagged and lifted all at once, alleviation mingling with delight. Three large steps brought them toe-to-toe. "Yep, right here." He placed small kisses on her damp forehead and down the bridge of her nose. His tongue smoothed over his lips. "Salty."

"Gross," she giggled. "I went for a run."

"To clear your head?"

"No, to keep from getting caught in your bed."

"That is too bad," he groaned. "How's Sophie?"

"Sleeping like the dead." She shook the cooking utensil. "But I checked. She's breathing just fine and doesn't have a fever."

"How are you?" he asked, tugging her closer.

Her teeth nipped his chest. "Hungry in every way."

"If you'd stayed, I'd have brought you breakfast in bed—and then eaten you."

"You're cruel." She whimpered against his shirt.

"I think you're the cruel one." Using both hands, he cupped her curvy butt over her thin, black workout pants, lifted, and ground her over his rigid length. "God, Carmen! Look at your nipples. You're ready for me. Wet and needy. Bet I could get you off in less than sixty seconds."

"I bet you could too, but I can't," she said with a gentle push. "What kind of role model would I be for Sophia?" Begrudgingly, he let her move back one step, but kept his hands at her waist. "We only just met, for goodness' sake."

"I agree." He sucked air between his teeth. "Doesn't mean I like it though."

Her chin levered back, providing the first good angle for their lips to meet. He took it, swooping in before she had a chance to speak. His hands coasted up and framed her face while he teased her mouth.

"Way to go, Mom," Sophie said from somewhere behind them.

He broke the kiss. The stunned look of a thief trapped in a safe contorted Carmen's pretty face. He soothed a thumb over her red lips and turned. "How you feelin', kiddo?"

"Awesome." A smile lit her entire demeanor. She stood just a bit taller than she had the day before. Devilish satisfaction lightened the way-too-intense burdens on her shoulders.

Sophie's eyes darted between him and her mother as she skipped lightly to the table. "So, Ma, what's for breakfast?"

Vail watched her calculating their relationship while she perched her intelligent head on her

palm. That girl, he loved her from the tips of her silly shoes to the tip of her nose. His hand clamped
over his mouth to keep the realization locked away.
Talk about moving fast. He could blame it on the
euphoric high from last night, but it would be a lie.
He'd been falling in love with that little girl since
she dressed him down with smart questions and
deciphered a scary situation with sharp wit instead
of fear. And her world-lighting grins didn't do much
to slow the progress of emotions.

Plans changed in his mind, adjusting to the
new course he'd set for himself. And Carmen and
Sophie. He turned to the swaying hips at the
counter. "So, what's for breakfast?"

Carmen's ponytail swooshed and she met his
gaze with her narrowed one that jumped between
him and Sophie. "You go sit over there and hold
onto your patience. I was going to cook gorditas de
huevos, but we don't have chilies or tortillas." She
grabbed two apples from the counter and tossed
them to him. "Will you cut these, please? The
spinach eggs will be ready in a few minutes."

He stepped closer. She stepped back, meeting
the stove with her bottom. "Stand still," he whispered. "This won't hurt a bit."

Her smile worked on his already sensitive
heart. He leaned around her, letting his arm brush
hers as he retrieved a knife and plate. Before with-
drawing, his lips brushed her cheek. He retreated
to the table and pulled out the chair next to the
red-cheeked little girl.

"You have mischief written all over your face."
He lopped off a piece of apple and handed it over.
"Shove this in your mouth so you don't get either of
us into trouble."

She plucked the fruit from his hand, pursed
her lips at him, and gave a slight headshake for

good measure. The apple crunched between her teeth. "So, what are we doing today?"

"Not fishing," he answered before the words were good and out of her full gnashing mouth. Carmen turned to say something similar, surely. Instead, she nodded in approval, and then turned back around.

He winked at Sophie and jutted his chin toward Carmen. "I was thinking, since the ice was pretty thick, we could sled the lake. You know, face your fears and all that."

Sophie covered her mouth and winced, while Carmen snapped around so quickly her ponytail slapped her in the face. His shoulder shook so hard he had to drop the knife for fear of stabbing himself. Then he looked at the woman feigning indignation and slid the knife to the other side of the plate.

They erupted in fits of side-cramping laughter.

When it died down, Sophie asked, "So, seriously, what are we going to do today?"

Vail cleared his throat and steeled his heart. "I need to go to DC to take care of some things—"

"Carlos?" Carmen asked.

"Yes, and I want you two to come with me."

Chapter Thirty-one

Sophie seriously wished her mom would relax and enjoy the road trip. The woman fidgeted as though she'd contracted OCD and a sudden drug dependency. The only time she stilled was when Vail held her hand, but then her eyes got whiplash jerking between her hand and Sophie's camp in the minuscule backseat. Sophie beamed brightly in an attempt to soothe her mom, but it only seemed to fluster her more.

The sparkle of big city lights pulled Sophie's attention out of the car once more. Spires and monuments cluttered the night sky. Cars dashed by, or rather they zipped past the other cars. Soon they veered off the interstate. A momentum pulling her just a little closer to the view. Her exhales lightly hazed the window. Unlike the jam-packed downtown, the buildings were spaced farther apart, but it didn't detract from their significance. Artful gardens and sprawling green lawns accentuated their formidable heights.

They passed several construction sites dotted with forklifts and large trucks masked in thick layers of dust. The cars slowed as they neared a fancy building with a surprisingly amicable mix of old world brick and modern glass architecture. She read Capital Hill Tower as they rolled past the front.

They turned into the structure's parking garage and parked next to a real-life monster truck.

Sophie hurried out of the car, ignoring her mother's alert, I'm-ready-for-battle stance and shifting gaze. The driver's side window came to eye level and she jumped to peek inside. Clean, dark-tan leather covered the seat and steering wheel. It complemented the slick, orangy-red paint on the exterior perfectly. She ran to her mom, threw her arms around her waist, and rested her ear on her back. The move tossed her mom and her sur-veillance off balance.

"I love you so much." Sophie grinned.

Mom dragged Sophie around to her front. The quirk in her brow said she knew something was up. "What do you want now?"

"That truck! It's awesome. Think about it this way, someone could hit me and I wouldn't even no-tice," she reasoned.

"Yeah, you wouldn't notice when you plowed over a car either." She peeled Sophie's arms from around her middle. "Come back when all you want is a hug. Now, let's get the bags."

Vail closed the trunk with one bag over his shoulder and two, theirs, in his hand. "Bags are gotten. And Sophie, maybe after work tomorrow I'll teach you how to drive it." He jut his chin in the di-rection of the massive truck.

"What! That's your truck?" She bounced on tiptoes, fists above her bent elbows, conservatively victorious.

Mom must have given him a look. He shrugged. "What? How not to run over cars will be first on the tap."

"She's twelve," Mom reminded.

His nose wrinkled like he smelled something rotten. Sophie's did the same. "Ah, maybe just a ride tomorrow?" He added with a whisper, "There's a bit of country not too far away where you can test her out." They fell into step together, headed for a bank of elevators. "What?" he asked again, this time with his free hand. "She can't bother anything out there. Anyway, how old were *you* when you first got behind the wheel?"

"Twenty," Mom said.

"No way," she and Vail said in unison as they all stepped onto the arrived car.

"Growing up, I had drivers." Her mom frowned.

"Why didn't we have drivers?" Sophie asked.

"I wanted to be able to go where and when I wanted. As much as I could," she admitted.

The doors opened and they exited into a neat hallway. Vail turned right, tugging Mom along by the hand. They walked and walked to the end of the corridor, and then waited for him to punch a whole lot of numbers on a keypad before unlocking the door and ushering them inside.

"Swank." She hurried through the foyer and into the kitchen, impressed by the walls of floor-to ceiling-windows overlooking the city. "Is that the capital building? And what monument is that?"

"Yep, that's the Untied States Capital and that's the Washington Monument." He pointed to each. "They had me on lock-down in here for weeks. I missed this view. Guess Khani called off sur- veillance since I wasn't here and my assailant has been found." He wiggled his brows and kissed her mom's hand before releasing it to set their bags on the sofa.

"Khani?" Mom asked. The crook of her mouth belied the casualness of her tone.

Sophie stretched to keep from laughing out loud. Her mom had no clue how beautiful she was or how totally over the moon Vail was for her. That was part of her charm. Sophie bowed, grabbed the edge of the granite countertop, and tugged on her cramped back muscles.

"She's second in command, a ballsy babe just about as tough as you are," Vail said. But she missed her mother's reaction as she sank deeper into the delight of movement.

When she straightened she noticed the scatter of papers across the otherwise spotless counter. Except for her fingerprints. Using the inside corner of her T-shirt, she wiped at the smudge and succeeded in smearing them into an even bigger mess. Her gaze snagged on a picture sticking out from the stack. A severed hand lay pale and limp in the dirt. Beneath it a dark, misshapen circle stained the ground.

Vail's hand slapped over the detached one and she jumped, nearly leaving her skin where she'd stood. He gathered the strewn papers into one file stuffed fatter than a taco at Renardo's back home. "I shouldn't have left this out. I'm sorry," he said. His gaze jerked hers from the bundle in his hand. His thick brows V'd in concern.

"I'm not a baby," she reassured. "I can handle it."

The file hit the counter with a *thump*. Vail stepped forward and framed her shoulders in his big hands. "I know you can, but you shouldn't have to see the horrors the world has to offer. Only the beauty."

"Why?" she asked.

"Often, it changes a person. Dims their inner light. I don't think that'll happen to you. You're too strong, but if I can protect you from it, I will."

Sophie's heart exploded with love. Or maybe it was her stomach. Because she couldn't catch the words that rocketed out of her mouth. "I love you."

Vail dragged in a sharp breath as though she'd stabbed him with a really big kitchen knife. Her mom's wasn't far behind.

Two for the price of one.

Her gaze dropped to her feet. She suddenly wanted a super-power. Invisibility or teleportation would have been handy. Or time augmentation. His finger crooked under her chin and lifted. She closed her eyes—not nearly as brave as her mother—terrified by the pity or disapproval she might see on his face.

"Sophie." Her shoulders dropped a bit and she opened her eyes. Vail smiled, not big and cheesy. This was a new one. Small and almost a frown at the same time. "I love you, so much."

She played the words over in her head to be sure she heard him correctly. His hand on her shoulder tugged just a little and she dove for him. He lifted her into the air as though she were no more than a few molecules of O_2. The oxygen in her lungs jarred as she met his hard chest and his arms encompassed her. She clung to him just as fiercely, squeezing with all she had.

He twirled her about, once. As the room spun her mom came into view. A wash of wonder and fear blighted her pretty face. Their dual declarations obviously poleaxed
her. Heck, Sophie was shocked and she'd initiated the whole thing. She latched onto the amazing feeling and the closest thing to a father figure she would ever have in her life.

After a minute more, his lips brushed her hair. He set her on the floor and stepped back. "All right." His hand ran from the crown of his skull to his forehead, flattening his already flat hair. "Let me show you to your room." Probably sensing Mom needed a minute, he skirted them both, grabbed her bag, and headed left through the open living area and down a short hall. She followed in a rush. "My bedroom is the only one in the opposite hall-way. You need anything, let me know. Bathroom is on your left, and here is your room."

He flipped on the lights and the massive win-dow continued through the room's exterior wall. Stepping inside he drew the thick curtain, blocking out prying eyes. "The bed is small, but so are you."

"This is twice the size of the one I've been sleeping on." She plopped her bottom on the mat-tress and dipped low before bouncing back onto her feet. "Wow, and twice as soft."

The white-on white-bedding invited her to snuggle in and stay for days. With the way her muscles ached from fighting for her life, she was tempted to try it. But first, she was more interested in seeing how things played out between Vail and her mom. So, when he turned to go, she followed him out.

"Nosey, huh?"

"Yeah." No use in denying the apparent.

"Well," he said, rounding into the kitchen, "I'll leave you two to snoop around while I shower."

Smart man.

She placated her mother—who hadn't stirred much from her shock—with a smile she missed staring at Vail. Just as well. If her parental sensors had been functioning at all, she'd have chastised Sophie for making him think she'd snoop. And she would. Snooping was how you figured things out.

"If you get hungry, there are granola bars in the cabinet. I have water, orange juice, and coffee. Not much else that doesn't need cooking."

"What kind of granola bars?" Sophie asked.

"There's no way you can be hungry. We bought that restaurant out an hour and a half ago," Mom said, snapping out of her funk.

"I'm a growing girl." She drew her shoulders back and straightened for effect.

"Almond and cashew, I think." Vail bowed his head and turned toward his room.

Sophie moved through the wide living room. She didn't dare sit on the smartly-put-together furniture or touch the neatly lined books on the minimalist shelf. Everything in the space had an assigned spot. It all coordinated and flowed like the photo on the cover of a magazine.

Everything except Vail.

He slept and ate here, but he didn't live here. There were no family pictures or wrinkles on the throw pillows. She folded her arms and looked out at the view. Instead of seeing the brilliant DC skyline, she saw her mother's reflection. The woe she'd felt for Vail doubled at her mother's stricken expression.

The edges of the paper she held rippled under her violent grip. Her chest heaved. A gaze fiercer than she'd ever seen on her mother—and she'd seen some doozies—could have spontaneously ignited the sheet.

"Mom?"

She set the page on the counter as though it roasted her hands and stepped away. "It's late, Sophie." Shaky hands smoothed over the fitted lavender shirt beneath her jacket. Sophie watched her approach in the reflective glass, losing her once in the cast shadow from the far off kitchen light. "Get some sleep, baby. You have to be tired from yesterday."

"I am," she admitted.

Soft lips kissed her cheek. Sophie grabbed her mother's hand and squeezed. "I love you, Momma."

She was suddenly crushed in an embrace so fierce it shifted her organs.

"I love you, baby girl." She kissed her once more and then hurried out to the balcony that wrapped the living room's full view.

Happiness and sadness dueled for seniority. She chaffed her arms and turned away from the window. The curious side of her wanted to run to the counter to see what had upset her mother. But the child still very much a part of her, though she'd never admit it, shied from the kitchen altogether. She'd boasted about her indifference to the severed hand, but visions of it would keep her nightmare department busy for a while.

If she wasn't mature enough to help her mother, she knew just the person who was. She hurried into the farthest room and gave a mini fist pump when a desk and wall of legal looking books greeted her. With a note pad and pen she wrote, "Heads up. Mom's sad about something in the file. She's on the balcony. Help, if you can." Her hand pulled back from the paper, lowered, jerked away again.

How should she sign off? Hugs, Sophie? Love, Sophie? Just...Sophie? She sighed, put the pen to paper, and hoped for the best. "I love you, Sophie," just popped out. So, she went with it, taking the entire pad with her to his door, and then sliding it underneath. He could miss a little sheet of paper. In the kitchen she grabbed a drink of water, dimmed the brilliant droplights, and then headed to bed to sleep forever. A.K.A. as long as her mom would allow.

Chapter Thirty-two

Every minute he was around her he loved her more. He smiled at the, "I love you, Sophie," complete with a balloon heart representing the I in her name. His line of sight traveled to the top of the note and his smile faltered.

Shit.

There was only one thing in that file that would hurt Carmen. And he'd wanted to be the one to tell her. Well, he never wanted to tell her, but it beat her reading it in a file. He scrubbed the towel over his head one last time hard enough to begin the balding process. At the dresser he retrieved flannel sleep pants and his well-worn MIT sweatshirt, and yanked them on.

She sat staring at the city, but seeing only the demons in her head. The wind toyed with the curls draping her shoulders and back. Her dried lips knitted. Tears welled from the biting breeze, emotion, or both.

He slipped through the door and walked to the railing. Cars crawled like lighted ants in the distance. The city noise melded into a soft din, muffled by howling gusts. His thumb tapped the rounded metal top.

"I should have told you."

"I should have known." Her voice was hoarse. Angry.

"You couldn't have known."

"Couldn't I? Everything in my life is evil. My own mother…the first and most successful cartel leader to date. Ha. You should take me in now. Put me behind bars before my true nature reveals itself."

Vail let it go. People said all sorts of things in enmity. He knew better and so did she. But he let her vent. Things kept inside only molded and decayed the soul.

"I should have never had Sophia."

He snapped around on that one. Tears streaked her face. Her white knuckles gripped the thin iron armrests. Her gaze found his and a sob broke free. "What if I gave her my tainted blood?"

In two strides he was on top of her. The metal on concrete scraped as he turned her from the patio table to face him. He bent at the waist and put his nose a few inches from hers.

"Think about your daughter. Is there any sign of evil in her?"

Carmen's hands slapped over her face. She wept long and hard. Vail tucked her head against his chest and rolled with the riptide of emotion.

"She's the sweetest thing in the world," she cried.

"She is." He agreed. Finally Carmen's tears subsided. "I don't know if it's nature or nurture. Probably they can both skew. But I know what I see. A loving mother and the beautiful person she's nurtured in an impossible situation. She's happy and healthy because of you."

"I've never seen her so happy…" She sniffled.

The look in her midnight eyes didn't make Carmen seem all that happy about it though. "And...?" he coaxed.

"And I'm terrified you're going to break her heart." She dragged each lip in turn through her teeth and eyes him.

"Hers or yours?"

"Both, maybe."

He couldn't tell her what he wanted. Not yet. But he could show her.

Vail attacked her mouth, their lips colliding with near bruising force. The chair screeched against the concrete from the brunt of his incursion. His hand fisted in the twine of hair, holding her to him. Not that she had anywhere to go trapped between him and the hard metal at her back.

Though every fiber in his being would rage against it, if she wanted, he'd let her go. Thank all that was holy and several things that weren't—like his carnal intentions—she opened to his seeking tongue. He kissed himself drunk on her rich flavor, parrying his tongue with hers, sucking the sweetness from her lips.

With one hand and his other arm supporting her back, he hitched her off the chair. Her hands dug into the fabric of his sweatshirt. It strained at his nape. She circled his torso with the biting grip of her legs. The soft heat of her core nuzzled the length of his growing erection. He stumbled over the chair in an effort to get to the door without breaking the kiss. What was he, seventeen?

Smooth, Tucker.

Yep, her hands were smooth all right, sliding skin-to-skin up his back. The cool breeze charmed his feverish skin. He bit at her lower lip and her moan carried off on the wind. With more tentative steps, he eased toward the door. Carmen rubbed her center up and down his plumped cock.

He ripped the door open, but, surprisingly, he had the wherewithal to protect his girls and lock it behind him. His steps to his bedroom were hurried. Since her legs were clamped so tightly a hurricane gale wouldn't knock her off, he released his hold on her bottom. The coolness of her belly met his fingertips as he glided over her ribs to her nipple.

Through the lace of her bra her soft bud distended. A flick and light pinch stirred her tender flesh. It hardened under his strident hand. He was going too hard. Too fast, like before. But still, not as fast as he needed to go. Only Sophie's presence inside the condo kept him from stopping at the dining table, stripping her bare, and filling her.

They fumbled their way into the bedroom. Again, Vail locked the door, ensuring Sophie's mental safety. Talk about scars. Walking in on your mom getting—well, getting properly serviced— would sure create some. He smiled against her mouth and she licked the edge of his lips. Light from the bathroom and closet crisscrossed the dark room, giving more than enough light to see his destination. He hurried past the plush bedding and gray accent wall to the translucent one on the far side.

Though he hated to lose her heat, the plans he had for her body heated him more. It took more strength than he expected to peel her legs from around his torso. He set her in front of him and the backdrop of the DC skyline. He bracketed her face and eased his lips away.

"Sometimes we don't see ourselves for the people we are. Impressions, polluted impressions, from others cloud our perception and we're forever lost to the madness. You don't deserve that, Carmen." Her swollen lips parted, but no words leaked out.

He grabbed the leather covering her shoulders. A gentle tug had the thing on the floor. Her gaze remained locked on him while he undressed her piece by piece. He untied her laces then slipped the boots and socks from her feet. Unable to resist he hugged her bottom to his face while he worked on the fly of her jeans. His hands actually shook as he wrestled with the button of her jeans. Anticipation had him on a hair trigger.

"I want you to see yourself through my eyes tonight." He spread the fly wide and worked the pants over her dreamy ass. He left them crowded at the base of her calves, liking the picture she made.

The outside of his finger grazed the side of her cheek. "The only way you're going to see yourself the way I see you is for you to watch me make love to you." She swallowed, inhaled to speak, but before she could object he turned her to the window.

"But they'll see," she gasped at her splendid reflection in the dark glass.

"They'll see shapes, not details, but most importantly they'll see the beauty you have to offer with your heart, mind, and body." He touched the center of her chest, the bridge of her nose, and then dragged his finger down to her pubic bone. Her breath caught. "I want them to see me love you. To be jealous that it's not them." Vail lowered his head to her ear. "Whether you know it yet, or not, they'll know...you're mine."

"Vail." His name was a cry on her lips. Of joy? Of sadness?

Interlocking their fingers, he stretched her arms wide overhead and flattened her palm against the cool surface. He bore his weight against her back, reveling in the contrasting texture of her form. "*Shhh.*" He kissed the proud corner of her jaw. "I don't know where this is going, honey, but it's going hard and fast. I suggest you breathe and enjoy the ride."

"I'm so scared."

"Me too."

He rested his forehead on the soft waves at the crown of her head. Her scent filled his lungs, clamped down on the chains of his heart. His head stayed there. He got drunk on her smell while his fingers slipped over her almond colored arms. The swell of her breasts tempted him to stray, but he remained steady in his goal. Total exposure followed by a steady advance, and then invasion.

His greedy hands followed the sloping curve to her hip. Slipping two fingers under the hem of her shirt, he snagged the end and peeled it off. When her hands fell to the side he whispered, "Hands up."

She obeyed eagerly. Utilizing every bit of will power he possessed, he kept his mouth off her smooth ass as he knelt at her alter. The black V of a thong slipped between the dimples of her cheeks.

"Sweet Jesus."

"Yes," she agreed.

Pants gridlocked at her ankles, he spread her ass wide, slid a finger underneath the string, yanked it to the side, and buried his face. His tongue speared her silky channel. The glass squeaked under her hands. Carmen groaned in unabashed pleasure and tilted her hips, allowing him better access. And he took it all. Thrusting like a man possessed, he coaxed her moisture to him while giving his own. Pants ricocheted off the window and echoed through his bedroom and his sex incensed brain.

Dipping his shoulders, he dove farther between her legs. At least he tried. Her jeans wouldn't allow him access. The red mist clung so densely he sat back to clear it, but as usual Carmen beat him to the punch. She bent, yanked at the bottom of each pant leg in turn, and discarded them to the scattered heaps of clothing littering the floor. Her hands outstretched high on the window once again and she opened her legs wide. His cock strained at the erotic X she formed.

Without a second's thought he dipped, and then turned. His lips suctioned over her cleft. He tempted her clit from its protective den, using steady pulls. Carmen's hips jerked against his face. She rocked. He slipped two fingers inside her liquid heat, letting his index finger nestle against the puckered entrance between her cheeks, and match the increasing churn of her body.

"Vail. Vail. Oh. Yes. Please."

He growled and lapped at her precious nub in retaliation for the fit of desire she forced on him. She fucked his face in long, flowing strokes that shortened with her breaths. Her core tightened, then convulsed around his fingers.

The sweetest song.

When he slipped from her legs and looked up, her head sagged against the glass. His lips slid along her backside. Damp curls clung to her shoulder despite the temperature outside. He shifted it to the side and continued his ascent.

"You know, I'm beginning to feel like this relationship is extremely one sided," Carmen said, a smile heavy in her voice.

"So, you admit this is a relationship?"

"They don't have a word for what this is."

Quick as a flash of jagged lightning, she encircled his wrist, pivoted, exchanging their places, and pinned his back to the glass. Her hands slipped under his sweatshirt and glided across his abdomen, gathering the fabric as she went. Up and over his head, she worked it until he was free.

She leaned forward, molding her breasts to his chest. Her tears had faded, but a hesitation crept into her features. He ran a reassuring hand along her jaw and over her back. Gradually her gaze returned to his. She held it as she dropped to her knees, pulling his loose pants down as she went.

"Men aren't supposed to be beautiful. But I can't find a better way to describe you." She swallowed. "You do things to my body without a single touch that I didn't think possible. And when you put a hand on me. Or mouth. My body isn't big enough to contain the pleasure you give me." Her hands sailed up the inside of his thigh. "I want to give you that same kind of thrill."

"The sight of you does that, honey. God, especially now."

A smile quirked one side of her mouth. She licked her lips and encircled his shaft with her dainty hand. "Well, let's see what this does to you."

Vail watched as the head of his cock disappeared between the swollen redness of her well-kissed lips. His heartbeat ratcheted. His abs clenched. With great care she sucked him in a few inches, and then popped off his tip. Adjusting her position, she came back for more, this time working him to the back of her throat. She gagged. Vail tried to pull out, knowing she'd likely never given head before. The glass barred his hips. Carmen refused to slow, only adjusted and took him deep again.

Soon slurps, sucking, and her moans addled his brain into submission. The world shrank to her mouth, his need, and her apparent delight in driving him mad. His hands fisted at his side. Heedless of his struggle for restraint, his hips pumped into her mouth. His head lolled. Too quickly the tingle at the base of his spine screamed in warning. He didn't want to stop. Couldn't stop.

"Carmen, you have to stop. I can't. God, I'm about to come."

Whether lost in the maelstrom or possessed, she worked him harder. Faster. He strained against the need for release. His restraint only intensified the climax. It evaporated the air in his lungs as it rocketed from deep within, tearing off a part of his soul with it. Vail muffled the roar of climax as much as he could, half insane with unrivaled euphoria.

She accepted all of him and pulled greedily for more. His dick refused to soften in her eager mouth. She licked him clean and kissed his head before working her way up his body to his heart. "Now they can see that you're mine, even if you don't know it yet."

Chapter Thirty-three

Carmen burrowed deeper into the fluffy comforter to ward off the blinding morning light. Lord, they'd passed out in a tangle of sex-sweaty limbs not an hour ago. Her arm snaked among the ultra soft sheets, seeking Vail's warmth. When she didn't find it her eyes reluctantly popped open. The other half of the bed lay empty. She groaned and stretched, not wanting to get up, but wanting to see her lover more. On her inhale the crisp scent of bacon enticed her to rise all the more.

The stickiness from their long, amorous night clung between her legs. Unwilling to think about the possible ramifications of their hedonistic actions, she shucked the covers and headed for the shower. With her bag still in the living room, all she could do was clean herself and wrap in a towel.

"Honey, are you trying to kill me?" Vail's gaze swept from her legs and hovered at the valley of her cleavage. "Because what a way to go." He wore the clothes she'd stripped from him last night and looked more delectable than the golden biscuits cooling on the rack. Using two fingers, he tugged her by the towel and kissed her full on the lips before pointing with his spatula. "You were supposed to stay in bed and be served."

"You served me plenty last night." She laid a kiss at the jumping pulse in his neck.

"Already had your fill?" He wrapped her in his arms while breakfast sizzled on the stove behind him.

"No, maybe never."

"That's good, because you may be stuck with me that long. I didn't wear a condom. I had some, but..."

Great, if they stayed together it'd be out of obsession and obligation. He loved Sophia, but it seemed she was another matter. He showed her love, but hadn't whispered the word outside of the bedroom. Even inside it he never used it in reference to loving her other than in the physical sense.

"I can take care of a baby on my own." She pulled away and turned to go. He caught her around the waist before she crossed more than a foot.

"Not mine you can't." He pressed her against his chest much like he had the night before.

Yet, this felt different. The emotions boiling at the surface of her mind had nothing to do with her treacherous family and everything to do with her uninhibited love for Vail Tucker. A love that had more potential to slice her in half than the sharpest blade.

His massive hands splayed over her belly. "Carmen, I never wanted another family. Something else to lose. Nothing was worth that liability until you crashed into my life. The thought of your belly full with our baby—"

"What smells so good?" Sophie hollered from down the hallway.

Carmen wrestled free of his grip, afraid of what he'd say. Or wouldn't say. Afraid of Sophia seeing her mother scantily dressed in Vail's arms.

She snatched her bag from the sofa and ran for cover.

What in the world was she doing toying with a man dangerous enough to rip her heart from her chest and make her live the rest of her days without it? An eternally damned but never dead zombie woman. She stared at her flushed face in the mirror and pulled back her impossible tangle of hair. Yep, the woman staring back loved Vail. But, maybe, if she quit now she could keep some bit of herself to carry her through the rest of her miserable days.

She'd lived so long without love. She still had Sophia, if she left before her daughter's affection for Vail outweighed Sophia's affection for her. It was time to get dressed and get down to business. Riffling through her bag, she found a soft purple cable-knit sweater and jeans, and prepared for the chill that would inevitably freeze her heart.

Sophia sat at the high bar talking quietly while Vail arranged the food onto plates. She poured orange juice into the three glasses lining the counter. "Are you planning on going into the office today?"

The butter knife stilled over the jar of fruit preserves. He slanted a glance at her. "Yes, after I eat and take a shower. I don't plan to be there long, but I need to take care of a few things."

"Carlos?" she asked.

Sophia perked and crinkled an eyebrow.

"Yes. I know they found and disarmed the other bombs, thanks to you. But I want to be in the room when the team moves on...the estate." He turned to her and forced her gaze up. "And I need to process him out to another facility."

"I want to go with you," she said.

"That's not a good idea." He waggled his jaw. "I've been there before."

"Precisely my point. It wasn't exactly on good terms."

"I can talk to Carlos. Get whatever you need out of him."

"Because that worked so well the last time?" He said it with a palm up as though trying not to incite her.

"He no longer has anything over me. I can convince him to talk."

Vail exhaled for longer than she thought humanly possible.

"You're not leaving me here," Sophia interjected plainly.

Vail kicked his chin toward her. "It's not exactly the kind of place that hosts take your family to work day."

Everyone paused as though life had hit its own freeze frame.

"Not that..." He scrubbed a hand over his face and sighed. "Never mind. Let's eat and get ready to go."

Chapter Thirty-four

Khani's wary gaze met Vail and his entourage at the double doors. Her mouth opened to speak.

"Woah, I love your make-up," Sophie gushed. "I can't wear any yet, but when I can I want it to look like yours."

"You must be Sophia. It's an honor to meet you, darling. I heard you're quite the warrior," Khani said.

"No, that's Vail," Sophie corrected.

Khani's gaze flickered over him, Carmen, and then danced back to Sophie. "Indeed, he is as well. There are many warriors in this little foyer."

"Where are you from?" Sophie asked.

"London," Khani answered. "And for the record, you won't need a spot of make-up ever with your gorgeous skin. I see you get it from your mother." Khani eyed Carmen for a pile of seconds.

Tension drew his lover's shoulders and he stepped almost imperceptibly forward and over, placing the very edge of his shoulder between the two women.

"Oh Lord above, not you too," Khani exclaimed. "It's a damn epidemic." She braced two hands in front of her, warding off the germs. "Not to worry, I've been vaccinated."

Nobody asked what she meant. Carmen hadn't taken a breath in at least a minute, which told him she got the gist of it too. Or maybe not. Their staff had experienced a wave of honeymooning. Khani seemed content to steer as far away from it as possible, but he certainly wouldn't consider himself in the getting-hitched category.

Who was he kidding...yeah, he was, if Carmen and Sophie would accept his old battle-scarred body.

Khani leaned around him. "I'm Khani Slaughter."

Carmen accepted the hand Khani offered. "Thank you for saving him."

His counterpart nodded. "Just don't hurt him again and we're square."

The love of his future gave a curt nod that made his eyes narrow. He didn't know if he believed her or not. And that hurt. She'd been distant since their talk in the kitchen earlier in the morning. He cleared his throat. "Let's go to my office and talk."

They headed for his office, but got waylaid by Rhonda. She rushed around her desk toward him. At the sight of Carmen she stalled. Then her gaze hit Sophie and brightened. "I'm so glad to see you up and around, and with two lovely ladies. Hi, I'm Rhonda Merk."

"Rhonda is my assistant," he explained. "She runs this place."

"Oh, no." Her hand flapped at the air. "Can I get any of you something to drink?"

"I'm fine, thank you." Carmen insisted. He, Sophie, and Khani waved her off also.

"Well, I won't keep you," she said, bowing back into her office. "If you need anything, holler."

He opened the heavy glass door for the ladies and ushered them inside. Khani propped against the wall to the right of his desk. Sophie took one of the two chairs in front, while Carmen froze just inside the door. He laced his fingers with hers, pulled her to the chair next to Sophie, sat, and tugged her onto his lap.

"Khani, please, sit." He nodded at his chair, and she did, with both brows up around her hairline and the hint of a smile on her bright red lips.

"Why is Carlos targeting the Sinaloa after nearly ten years of relative silence?" Khani asked, pinning Carmen with a direct gaze.

Her scoff rumbled in her chest. "He's always been indignant about the AFO's apparent weakness. As you know, the Tijuana boarder, as well as the entire Baja District, was under AFO control for the greater part of two decades. Almost a decade ago, the Sinaloa overthrew my father and took the resources, the people—the ones they didn't kill—as well as the land, and then exiled my family."

Carmen's grip on his hand tightened. "If you think Carlos was ever quiet about it, you're mistaken. He raged for hours on end, throwing things about the house, bullying his men. Finally he'd had enough talk and decided to take precise steps to retaliate against the Sinaloa Federation."

Khani inhaled, her mouth open with the next question. Vail knew what was about to come out of Khani's mouth. The closest thing Khani had to children was her brother. From where she sat it was cut and dry. Carmen should have stopped Carlos. But she didn't take all the facets of the situation into account. Namely, Sophie. Guaranteed though, were it Zeke's ass on the line, she'd do everything in her power to save him from harm. Even let the bad guys distract themselves with hurting others. For a while at least.

"Well, why wouldn't you—" Khani stopped.

An eerie silence settled over the room a second before the unmistakable *pop, pop, pop* of gunfire exploded from the hallway, snapping Vail's heart like a twig.

He stood, Carmen in one arm. His other hand encircled Sophie's upper arm. He hauled them around the desk and kicked the alarm with the toe of his boot. The mechanism sealed every external entryway with two inches of steel and sounded a siren shrill enough to deafen.

"Mother fucker," Khani said, racking the slide on her pistol.

He was so caught up in fear for his girls he hardly registered the curse. He sat Carmen on her feet and brushed a kiss across her forehead, and then Sophie's hand, before releasing them.

Carmen immediately encircled Sophie in her arm. "I need a gun."

Vail was already at his wall safe punching numbers. He opened the small door, recovered two wood-gripped Ruger 1911's and two extra magazines. "The door is bullet-proof, but it doesn't mean they can't get in through the security system." Her gaze flew to the vent. "It's been sealed."

He handed her the gun and extra mag, and stuffed his extra into his back pocket. The cold metal of the slide wrenched under his grip. Not daring to take the time for goodbyes, he ran for the door.

Khani stood to the side of the opaque glass. Vail gave the signal. She pulled it wide. He went low, centering the forehead of a sweat-soaked gorilla donning a full tactical vest and double-drawn pistols. He hugged the trigger, spraying red on the wall. His barrel slid right, taking out the guy rounding the corner before he made the turn. The body fell like a log.

His partner advanced, clearing Rhonda's office and holding down the hallway while he made certain the door was locked behind him.

Khani jerked an almost invisible nod. "Not there," she mouthed.

They moved as one deadly unit to the end of the corridor, stepping over the bodies as they went. A body sprawled in the main hallway. Her skirt hiked around her thighs. Her sand-colored hair soaking in a pool of crimson. They bolted up the hall, Khani going low this time. His blood steamed to a vicious mist of rage.

"She's still alive," Khani breathed.

"Can you keep her that way?"

"Do my best. Shot to the neck and she's in shock. End this fast."

"Count on it."

He advanced in a crouch, clearing every office he came to. The clear glass of the conference room allowed him to see it was vacant. But the long T of the corridor holding the cells would leave him wide open to attack. He centered, coiled. At the thunderous echo of footsteps, he swung the opposite direction. Vail was ready to rain hell on the men barreling toward the thick metal door of the stairwell.

The metal latch *clacked*. He came face to face with a sea of M-4's, pistols, pissed, and quite surprised operatives.

Thank fuck.

"Well, I didn't believe in ghosts." Tyler nodded.

"Tyler, help Khani with Rhonda. Boudreaux, get the ambulance and call the doc, let him know what's on the way. Abernathy and Hebert, guard my office door, but do not go inside. Oliver and Hunter with me. Everybody else, search the building and surrounding area. No one gets away."

"Good to have you back, Commander," one of the men said. The others gave barks of agreement.

Except for two, the herd scattered. Vail signaled them eyes out, down the hallway. One across the hallway. Oliver high. Him low. Go.

In the wide open of the long expanse of bare walls, three men worked diligently on the door to Carlos's Ruez's cell. Another kept watch. He fired first, his bullet *zinging* close enough that Vail's old wounds tingled with remembered agony.

Shots filled the narrow space. Men screamed. Blood poured. Splattered. Dotted the concrete. Vail flashed back to the night when his own stained the floor. But this was not that night.

A pile of men lay slain at Carlos's door. His men stood tall, eyes still on, ready for anything. Vail only wanted one thing more than to drag Carlos from his cell, toss him down on the pile, and put a bullet in the man's head.

"Take care of them and then check the cells. I'll be back." And he ran for the one, no, two things he could never lose.

Chapter Thirty-five

Fear had levels. Carmen thought she'd experienced them all. But this. This petrifying rack of her nerve endings outdid them all. The two people she loved were in jeopardy. And all she could do was sit and wait. Cling to her daughter and the gun in her hand, and wait.

They'd jumped at the quick shots Vail had taken before he'd been fully outside the door, but she'd seen him move swiftly after that and hadn't heard any more shots. So, he was okay. He had to be okay.

Neither of them cried, too on the brink of fight with no room for flight in this scenario. Sophia's heart pattered against Carmen's chest, but her little jaw jutted in defiance. Her daughter's strength filled her with maternal pride. It pissed her off that fear shared in the beauty of that joy.

"I love you, Baby Girl."

Those thin, mighty arms cinched around her waist. "I love you so much, Momma. And Vail too."

The wistfulness in her tone snapped her like a twig. "I know you do, baby. He's a warrior, remember. Strong and mighty. Keen and resolute. If anyone can handle the situation, it's him."

"I know you love him. Why won't you just say so?"

She levered back to get a better look at Sophia's intelligent eyes. Carmen dragged in a breath, flicked her gaze to the door, and then looked back to her daughter. "I'm afraid."

"You're not scared of anything."

"Sure I am. I'm terrified of losing you and never really having him."

"Then tell him. He loves you, I know it."

"You don't know it. Him loving you means something different than him loving me. It's bigger and more complicated."

"You've always told me that everything worth having is complicated. Like an education, remember?"

Carmen kissed Sophia's cheek, brushed her hair from her face, and then brushed another across her forehead. "When did you get so wise?"

Sophia gave a tight smile, her gaze shifting to the door and back again. "Yesterday."

The instinct to laugh at her daughter's cuteness was only overridden by the ridiculous fear choking her. What if Vail didn't come?

A shadow cast over the doorway. Carmen's gun came up, but she held the trigger loosely. Her heart beat in her throat. "Over in the corner," she whispered. With a hand she guided Sophia to where the sidewall and the front wall met, out of the line of sight, and in a perfect position to pick off an intruder.

Carmen placed herself between the door and Sophia. She leveled the gun at chest height and waited. Four shots rang in quick succession. The barrel of her gun wavered.

Dread filled her. There were too many shots too close together. Too much room for error. She wouldn't leave Sophia unguarded for anything. But for the first time, she wanted to leave her daughter and go protect Vail.

"It's okay, Sophie. It's okay." She repeated the mantra to comfort Sophie, and herself.

"Mom?"

"Yes?"

"You just called me Sophie."

She laughed, despite everything. It was short and harsh, but it was a laugh. Vail had somehow snuck into her heart and mind. In a matter of days he'd undone the habits she'd honed over twelve years and then some.

"Yes, I did. Do you like it...or not?"

"I love it."

"Okay then."

A single set of shoes boomed against the concrete, screaming for the office door. Carmen braced the 1911 with her left hand and exhaled long and steadily.

"All clear, Carmen. Don't shoot," Vail hollered through the glass. The door opened, but only his arm breached the room. "Carmen?"

"Vail!" She flipped the safety, lowered the gun, and ran.

He stepped into the room a beat before she reached him and launched herself into his arms. The crushing weight of his hug filled her with such relief tears—happy, ecstatic, crazy, tears—streamed from her eyes. Her mouth landed hot on his. He opened for her. Their tongues mated in a desperate dance of love.

She panted with a wild need that was nowhere near appropriate with her daughter present, but she couldn't bring herself to stop. Vail apparently had more sense and broke the kiss.

"What about being a good role model?" he asked, the impetuous hint of a smile on his lips.

"Just kiss me," she begged.

His lips grazed and nipped, and then he pressed his cheek to hers and hugged her impossibly tighter. He leaned back and a fine mist fogged his eyes. "I don't know what I would have done if..."

"I love you."

She grabbed his face to make certain he heard the word. If he never said them, if all she had in life was his time and his baby in his world then that would be enough. He would be enough.

His lips crashed onto hers time and again. Sophie coughed and they both slowly disconnected. He set her on her feet. His hard hand slid to her neck. His head shook back and forth.

"Carmen, love isn't an adequate word for the way I feel about you. I adore your happiness. I cherish your anger. I wait in this state of rapt anticipation for your touch. To hear your thoughts. I love you. I do, but the word just doesn't cut it."

Sophie bum-rushed them, slipping her head into the middle of their love fest and locking an arm around each of their waists. Vail scooped her into his arms and tugged Carmen close.

"This," he whispered. "Just this." The muscles in his jaw tightened and flexed. "I need to know how you found this facility."

"The man who did our fake identities all those years ago...well, it was rumored that he ran a mercenary group in the States. You know, ex-military types and such. I put out the request to find Carlos with a hefty portion of my inheritance attached. It took four weeks, but one day I went to the tennis courts to vent some anger and found a sheet of paper at the bottom of the ball basket with this address, the floor plans, and the entire building schematic." She shook her head. "I don't know how he got the information, but then, I didn't care. Now it means..."

"I know. I want nothing more than to stay with you two, but I need to take care of a few things."

"Was anyone hurt?" Carmen asked.

"Rhonda. But Khani is the best medic I know. She and a couple other operatives have already started transport to a medical facility."

"Can we go with you?" Sophie chimed.

"What I'm about to do isn't for... Actually, yes. I want you close to me." He turned to Carmen. "Both of you." His lips skated over the back of her hand. "Beating Carlos didn't get the information we needed before. So, as much as I'd like to knock the life out of his body, I'll restrain myself. Because I have a better idea."

Chapter Thirty-six

The observation room rocked. A panel of giz-mos attached to a desk in front of a ten-by-five slab of one-way glass. If she had popcorn and a place to prop her feet, it'd be like a movie theatre. Cool. Dark. Quiet. Beside Sophie, her mom sat, fingers strumming frantically over the arm of the cushy chair. Of course, her mother didn't want her to see anything gory. And honestly, neither did she. But she trusted Vail.

Beyond the mirror, Carlos paced in a vibrant orange jumpsuit. His fat belly had grown and his nose slanted almost sideways on his face. It hadn't looked like that the morning he'd stood by as his men wrestled her out of her home and stuffed her into the hot, dark trunk.

If she smiled, did it make her a bad person?

Vail opened the door to the cell where her un-cle paced. His large black boots thumped on the floor. It amazed her how quietly such a big man could move when he wanted. But there was nothing stealthy about this. He didn't even bother closing the door.

Carlos Ruez, her blood, her enemy, spat on the ground. "Fuck you, American shit." Her mom's eyes widened, but they both knew she'd heard that and worse living at the estate. "I'll get out. It didn't work this time, but it will. I have—"

The man she wanted to call Dad more than anything hurled himself across the feet separating them. His fist balled, drew back, and sank into the side of Carlos's cheek. The waylay cut off his pitiful tirade. He slumped to the floor in a disheveled pile, looking more like a garbage bag on the side of the road than the ringleader of a cartel.

Two men entered the room behind Vail. Both were younger by twenty years, maybe. And they were cute, but not near as good-looking as John Batten. Try as she might she still saw his smile every time she closed her eyes. She'd probably never see him again. Didn't know what she'd say, if she did, but he was a perfect fantasy boyfriend. The boy who'd been so funny and charming at a time when she'd needed it most.

One of the men dropped a length of rope in the center of the room and then moved to the wall, fastening a piece of metal to the concrete with long screws. The other guy lugged a ladder. He propped it up and climbed to the top. She and her mother both leaned forward. He pulled an eye bolt from his pocket and screwed it into a hole in the ceiling she hadn't noticed before. The guy on the ground handed up the rope and the one on the ladder looped it through the metal circle.

Wordlessly, Vail caught a roll of duct tape the rope guy tossed and went to work securing her traitorous uncle's hands behind his back. When he finished he moved to his feet. The wide adhesive bound them together like two Popsicle sticks. As though moving a corpse with no care to its wellbeing, Vail dragged him by the feet to the middle of the room. With a nod he dismissed the other two, looped the rope end around the tape at his ankles, tied it off, and used the long end to hoist the unconscious man into the air.

From beneath his short sleeves his muscles bunched. His face strained. The rope slipped once and Sophie rubbed her hands together, thinking it must have hurt. But he only rearranged his grip and continued to heave. When her uncle reached eye level to Vail—really high in the air—he turned to the cleat on the wall and wound the black rope about the metal. When he stepped back and released the rope she and her mom both gasped, waiting for Carlos's body to crash to the ground.

She most certainly did not want to see that.

It held.

"You thought it was going to fall," her mom said.

"You did too."

"Maybe," she conceded.

Vail pushed Carlos's forehead and his body swung slowly. He waltzed around the room. Looking for what, she didn't know. But when he reached the one-way mirror he turned, kissed the tips of his fingers, and pressed them to the glass.

"So, can I call him Dad?"

"Sophie," her mother scolded. But then she picked up Sophie's hand, squeezed, and giggled like no one in an observation room with their heinous brother hanging literally in the balance in the next room had a right to giggle. "I'm sure you can. One day."

His silver hair flashed in the room's bright light as he turned and walked back to Carlos. "Good morning, sunshine. Have a good nap?"

"Damn you, Tucker. I'm going to fucking kill you and that whore of a siste—"

Vail's hand clamped over his throat, choking off his air supply. "You're going to listen, Carlos.

That's what you're going to do." He released him when his face turned light blue.

"You can't...break me. Beat me all you... want," he hacked.

"I'm not going to lay another hand on you. I'm here to impart some information and let you make a decision."

"Screw you," he yelled in return.

Her mom's fingers tightened around hers.

"It's okay, Mom. I've heard worse and I know not to repeat what I hear."

"You're such a good girl."

"I do have my moments," Sophie agreed.

Mom shoved her shoulder.

"Everyone has choices, Carlos. Today you choose your fate. One will send you to prison for the rest of your life. The other will leave you begging for death for weeks on end." Vail folded his arms and bore his gaze into Carlos. "Tell me what else you're planning against the Sinaloa with your next breath, or I press record." His jaw pointed toward the booth that, hanging like he was, her uncle couldn't see. "I say, 'This is Carlos Ruez, the man who single-handedly destroyed the Sinaloa Federation.' I fly you into Sinaloa territory. Deliver you into their hands. And never look back."

Vail had said he wouldn't mind seeing the Sinaloa facilities blown to bits, but he wanted to do it. If Carlos did it, he'd only step in where the Sinaloa left off. Just as ruthless, just as deadly, and the transition of power would inevitably claim hundreds of innocent lives. Not to mention their crappy demolition skills would kill just as many unassociated with either organization.

Vail shrugged. "Last chance."

Silence stretched until Sophie wiggled in her seat, anticipation getting the best of her. Vail didn't move a muscle. Neither did her mother. A full minute had passed with her uncle swinging back and forth.

Gradually she saw the shift in his demeanor. He drooped like a corpse, losing all tension from his muscles. "I've got a stockpile of explosives in the garden house at home." His voice was harsh and raw. "I'm going to blow the rest of the Sinaloa's facilities sky high."

"You were," Vail corrected. "Now, you're going to jail until you're carried out in a body bag."

Chapter Thirty-seven

His team sat around the table of the conference room, their stoic features showing none of the adrenaline raging through their veins. They were professional. The best of the best. He'd always been a professional. Centered. Unflappable. Until Sophie and Carmen. The need to roar from the rooftops and beat his chest in victory overwhelmed his senses.

"Carlos Hersio-Ruez is still very much a threat. I've said it before and I'll say it one more time. I want him secured first. The explosives second. Take out his men as you go. Your entry is tight. Stick to the plan.

"Your response was impeccable today. The four men you apprehended outside the facility are being processed. Clean up is on target. I spoke with Lieutenant Commander Slaughter. Rhonda is stable in large part thanks to you. Well done. Had you not been so quick to react she'd have bled out on the floor like I almost did last month."

Vail leaned forward, pressing his hands onto the conference table. He hated this next part. But he loved this job because it was a challenge. Every. Single. Day. He watched their faces. The shift of their eyes. The restlessness in their bodies. The sweat on their brows.

"After the two breaches it's obvious one among us is a traitor. I honestly don't know who you are, but this is your one opportunity to come away from this unscathed. You'll spend the next forty years of your life getting comfortable with your cellmate and the wonders of prison food, but you'll be alive.

"Wait. Make me ferret you out. I'll ship you to Cambodia and visit each year to see the advancement of your starvation and gangrene. Make another move against your fellow operatives, and you'll be a whisper of a memory, nothing more."

Two sets of eyes saucered in surprise, but most remained neutral, watchful. If his people were half as good as he knew they were, this thought had at least grazed their brains. Dan Arney, The Foot Tapper as Sloan called him, tapped his foot, but there was nothing unusual in it. He'd done it since day one a year and a half ago.

"No one?" He straightened and folded his arms. "Your days of cable and sunlight are slipping through your fingertips." He shrugged. "I said I didn't know, and I wouldn't lie to you. I don't know. But...someone does."

With a nod, Carmen walked down the hallway with a slow, measured stride. As she came into view through the clear glass some of his people smiled. Dan's foot-tapping reached Mach speed. A room full of eyes shifted in the guy's direction. Across from him, Johnson's hand moved toward his sidearm.

"Everyone's hands on the table," Vail barked. "No one else is getting shot here tonight. It doesn't mean I won't strangle someone though."

The young man and his team presented their hands. All but one.

Dan's gaze jumped around the room like a hen in a fox den. He rubbed his palms together as though trying to wash away his sins. "It was so much money. I...I just couldn't..."

Vail stopped Carmen's advance with an imperceptible wave. She nodded and headed back for the break room and Sophie.

"I don't think you'll be able to spend it in hell. Oliver and Hunter, relieve Arney of his weapons and secure him in cell two until I can figure out where he'll vacation. Everyone else, you have your mission. Rely on one another. Execute it. And get your hind quarters back here. There's always more work to do."

An ensemble of, 'Yes, sir's' filled the room. He watched the two operatives efficiently divest Dan Arney of his pride, haul him out of the room, and walk him down the hall of horror. The closer they came to the metal door, the more violently the man thrashed.

Choices. It's all about the decisions we make.

Vail shook several hands on his way out of the conference room. Unlike Dan, his pace increased the closer he drew to his destination. He rounded the jamb to find his girls snuggling on a love seat together, Sophie's eyes at half-mast. He hated rousing her, but it was time for all of them to go home.

"You got him," Carmen whispered with a knowing smile.

"Yeah, and Rhonda is going to make a full recovery," he returned in a hushed tone.

"That's great news." Sophie popped up, yawned, and stretched like a little kitten.

"It is," he agreed.

"What about my father?" Carmen asked.

"A team is en route. Within twenty-four hours you'll be free and clear of it all."

She nodded, but her smile fell. "I want to go."

"No," Vail and Sophie said in the same vehement tone at the same time.

"It's my family. My mess," Carmen explained.

He crossed to his girls, dropped to one knee, and grabbed one of each of their hands in each of his. His gaze focused on Sophie. "Will you have me as your father to love and cherish and protect you, even from your boyfriends?"

She covered her mouth with her tiny fingers. "Yes." Tears fell from her lashes and onto her cheeks, apple-round with a huge smile.

He kissed her hand and let it drop to warm Carmen's in both of his. "Carmen," he breathed. "Marry me? Leave the past where it lies and begin your new life with me. Be my family and let us be yours forever."

She was quiet for several too-long seconds and his pulse lurched. "Yes," she whispered.

"Yes?"

"Yes!" A rich laughter sang from her throat. She tugged him close and melded their lips. "Yes," she mumbled against his mouth.

"I have one request," Sophie interjected.

"Name it," Vail said, his face wider than the moon.

"I want a sister...or brother," she announced. "Maybe one of each," she added with a thoughtful nod.

"Done," Vail agreed.

"Oh is it now?" Carmen smiled.

"If it's not, it will be soon," he promised.

DANGER MINE
A BASE BRANCH NOVEL

One determined to avoid it. One determined to conquer it. Both on a wayward mission and unable to deny it.

Khani Slaughter has dealt with danger from the day of her conception. Thirty one years dealing with the bullshit and she knows how to attack it, defeat it, and avoid it. Yet, for some unfathomable reason, she gravitates toward it. When you're the head and sometimes deadly hands of the Base Branch, the special operations force for the United Nations, hazard pervades. Her personal life, though, is restricted territory for trouble. No strings flings. That's what she went for. Uncomplicated rolls in the sack. That was all she allowed. Or it had been until, the rookie showed up.

Base Branch operative, King Street takes danger and molds it to his benefit. Only, there's not much advantage in screwing the boss when regret sends her across an ocean. The desire to make her see him for more than a mistake on her and humanity's part places his wide frame directly in her path.

He is cocky and way too brash. Not at all what she wants. But when her brother goes missing he is who she needs. Someone willing to navigate a wasteland, dodge bullets and her prickly demeanor to help rescue her only family. Just maybe, in the process they can save each other from their painful pasts.

VERSIONS
A BLACKLIST NOVELLA

The truth doesn't have versions. Or does it?

Rin Lee covered her childhood in dirt and danced on its grave. Only she pranced a little too hard and spent her young-adult life tiptoeing the straight and narrow. Things finally paid off in the form of a job with the Department of Defense, a home of her own, and a boyfriend muscled enough he put Zach Efron to shame. Until one text reveals a hideous truth that splinters her world.

Suddenly she can't trust Nate or their surrogate family of friends. Can she possibly trust Luck —the man who mirrors her soul, scares her beyond the neat confines she's erected around herself, and makes her scrutinize the versions she's always been too angry to see?

Luck turned to the streets out of necessity, while Rin slapped on blinders and ignored those willing to help her. A stupid move for a sultry young woman. But the skills she learned in the rough and tumble underbelly of DC will serve his latest assignment well. Because people like them have the instinct to survive.

Megan Mitcham was born and raised among the live oaks and shrimp boats of the Mississippi Gulf Coast, where her enormous family still calls home. She attended college at the University of Southern Mississippi where she received a bachelor's degree in curriculum, instruction, and special education. For several years Megan worked as a teacher in Mississippi. She married and moved to South Carolina and began working for an international non-profit organization as an instructor and co-director.

In 2009 Megan fell in love with books. Until then, books had been a source for research or the topic of tests. But one day she read *Mercy* by Julie Garwood. And oh, Mercy, she was hooked!

Megan lives in Southern Arkansas where she pens heart pounding romantic thriller novels and window-steaming erotic romance. For information on releases and giveaways subscribe at meganmitcham.com!

Facebook: @MeganMMMitcham
Twitter: MeganMitchamAuthor
Pinterest: MeganMitcham5
Goodreads: Megan_Mitcham
Website: www.meganmitcham.com

FOR INFORMATION ON NEW RELEASES & GIVE-
AWAYS, SIGN UP FOR MEGAN'S NEWSLETTER AT
WWW.MEGANMITCHAM.COM.